## NO SIGHT FOR SORE EYES

"Uncle Billy?" Sara Sims's voice was muffled by dust and bales of hay.

Sheila saw a slight movement in the corner nearest the dirty windows. She moved slowly toward something swinging in the shadows.

Then she saw what it was.

"Oh!" Sheila couldn't move. It was a horrible sight.

Uncle Billy hung from a noose swung over a rafter. An old chair lay on its side just beyond his dangling feet. Even in this poor light, they could see that his face was purple, his tongue swollen out of his mouth.

With eyes bulging in their sockets, he looked as horrified as Sheila felt.

——————————— ★ ———————————

# PATRICIA HOUCK SPRINKLE

## Somebody's Dead in Snellville

**WORLDWIDE.**®

TORONTO • NEW YORK • LONDON
AMSTERDAM • PARIS • SYDNEY • HAMBURG
STOCKHOLM • ATHENS • TOKYO • MILAN
MADRID • WARSAW • BUDAPEST • AUCKLAND

**SOMEBODY'S DEAD IN SNELLVILLE**

A Worldwide Mystery/August 1994

First published by St. Martin's Press, Incorporated.

ISBN 0-373-26149-7

Printed in U.S.A.

To Button Gwinnett, who unwittingly started it all

# FOREWORD

GWINNETT COUNTY, named for one Georgia signer of the Declaration of Independence, is merely a thin layer of red clay over Stone Mountain's granite roots. For two hundred years Gwinnett dozed, growing cotton, corn, pine trees, and a smattering of towns along the railroad track.

Then in the 1980s Atlanta crept northeast. The nation followed at a gallop. Almost overnight, obscure Gwinnett became the fastest-growing large county in the nation.

At a dizzying pace meandering gravel roads sprawled into five-lane highways. Pastures sprouted subdivisions. Fast-food chains competed for cornfields. Country families, beleaguered by developers, found that red clay farms had turned to gold.

In one family, seeds of murder were planted.

Author's Note: These characters are real only in the sense that any fiction is real. The family is not based on any family I know—yet.

# ONE

*The First Week*
*Sunday—Mother's Day*

"DUDLEY TAIT, you haven't heard a word I've said!"

Martha Sloan's voice crashed into Dudley's thoughts like a falling bough. She was right of course—he hadn't. Standing by their bedroom window, he had been contemplating the Georgia spring. He felt a kinship with the hickory trees.

In the bright sunlight, dogwoods fluttered new leaves and poplars towered in mature dress. One magnolia dowager stood majestic in her glossy year-round wardrobe. She reminded him of Martha Sloan—large, confident, and careless about the mess she strewed around her. Eye-level with the hickories, however, he could see tentative buds only beginning to dot their stark branches. Dudley, too, had been slow to bud. Now, at fifty-five, he had begun to fear he never would.

"What on earth are you thinking about?" Seated at the mirror in her slip, Martha Sloan glared at his reflection as she contorted her lips to smooth them with red gloss.

Dudley rubbed one hand across the top of his head. Each time he did that lately he felt the scalp getting nearer. With a sigh, he dropped his hand to adjust his tie over his large Adam's apple.

"Sorry, Martha Sloan." He crossed the room and patted her still shapely shoulder. "I was daydreaming, I guess."

"About what? Lately you're as moony as a coon dog in mating season. What's going on?" She rose from the dressing table and headed for her closet in a cloud of Chanel. "What on earth am I going to wear? It's too hot for my beige suit, and too early for my white dress. What else will match that damn red corsage Aunt Ruby is sure to bring to church?"

Dudley had been married too long to think she expected an answer—or that he was reprieved. He padded across the floor in bare feet, wishing as he always did that Martha Sloan hadn't covered his mama's heart-pine floors with carpet as soon as Mama was safely in her grave. That wasn't the only change Martha Sloan had made as she modernized the old house he had grown up in, but it was the one Dudley regretted most. He had always loved the hard, cool feel of wood beneath his soles. He pulled on socks and slid his feet into black loafers while he waited for her to continue.

Sure enough, as soon as she had pulled a pink silk dress over her head (careful not to muss her hair), Martha Sloan returned to the attack. "Tell me, Dudley, what you were thinking about! Oh, Lord, I've got to change lipstick. This is too orange for the dress." She again seated herself before the mirror, began to scrub her lips with a tissue.

"Tell me," she commanded indistinctly.

Cornered, he clung to his private thoughts by blurting what he never should have said. "Something happened Friday at the county commission, but I can't really talk about it yet."

"Come on, Dudley, you can tell *me*. I'll be silent as the grave. Is it something good?" Teasing him, her large brown eyes glowed.

For an instant she looked like the girl who had bewitched him into marriage thirty years before. These days, she wore costly frosted curls instead of a bouffant bubble. Her soft pink mouth had become a slick slash above her firmly controlled chin. Rosy nails had been sculpted to talons, and her body had grown thicker in the waist and hips. But her eyes were the same. They had charmed him years ago. This morning they persuaded him to disclose more than he intended.

"It's Grandma Sims's farm. Developers want to buy it for a mall."

Martha Sloan's mouth fell slack, lipstick forgotten. "Are they crazy? Who'd go way out there to shop?"

He shrugged. "Most new construction in the county is east of Lawrenceville. By the time a mall can be built, that part of the county should be ready to support a mall as large as Gwinnett Place up in Duluth."

Her eyes widened until her artificial lashes almost caught on her bangs. Jumping up, she shook him in playful disbelief. "How much will they pay? How much?"

He shrugged. "I don't really know, honey. Somewhere in the neighborhood of a hundred thousand an acre—maybe."

Martha Sloan calculated on her long red nails. "One hundred acres times a hundred thousand dollars..." Her jaw dropped in amazement. "Dudley! That's a million dollars!" She hugged herself, jigging in stockinged feet like a child.

He smiled indulgently. Seldom these days did he give her this much pleasure in anything. "It's ten million, Martha Sloan."

She stood stock-still, eyes wide, mouth wider. "Really?" she asked in a hushed voice. *"Ten million dollars?"*

"It's your grandmother's, not ours," he reminded her. With the caution common to all attorneys, he was compelled to add, *"If* the deal goes through, of course."

That moved her. She grabbed his arm, shook it fiercely. "What do you mean 'if'? You make it go through—you hear me?"

"I can't 'make it go through,' Martha Sloan. I can't even vote on the issue, since it's your family's farm. It will be weeks before they are ready to vote, anyway. This is just a preliminary proposal."

She chewed her lower lip, eyes narrowed in thought. "You've got to get Grandma Sims's power of attorney, Dudley. She's not able to make a decision on anything this big, and heaven help us if Aunt Ruby and Uncle Cline get their fat hands on the deal.''

She returned to her mirror. He said nothing. The only sound in the room was a fly buzzing near the open window.

He was shaken by that fleeting memory of Martha Sloan as she had once been—a vivacious, pretty girl waiting for the right man to shape her into the twin mysteries of "wife" and "mother." For a brief, humble moment he regretted not having been a better man, one who could have brought out the best in her. When, he wondered, did we get so caught up in getting that we forgot about giving? Her next remark shattered his reverie, made him wince.

"You've got to get it, Dudley. Her power of attorney, I mean. Tomorrow, if you can." When he did not answer, she coaxed, "You got us Mama's."

"That was different, honey. Your mother is ... special. Grandma Sims is perfectly able to transact business. I'm not even the executor of her will. Bubba is.''

"Bubba!" Her voice was rich with disgust. "When is he ever sober enough to execute anything? I'd like to execute him!" With that pronouncement of sisterly love, she slid one more coating of pink across her mouth.

Dudley's eye fell on the clock. Glad to end the conversation, he hurried to pull a gray jacket from its hanger. "We're going to have to hurry if we're going to get to church before the first hymn's over. Cline said they're bringing Grandma Sims, since it's Mother's Day. Remember, now, honey—not a word of this to the family at dinner." He joined her at the mirror to run a brush over what remained of his hair.

Thin, tall, and faded, he thought with a silent sigh as he considered his own reflection. Behind his round glasses, his eyes were a faded blue. His hair was a faded brown. Even his skin looked too white. "I'm glad we're going to Nassau in June." He needed the sun like a hummingbird needs nectar. His bones longed to feel warm again. His soul yearned for ... He sighed aloud.

"Me, too." She absently touched her hair, inspected the chic finished product that was her face. "Next year—who knows? Maybe we can afford the Orient! *If* we can figure out a way to get a chunk of our inheritance by then."

"You don't have an inheritance yet," he reminded her.

She shrugged. Reality never got in the way of Martha Sloan's plans.

She picked up her purse from the dresser and looked through it. "Comb, Kleenex, wallet, diet pills to keep me from eating too much and Valium for when my headache starts. That ought to get me through church and dinner at Aunt Ruby's. Oh, Dudley!" She jumped up and gave him the biggest hug he'd had in years. "Honey, you can do it. I just know you can!"

Downstairs he collected his oboe, followed her to the carport, and helped her into the passenger seat of her yellow Cadillac. As he circled to the driver's seat, he noticed her fading bumper sticker: EVERYBODY IS SOMEBODY IN SNELLVILLE.

Smellville, Snailville—Martha Sloan had not grown up, as Dudley did, with the jokes. He could still remember when Snellville was a crossroads, a few stores, and large tracts of vacant land. Some days he wondered whether it was progress or something else entirely that had dotted the countryside with subdivisions and lined Highway 78 with businesses. He regretted the loss of space to tramp through fields and woods for hours and seldom meet a soul. Martha Sloan, on the other hand, minded most that other Gwinnett towns were centered on charming stores and oak-lined squares, while Snellville did little more than straggle along the Atlanta-Athens highway in an endless chain of national franchises. She often fumed at the post office for zoning the old Tait homestead into Snellville instead of Lawrenceville. But since she was stuck in Snellville, Martha Sloan defended its image with zeal.

One word stuck in Dudley's mind as he started the engine: *Somebody.* "Somebody loves me, I wonder who?"

"It's a tough job, but somebody's got to do it." He was uncertain what "it" was that Martha Sloan thought he could do, but whatever it was, he was the somebody who would probably have to do it.

# TWO

TWENTY MILES AWAY, Sheila Travis was hoping she'd get home before she died.

With a quick glance in her rearview mirror, she steered her black Maxima into the far left lane of Atlanta's perimeter highway and let the speedometer climb past seventy. Surely police officers would be in church at eleven a.m. on Mother's Day.

She felt feverish, punched the air conditioner onto high, then stole another look in the mirror. Red nose, eyes watering, hair frizzing from the humidity—had she ever looked worse in her nearly forty years? She wished she'd thought to take off her light wool jacket before leaving the airport. Just right in New York, it now bound her worse than a child's snow suit. She squirmed, but dared not try to remove it at this speed.

In the past eight days Sheila had sat through six meetings in four cities, then visited a college friend who shared reminiscences until late at night—and a very bad cold. On the plane Sheila had tried to concentrate on a book she had picked up in the airport, Anne Delly's *Armchair Gourmet,* a current best-seller combining humor, time-saving tips, and a few actual recipes. Today, however, the very thought of food made her queasy, and by the time Delta circled east to approach Atlanta's airport, she ached as if she had been beaten with a thick stick. Ruefully she had watched Gwinnett County and Stone Mountain pass beneath her window. If she bailed out, she had reflected, she could save herself a forty-mile drive around the perimeter. The way she felt, she wouldn't even mind being killed in the attempt.

As she grabbed another tissue, she promised herself that if she should live long enough to reach Peachtree Corners, she would collapse into bed and sleep for a hundred years. Hosokawa International—and Mr. Hashimoto, her boss—could stagger on without her report on last week's meetings. Porter Phillips could find himself another date for the reception at the High Museum of Art Tuesday night. She had barely enough energy to brace herself for the thorough face washing that Lady, her sheltie, would consider de rigueur for a returned traveler.

At last she turned into the large apartment complex she now called home. Nestled into wooded hillsides, it was serviced by professional landscapers who spent a good deal of time—and scandalous amounts of money—making certain Nature looked natural. In the week since Sheila left, last month's bed of red and yellow tulips had been replaced by pink geraniums. The bulbs had probably been trashed. Sheila and the management had already had two run-ins over their waste of perfectly good flowers, but today she couldn't summon even a proper fume. Only one thought pressed her foot on the gas pedal hard enough to climb the curving road to her apartment at the top: her own soft bed.

She pulled into her parking space, surprised to see Sara Sims Tait, her young neighbor, standing in the breezeway between their apartments. As bad as she felt, Sheila could still wish Sara Sims would cut or perm her hair and stop wearing floral prints, ruffles, and full skirts. Today's dress—a voile of wine-and-navy flowers, with a wide sash and lace trim—did nothing for the woman's tawny hair and deep brown eyes, and the ruffled neck and hem made her look four feet tall and plump instead of petite and nicely rounded. In a city full of beautiful, polished twenty-two-year-old women, Sara Sims was still a dowdy girl.

Her roommate Beth, a Delta stewardess, was seldom at home, and since Sara Sims was constitutionally incapable of having experiences without sharing them, Sheila saw a good bit of her. But she was a kind child, watering Sheila's bonsai and keeping Lady whenever Sheila was out of town, showing up at Sheila's door two and three times a week with a cake, pie, or loaf of homemade bread. Usually Sheila considered she got the better half of the deal. Today, as she wearily opened her car door, she wondered how long she could tolerate constant cheerful chatter.

Sure enough, Sara Sims started talking before Sheila had dragged her lanky limbs up the few stairs to the breezeway. "Brace yourself. I've got some bad news."

Sheila hadn't known she could feel weaker. Now her knees were made of cooked noodles. It must be the cold—surely she wasn't getting sentimental about a dog! This particular dog had been dumped on her several months ago while she investigated a murder, and she'd been promising herself to find Lady a new owner soon. It was surely a sign of how sick she was that she hurried up the steps croaking, in spite of herself, "Is it Lady?"

"Oh, no, I've got Lady in my place. It's your kitchen. The man underneath you had a fire this morning, and burned up your floor. They say it can't be repaired until Tuesday."

As Sheila turned toward her door, Sara Sims caught her elbow. "It's really bad. Not much was burned, but it smells terrible, and the firemen made a mess. I didn't know what to do, so I called your aunt. She said—"

"—she's going with friends to Morrison's Cafeteria for lunch after church, and will be home about three." Sheila fumbled wildly for a tissue, sneezed, waved away Sara Sims's automatic "Bless you" and added, "She's done it every Sunday for forty years. A fire at her own apartment probably wouldn't stop her, much less one at mine."

Sara Sims gave her an unflattering appraisal. "You sound almost as terrible as you look. But I've got some antihistamine that'll stop your nose in a minute, and I told your Aunt Mary you can go to my Aunt Ruby's for dinner. You didn't eat on the plane, did you?"

Sheila shook her head and fumbled through a week's debris for her keys—which she had, of course, tossed automatically into the purse when she left the car. "I'll be all right. I can't smell a thing. I'll just heat up some soup for lunch, and sleep."

She ignored Sara Sims's "You'll see" and staggered inside. But when she saw the gaping hole in her kitchen floor, water still dripping from her cabinets, and her sooty sofa—and when the thick smell of smoke penetrated even her stuffy nose and made her sore eyes burn—she had to agree that she could not stay even for the few hours until Aunt Mary got home.

"I told you," Sara Sims reminded her. "Come on." Without waiting to see if Sheila followed, she headed out, still talking. "I've called Aunt Ruby. We always eat over there on Sundays, and she's expecting you. Kevin's coming, too," she added, so casually that it had to be significant.

As if conjured, Sara Sims's new male friend appeared at the door.

Sheila had met him twice before. She liked him no better when she was about to die than she had when she was merely in a hurry and blocked by his sporty pearl gray car.

In her opinion, he just missed being handsome. His face was almost square, but with a slight tilt, as if someone had modeled it, then given it a small push before it dried. His hair was thick and dark, but neither quite brown nor quite black. His muscles were maintained not by work, but by determined recreation.

His looks, however, she could tolerate better than his personality. Thirty-five to Sara Sims's twenty-two, he treated her in a casually superior way that made Sheila want to kick him. Yet Sara Sims adored him, glorying in the broad shoulders that they both assumed all women wanted to lean on. Today Sheila felt fresh exasperation as Sara Sims reached for his hand and swung it with a glowing smile. Did the child want to be in love so badly she couldn't wait to find out if the man was worth all that devotion?

You couldn't, her conscience reminded her. At her age you had already walked down the aisle with Tyler.

Well, I've come a long way in the eighteen months since Tyler's death, she reminded her conscience. I will never obey that peremptory male tone again.

Kevin interrupted her silent dialogue. "Let's get a move on. Didn't you say they live out beyond Lawrenceville?" Without waiting for a reply, he turned to Sheila. "You look terrible. Sara Sims, get her some of that antihistamine I brought you last month. She'll be fine before we get there."

Sheila gave him what she hoped was a baleful glance and opened her mouth to say she was going absolutely nowhere. At that moment, Lady slipped between Kevin's legs, hurled herself at her mistress with a volley of barks, and shredded Sheila's last good pair of panty hose.

While Sheila picked up the dog and ducked ecstatic caresses, Kevin carried Sheila's bags and briefcase into Sara Sims's. He returned with a bright orange pill.

Sara Sims followed with half a glass of water and, of all things, a violin case. Did she think Sheila could swallow better to music? Apparently not, for she set down the case and handed Sheila the water with a confident smile that could earn her a lifetime television commercial contract. "Kevin's pill will do wonders for your cold. You'll forget you ever felt bad."

Sheila would never forget. She wanted to lie on the floor whimpering until they left her absolutely alone.

Later, when the month had dissolved into horror, Sheila would assure herself (and anybody else who asked) that she only got involved because she was too ill that first day to resist. It was a measure of exactly how weak she felt, she would insist, that she swallowed the pill, let Sara Sims shut Lady inside, and obeyed Kevin's abrupt "Let's go."

But she would never forgive herself for folding her long limbs into his minuscule backseat without a single word of demur.

# THREE

THE ANTIHISTAMINE WORKED. Within minutes Sheila felt well enough to comb her hair and powder her nose. She also felt drowsy enough to rearrange herself in the backseat—an exercise, she thought sourly, not unlike turning in the womb—and doze, tuning out Kevin's conversation on his car phone and Sara Sims's singalong with the radio. Gwinnett County is large. Sheila was able to get over half an hour of sleep before she heard Sara Sims exclaim, "Slow down—we're almost there!"

Sara Sims was keyed up like a little girl eager to show the family a new trophy. Sheila, with no doubts about which guest was the trophy, slowly opened her eyes. They were passing an elegant new subdivision of large brick houses backed up to a pasture where cows rested by a pond. Were people in those houses ever tempted to climb the fence to save themselves a four-mile drive for milk? Would any of them know how to milk a cow if they did?

It was another half mile, however, before Sara Sims spoke again. "There! The house between Grandma Sims's and Nana's!"

Three houses sat surrounded by acres of pasture, cornfields, and pine woods. First came a small white frame house with a silver tin roof, dwarfed by an ancient sycamore. The front porch was almost hidden by enormous Formosa azaleas. Much of the yard was bare dirt, ringed with clumps of tall grass. Beside the house hunkered an old black Chevy on four flat tires. Down the side yard, two ruts through long grass led to a barn painted only by wind and rain.

The next two houses were brick, surrounded by neat lawns and flower beds, but they had more in common with the small white house than with their superior neighbors up the road. Behind each was a clothesline, a chicken house, and a newly planted garden, and beside the drive of the center house a small vegetable stand awaited the harvest.

Kevin parked on the grass beside several other cars, and Sheila willed herself to unfold and walk. She followed the others through the back door in a soft, fuzzy blur.

"Hello, Mrs. Witch, I came with Hansel and Gretel here."

She didn't actually say it—at least she hoped she hadn't. But she was tempted. The dumpy woman had a moist, flushed face surrounded by grizzled hair. A large wart adorned her nose, and thick lenses magnified her eyes into chocolate drops. The room seemed full of ceramic animals, Avon collectibles, and plastic flowers. The air was thick with the odors of fried chicken and pecan pie. Sheila was almost sorry when, instead of inviting her to put her head inside to test the oven, the woman wheezed, "I'm Ruby Shaw, Sara Sims's great-aunt. We're mighty glad you could come. Let me help you take off that hot jacket. We didn't know if you'd need a red flower or a white one, so Cline picked pink." Her own flower was red, pinned on her apron's bib.

Without waiting for an answer she helped with the jacket and jabbed a straight pin through Sheila's silk blouse to attach a spray of sweetheart roses. She wiped her face with an already damp tissue and crammed the tissue back into her apron pocket, then handed Sara Sims two red carnations. "You all eat in the kitchen here, with Bubba's crew. I've put Sheila in the dining room."

Sheila's head had begun to whirl. The house was hot from a long-used oven and too many people. Even though all the windows were open, a desultory breeze merely riffled the curtains and turned away. She scarcely heard her hostess's introductions, registered impressions rather than faces.

"...my nephew Harley—we call him Bubba—and his wife Evelyn." A woman with a bristle of red hair, peeling tomatoes by the sink. A short stocky man rising heavily to his feet, exuding a strong smell of peppermint. His red carnation looked strange on a khaki jumpsuit, but his handshake was friendly.

"...their son, Roger, and his wife, Erika..." A young man with a handsome face and a petulant mouth, not yet as stout as his parents—nor as polite. He gave Sheila the barest of nods before returning to filling his plate. His wife, pretty in a pallid way, smiled mechanically and bent to restrain her prancing daughter.

"...*their* children, Tad and Michelle." A boy scarcely six stuck out his tongue and a tiny girl neighed and informed Sheila, "I'm not a girl, I'm a pony!" Her little red flower bobbed on her flat chest.

In the dining room, Sheila sank into an offered chair and noted gratefully that except for a fat golden cocker spaniel, she was the only one at the table under fifty. She could not have endured children. As Ruby performed brief introductions, people seemed to swell forward and recede like balloons at a parade. She gave each a weak smile, but said nothing. What difference did it make if they thought her rude? She had no intention of seeing any of them again, and if she shared her germs, they would never want to see her again, either.

"My husband, Cline Shaw..."

The pride and affection in Ruby's voice were touching, especially since the man was so ugly—stout, red of face and hair, eyes green behind thick bifocals, an American flag glittering in his lapel. He sat on Sheila's left, his thick thigh in a wrinkled brown Sunday suit too close to her own.

"My brother, Billy..."

Across the table, a mat of thick white hair with a crooked part, bent so low over his plate that his chin nearly rested on his blue overalls. He did not look up.

"My mama, whom everybody calls 'Grandma' Sims..."
*Grandma* was pronounced rapidly, "Gramma."

Sheila's astonished gaze met eyes that were black and
fierce, startlingly alive in a face that was little more than skin
stretched over bones. Ruby was old. How old must her
mother be? And how dared Sara Sims and Ruby expose this
frail old woman to germs? She felt such a rush of anger, she
nearly missed the next name.

"Aubrey Wilson, who was married to my sister Emma,
who died."

Lean, tanned, handsome, with silver hair in waves above
a high forehead and vivid blue eyes. His smile was too wide,
though—it showed that his teeth were false. And deep lines
of discontent were etched around his mouth.

A manicured hand was thrust impatiently down the table
in a jangle of gold bracelets. "I'm Martha Sloan Tait, Sara
Sims's mother." The modish woman attached to the hand
paused with an expectant smile.

It took Sheila's fuddled mind too long to realize she was
supposed to protest, "Oh, surely not." She was too busy
wondering whether Martha Sloan had first dressed Sara
Sims in ruffles and lace because she hoped to create a fem-
inine beauty out of a short, plump child, or because a
dowdy child set off the mother's own good looks. Dressed
properly, Sara Sims could look interesting, even pretty, but
she would never shine next to her mother. Stung by sudden
pity for her neighbor, Sheila wondered how Martha Sloan
looked with her face clean and her hair wringing wet.

Martha Sloan ignored the pause with a determined smile.
"And this is my husband, Dudley. He's a lawyer, and sits on
the county commission."

Dudley Tait laid a hand on his wife's forearm, as if to restrain her, before giving Sheila a small, embarrassed smile.
"I hope we won't overwhelm you, Sheila."

"Courtly" was the word that came to mind as she looked
at the slender man with mouse-brown hair carefully combed
where it was thinning. She suspected that it was from him

that Sara Sims had gotten her smile and kindliness. He looked like a man who would go to a lot of trouble to please others.

The last chair, between Dudley and Sheila, was vacant. Introductions complete, Ruby sank into the chair nearest the kitchen with obvious relief. "We're all here except Wart. Aubrey, will you return thanks?" Sheila prayed they would all ignore her.

Even the Almighty, however, has a hard time stemming Southern curiosity—often mistakenly called Southern hospitality. Within the next ten minutes they fired questions at her as rapidly as they passed fried chicken, mashed potatoes, cream gravy, corn, beans, tomatoes, hot biscuits, and cholesterol-free spread.

Martha Sloan, adept at tracing family trees, soon related Sheila to the wealthy Mary Beaufort who had contributed so generously to the new civic center. Dudley placed her as the widow of Tyler Travis, formerly with the U.S. embassy in Japan. When she told them she had also been born and raised in Japan, she felt them stiffen, but when they learned that her parents were from Alabama and South Carolina, that she had gone to high school in Atlanta and had now come back to Atlanta to work, they relaxed. No need for company manners when she was almost home folks.

The men and Martha Sloan slid into a good-natured wrangle about whether the University of Georgia's quarterback could carry the team next fall. Grandma Sims and Billy concentrated on their plates, and Ruby apologized unnecessarily to Sheila for putting too much salt in the excellent gravy.

Later, when it was important, she tried to remember what had been said and done next. There had been tensions, certainly. Most of them, however, had had little to do with her.

First Cline had beamed at her, pressing his thigh closer and wafting fumes of cigars and Old Spice. "What do you do, little lady?"

She hesitated. The stars and stripes in his lapel were only small replicas of the large flag hanging beside his front door. Even the Shaw's mailbox, she remembered, was red, white, and blue. But since he was waiting, she told him. "I am a director of international relations for Hosakawa International. Our U.S. headquarters are over on Beaver Ruin Road. I coordinate—"

He jerked his thigh away as if hers burned him. "You work for *Japs?* If you'd seen what I saw in World War Two—" His face mottled with indignation. "And now they are pure-tee buying up hunks of our country! Where's your loyalty, woman?"

Sheila bit her lip and took a deep breath. What would she accomplish by pointing out that the United States had been buying up hunks of the rest of the world for years? "I was raised in Japan, Mr. Shaw," she said levelly, hoping he could not see her hands shaking in her lap, "where my parents taught that all men and women are brothers and sisters."

"Well, yes," he faltered, "that's true on one level. But..."

"Cline, honey," Ruby laid a liver-spotted hand on his.

"Okay, sugarplum." He subsided, stroking what was left of his hair. "But the U.S. of A. is good enough for Cline Shaw. I worked for the railroad, little lady, and me'n Ruby've seen might near all the places you can get to by rail."

He launched into a travel story. Martha Sloan interrupted to brag about an upcoming trip to Nassau. In a lull, Aubrey Wilson fixed Sheila with a genial smile that did not touch his eyes. "Where do you go to church, Mrs. Travis?"

In that company there were several right answers—all Baptist. That was not an answer she could give.

When she hesitated, Dudley hurried to her rescue. "We can't expect Sheila to come all the way to First Baptist from Peachtree Corners, Uncle Aubrey. How's the building fund coming along?"

"We've got a ways to go yet," Aubrey, diverted, shook his head in regret. "We sure could use a big donor or two."

Had Martha Sloan started to speak then, and Dudley put a hand on her arm?

Or was that when the tiny woman across the table said querulously, "I need another biscuit"? She had bored into Sheila with those eyes until Sheila felt absurdly guilty, as if she'd secreted the biscuits about her person.

Ruby placidly slid one into the waiting hand, on which veins stood out almost as thick as the fingers. "Here you are, Mama. Want me to butter it?"

"I been buttering my own for ninety-seven years. Reckon I can do one more." When Ruby flushed at the tart reply, the old woman's mouth curved into a triumphant smile wholly without mirth.

Once Billy raised his face to Sheila, his eyes sly and curiously young. She realized that he was not shy, as she had supposed, but retarded. "Wanna hear a joke?" His smile was a leer.

Martha Sloan's hand darted out, as if she would like to grab him. "Hush, Uncle Billy!"

"Let me give you another ear of corn," Ruby offered. When he was munching it, joke forgotten, she wheezed to Martha Sloan, "You having Memorial Day as usual?"

Sheila wondered how anyone avoided having Memorial Day.

"You better," Roger called in from the kitchen. "I already bought a new bathing suit."

"Me, too!" his son echoed. "With Ninja Turtles on it!"

"I guess so," Martha Sloan sighed. "But I've been so busy with the Arts Council, I haven't even thought about food."

"Ruby can't make my grocery money go anywhere these days," Grandma Sims quavered. "She says prices is rising, but it don't seem possible they can rise that fast."

Before Ruby could defend herself from that oblique slander, Martha Sloan turned to the old woman with teas-

ing eyes. "Money's short, is it, Grandma Sims? I'll bet—"
She broke off, gave Dudley an astonished glare. "Stop
pinching me," she hissed.

The back door slammed. "Here's Wart," said Ruby.

Martha Sloan subsided with the expression of a waiting
cat.

# FOUR

SHEILA KNEW IMMEDIATELY that the young man who limped in was a Sims. He was short, like Ruby and Sara Sims, and so round that his stomach kept appearing between the buttons of his camouflage shirt. His small eyes were button black, like Grandma Sims's, and they bulged slightly like Bubba's. Sheila wondered if his nickname was a condensed form of something or if it had been given to him because of the way he turned his head stiffly from side to side without moving his shoulders, which made him look like a malignant toad.

She also knew that her pill was still working. He smelled strongly of manure.

"Take off them barn boots!" ordered Grandma Sims.

"No barn boots in the house! No barn boots in the house!" screeched Billy.

"Okay, Uncle Billy, keep your shirt on." The young man swatted the old man not very kindly on the shoulder, went back out, and returned in sock feet. "That better?" Yanking out the empty chair beside Sheila, he dropped into it, emitting a stench of sweat, dirt and lingering manure. He propped his forearm, tatooed with a green and black snake, close to Sheila's plate and belched, then grinned.

"Not much," Martha Sloan said sourly.

Sheila, striving to breathe only when necessary, agreed. It was clear that neither cleanliness nor godliness ranked high on this young man's Sunday schedule.

"Take off your hat," Ruby wheezed, taking another helping of green beans. He did, revealing dark hair cut close to his scalp.

He filled his plate, shoveled in several bites, then wiped his mouth on the snake.

"Use your napkin," Martha Sloan commanded. "We've got company."

He turned his toad's gaze on Sheila without expression. "So I see." He half drained his glass of tea and held it across her for a refill. She nearly retched from the odor.

"This is our cousin, Wallace Sims," Dudley told Sheila, "known as Wart. Wart, meet Sheila Travis, Sara Sims's neighbor."

"Yeah." He jerked his head up and down a couple of times in acknowledgment, then returned to his main interest, food.

For several minutes nobody spoke. A robin chirped beyond the open window. When a distant train whistled, Cline automatically consulted a large pocket watch. Forks scraped plates, feet shuffled beneath the table. A breeze stirred the curtains, and Sheila welcomed a whiff of honeysuckle overlaying the smell of Wart.

From the next room came laughter and the happy giggles of children getting attention from their grandparents.

At last Wart was done. He shoved back his chair, stood, and limped out into the kitchen. He paused by the table. "You going up to Forsyth County in two weeks, Kevin? The boys want to know." Sheila could not hear Kevin's reply. "Well, think about it," Wart said. "We could use you." His halting steps resumed. When the screen door slammed behind him, Sheila joined the silent but collective sigh of relief.

As dreadful as he was, however, she was glad that instead of apologizing for him, Cline merely swiped up his last traces of cream gravy with a wad of biscuit and asked mildly, "Did you all see that Washington has finally admitted we're still having a recession? It beats all, the way those folks are always the last to know what's going on."

"They don't have to count pennies like the rest of us," Ruby replied, taking another biscuit and spreading it with butter.

Martha Sloan made a funny little noise, somewhere between a whoop and a gulp. "I can't stand it any longer, Dudley. I have to tell them!" Her eyes danced, raking them all into a net of suspense. "The most exciting thing has happened! You'll never guess!" She did not pause long enough for anyone to try. "Developers want to put a mall right here!" She patted the table several times. "They may pay ten million dollars for the land! What do you think of that, Grandma, honey?"

The old woman said nothing. She was no more fooled by Martha Sloan's sudden rush of affection than anyone else in the room. Sheila had recently attended a showing of representative sculpture. If she had to make one of Martha Sloan, she would mount fish hooks upside down in the bottom of a bowl and cover them with pink whipped cream.

The words had carried. Those in the kitchen, finished with dinner, were suddenly aware they were missing something.

"What'd you say?" Bubba demanded, leading the crowd.

Martha Sloan turned her brilliant smile on the newcomers. "Grandma's going to get a hundred thousand dollars an acre for the farm! *Ten million dollars!* Isn't that wonderful?"

"*May* get," Dudley corrected her with a helpless wave of one hand. He might as well have tried to hold back a riptide with one small oar.

Roger was already celebrating. "Ten million dollars? Whooee, Grandma! We're going to be rich!" He rubbed his hands in glee.

"Rich! Rich!" his children clamored, jumping up and down.

"Don't get them all excited, they need to nap," Erika told their father. Roger ignored her. At last she towed them out. "We'll be at Nana's," she called back. Roger didn't reply.

The old woman had still said nothing, but her sharp old eyes darted from face to face, like a bird's.

Bubba headed for the kitchen. "This calls for a celebration. Aunt Ruby, you got anything to drink?"

"Got more iced tea, Bubba."

"And that's all you're going to get, hon. You're on the wagon, remember?" Evelyn added.

"Damn." He stomped out, sulking, brought back a glass of tea.

"Besides," Evelyn reminded the others, lightly resting her hand on the thin old shoulder, "it's Grandma Sims who's getting rich."

The elderly woman looked up with the first sign of liking Sheila had seen, but she shook her head and croaked. "Not me, Evelyn. I ain't selling my land in my lifetime. Call Wart and tell him I'm ready to go. As usual, Ruby ain't done nothin' about it."

Ruby raised her head quickly as if to protest. Instead, as Evelyn went to the back door and called, she added another small helping of mashed potatoes and gravy to her plate.

Dudley raised one hand again. "It's not a sure thing, now. They are just taking preliminary surveys to see if this is the best site."

He obviously regretted that the subject had been introduced in front of visitors. Suddenly the others also remembered that two persons present were not family. An awkward silence was broken by Evelyn's return. "Wart's coming, Grandma."

Grandma Sims shoved away from the table. Taking a stout black cane from the back of her chair, she struggled to her feet.

"May I help you, ma'am?" To Sheila's surprise, Kevin hurried to take her elbow.

Grandma Sims peered up at him, uncertain. "Who are you, now?"

"He came with me, Grandma Sims," Sara Sims told her. "His name is Kevin Bradshaw." She didn't try to conceal the pride in her voice.

"Thank you, Kevin Bradshaw, but Wart will see me home. Wart?"

Wart brought a walker and, with surprising gentleness, positioned it before the old woman. "Here, Grandma. Let Kevin help you through the kitchen while I fetch your wheelchair."

While the two of them steadied her on the walker, Sara Sims bent to murmur into Sheila's ear. "Wart introduced me to Kevin. Kevin's in the army reserves, and Wart was in the marines until he hurt his leg. They met out in Saudi Arabia. I just hope they don't want to go play war games this afternoon."

"War games?" Sheila repeated blankly.

"Yeah. They run around the woods shooting each other with fake bullets full of red paint. It's their idea of a fun time."

She gave a mock shudder. Sheila's was real.

Evelyn spread a white sweater over the old woman's shoulders and handed Kevin the cane. With him hovering just behind her, Grandma Sims made a laborious exit. At the door she paused. "Mind what I said, now. I ain't selling none of Pop's land in my lifetime. You tell 'em, Dudley—you hear me?"

"I hear you, Grandma."

She departed, hunched over the walker, resolute as a duchess.

When she had gone, Sheila felt the room breathe another collective sigh of relief. Eyes sought one another, looked away. She hoped they would adjourn to the living room to talk. She planned to retreat to the kitchen—even at the price of a pan of soapy water. To her regret, they pulled in chairs from the kitchen and crowded around the table. Sara Sims pulled hers behind Sheila's, but the chair between Sheila and

Dudley remained vacant. She hoped Wart wasn't expected to return. She was fond of breathing.

"Look at Roger," Sara Sims whispered. "Itching to talk about all this." Sure enough, the young man was squirming in his seat.

"What are you whispering about?" Martha Sloan demanded.

"Filling Sheila in on the family," Sara Sims lied. "Not that she'll get us all straight in one afternoon. Kevin still hasn't."

"I hope he won't need to. I wish you'd drop him, and find yourself a good lawyer, like your daddy. Or at least somebody in business."

"Kevin's *in* business," Sara Sims retorted with force.

Martha Sloan's lip curled. "If you call managing somebody else's sporting goods store 'being in business.' He's..." She broke off as Kevin reentered the room.

"She's on her way," he said briskly, as if he'd just launched the *Queen Elizabeth II*. He lifted a chair and set it close to Sara Sims's. If he had heard Martha Sloan, he gave no sign.

Martha Sloan turned to her husband. "Did you hear what she said? She could live for years, honey! Developers won't wait. You've got to talk to her, make her see sense."

"What *is* sense?" Ruby wheezed, rosy cheeks growing pinker. She tore at her fingernails, which were already swollen stubs. "Cover up good farmland with concrete so people can buy more stuff they don't need—is that what you want Mama to do with the farm? What about our house—and Bessie's, next door?"

Martha Sloan had no time for unenlightened viewpoints. "You can buy other houses. Mama's is too much for her already."

Cline leaned over to give Ruby a pat. Sheila suspected he often played peacemaker between his wife and her niece.

But today Ruby was not ready for peace. She leaned back and folded plump arms over her plumper chest. "You wanting to move at our age, Cline Shaw? With the garden already in?''

"I wasn't aiming to go tomorrow, honey bunch. We can harvest your tomatoes, even the pumpkins.''

"To hell with your pumpkins!'' Martha Sloan's fist slammed the table by her plate. "That tacky little shed makes this property look like something straight out of *Dukes of Hazzard*. Anyway, we are talking, Aunt Ruby, about ten million dollars. Ten mil-lion.'' She repeated the last two words slowly, for emphasis. "That could buy all the pumpkins in Gwinnett County and most of Georgia. But if Grandma won't sell, they'll find someplace else to put their mall. Dudley, you've got to talk to her!'' Her voice rose in a wail.

Ruby turned back to Cline. "What would *you* do with a million dollars, Cline? What do you need that you don't already have?''

Cline rubbed his hair where it was beginning to thin at the crown. "I don't need anything, honey, but I'd like to give something to Merle, invest some for the girls.''

"Humph,'' Ruby said, unimpressed. "Like you invested in Eastern Airlines? Faye would be better off...''

"Did I hear my name?'' A woman came gracefully from the kitchen and set a cello case beside Sara Sims's violin. "Hello, Mammaw, Pawpaw.'' She bent to hug first Ruby, then Cline.

If Wart was a toad, Faye was the family's doe. Her arms, legs, and fingers were thin, delicate, and as brown as if she'd lain in the sun for weeks. Her face was long and free from cosmetics, with a pointed chin and large brown eyes. Her hair curled gently on her shoulders, its brown touched with Cline's and Evelyn's red. Beneath her yellow cotton sweater, her breasts were small and high. She could be any age between twenty-five and forty. Giving Sheila a fleeting smile, she slipped into the next seat and shoved Wart's dirty plate aside. Then she smiled around the table. "Hello, everybody else.''

"Hello, princess," Cline said, his voice gruff.

"Mrs. Travis—Sheila," Ruby corrected herself, "this is my granddaughter, Faye Baines. Faye teaches at the high school up the road. But they go to church in downtown Atlanta, so they are always late getting here."

As Faye extended Sheila a thin, limp hand, Cline asked, with worried eyes, "Where is your mama, honey?"

"It's one of her bad days, Pawpaw. She decided to sleep this afternoon. We'll have to have a trio, Uncle Dudley."

"We'll manage, Faye. Have you eaten?"

When she shook her head, Ruby started to haul herself to her feet. Evelyn beat her to it. "I'll get her a clean plate, Aunt Ruby. You sit and rest."

"I'll come see what I want. I'm not very hungry." Faye followed Evelyn to the kitchen.

Ruby murmured to Sheila, "Faye's mother has cancer. Real bad. The doctor gives her six months."

Cline rose. "I think I'll take Rags for a little walk. Come on, boy." The fat old dog rose and waddled after him.

Ruby whispered when he was barely out of earshot. "It just tears Cline up. He adores Merle. She's our only." She heaved a deep sigh. "And Cline's right. Merle could use some money for the doctors, and to feel she had something to leave besides debts."

"Who couldn't use some extra money?" Aubrey asked. "I wouldn't mind leaving an appropriate memorial to Emma. The education building at the church, for instance. Even though we never had children, Emma was always crazy about young people."

"Aunt Emma's dead," Martha Sloan objected. "You can't expect Grandma to leave money to her dead children."

Aubrey raised one thin eyebrow. "That's too bad. I guess you and Bubba won't be getting anything, either, with your daddy gone. Grandma'll have to leave it all to Ruby and Billy here."

"I gotta go." Uncle Billy stood up and fumbled at his pants. Ruby started to rise, but Evelyn hurried from the kitchen.

"Here, Uncle Billy, come to the bathroom. Come on, now."

He shuffled to the door, docile as a child. Sara Sims bent toward Sheila and murmured, "Uncle Billy is simple, as you have probably guessed. He and Ruby are Grandma Sims's only living children, which is what this ruckus is about."

Sheila had already deduced that. What had taken her longer to realize was that the elegant Martha Sloan was sister to Bubba, the reluctantly recovering alcoholic, and Evelyn only a Sims by marriage. Would Evelyn have married Bubba if she'd known she'd follow Aunt Ruby as family dogsbody?

Ruby turned to Martha Sloan in an obvious attempt to change the subject. "Can you stay with Mama Tuesday so I can get a perm?"

Martha Sloan shook her head. "I have to bake all day for the Women's Club tea. I can come for a while on Thursday." She then continued as if no interruptions had taken place. "Since Daddy had two children, we'll share his portion."

"Which means," Roger said sourly, "that Uncle Cline and Aunt Ruby get one fourth, Uncle Billy gets a fourth, you and Daddy *share* a fourth, and Wart—" his voice rose with incredulity "—Wart also gets a fourth!"

Faye had taken her place again with a half-filled plate, and had been eating as if lost in her own world. Now she looked around the table in bewilderment. "What on earth are you all talking about?"

They all hastened to tell her. "So," Roger concluded, "since both his daddy and his granddaddy are dead, good old Cousin Wart gets two and half million while some of us get the crumbs our parents choose to drop!"

"Don't be tacky," snarled Martha Sloan.

"I'm being realistic," Roger insisted. "If there's money in the family, I want mine now, while I'm still young enough to enjoy it. I don't want to wait around for Daddy to die."

"Take Uncle Billy's share, then," Bubba growled, visibly offended. "He can't spend a million dollars if he lives a million years. How much can a man spend on overalls and chewing tobacco?"

"How much can you spend on liquor?" his sister snapped.

"No more than you'll spend on clothes and doodads."

Martha Sloan narrowed her eyes and chewed one corner of her mouth. "Maybe Roger has a point. Maybe instead of dividing the money among her own children, Grandma ought to give one share to each of her living relatives."

Roger was quick to protest. "No fair!"

Sheila was surprised. She would have expected him to put forth that idea himself. But before he could enlarge on his reasons for objecting, Faye asked softly, "What do you think, Uncle Dudley?"

He sighed. "I think I should have kept my mouth shut."

"Did you start all this?" she asked, distressed.

He shook his head. "Not on purpose, Faye. Not on purpose."

"Let's don't discuss this any more right now." Ruby waved her tissue to shush them—exactly, Sheila suspected, as she had been shushing them for over fifty years when they misbehaved in front of strangers.

But what were the strangers supposed to do? She looked at her watch. "Would Kevin take me home?" she murmured to Sara Sims. "I need to get a few things together and go on to my aunt's."

Sara Sims touched Kevin on the knee and spoke in a low voice.

"What are you whispering about now?" her mother demanded. "How many times have I told you it's rude to whisper in public?"

"I was asking Kevin to run Sheila home. She wants to go." Put baldly, it sounded like the ultimate in bad manners. Sheila did not care. Rudeness would be a small price to pay for escape.

"Oh, you can't go yet, honey," Ruby pulled herself with some difficulty to her feet. "We haven't had our pie yet, and then we always have some music." She waddled toward the kitchen.

Sheila was not prepared to face an afternoon of amateur music. Probably gospel hymns, she thought irritably. Her head was getting stuffy again, and her throat felt like she had been swallowing swords and flaming torches. Determined, she followed Ruby into the kitchen, pleading her cold as an excuse for leaving early.

When Ruby made a ritual protest, Sheila discovered she expected each phrase and could reply almost automatically. My goodness, she thought, my Southern roots must be sprouting!

As she and Kevin were at the back door, she heard Roger cry, "What difference does any of this make, anyhow? Looks like we'll only sell the land over Grandma Sims's dead body."

She also heard Martha Sloan's chiling reply. "If necessary, that's exactly how we'll do it."

# FIVE

THE SUN HAD SET, leaving long streaks of pink and purple across the sky. A faint breeze passed through the sycamore and poplars. It darted around the old barn and lightly touched the shoulders of two people standing in Ruby's back yard.

A voice broke the silence. "If only she would die!"

The other did not immediately reply. In that instant the cicadas began to whir, as if voicing divine protest.

The silence swelled. Finally the other spoke. "There's no point in wishing that."

"But if she did ...?"

They were silent, contemplating the possibilities. The twilight deepened. The cicadas kept up their shrill protest.

At last they turned to go inside. They did not see the place by the mower shed where the shadow was thick. Someone else stood there in the darkness, enjoying more than the evening.

# SIX

*Tuesday*

MARTHA SLOAN TURNED impatiently from the microwave. "Don't you change that channel again! I told you, I want to watch Channel Three." She returned the television to the public channel, then expertly pressed microwave buttons to bake brownies. "What's the matter with your own television?"

Uncle Billy ducked his head and clutched the strap of his overalls. "Broke. Mama's gonna get it fixed. Wart's gonna take it this afternoon." He pronounced the last word in the country way, accenting the first half.

She sighed. Which was most exasperating—his old-fashioned habits, the slime of tobacco spit at one corner of his mouth, or just the fact that he was here, in her clean kitchen, on this Tuesday morning when she had to bake and ice dozens of brownies for the Women's Club tea? She moved away, out of range of his smell. Grandma made him put on fresh overalls each morning, but his hygiene was slovenly. By midmorning, he stank so that only Grandma Sims, who couldn't smell anything anymore, could stand him.

"Well you can't watch cartoons in here. You can go into the den if you want to," she added ungraciously.

"Can't work that TV," the old man lamented. "It's got no buttons."

"Oh, for heaven's sake." She took him by one arm and more dragged than led him into the den, pushed him into Dudley's leather recliner, and reached for the remote control. "What channel do you want?"

He told her, wriggling to get comfortable. "Got a Coca-Cola?" Seething, she brought him a can.

She had scarcely begun to mix the next batch of brownies when Uncle Billy shuffled back into the kitchen.

"I'm hungry. You got cheese?" He pulled the longest knife from the block and touched his forefinger to the edge.

"Stop that! You'll cut yourself!" She opened a drawer and took out a cheese cutter, pulled a block of cheddar from the refrigerator. "Put the knife away, and I'll get you some cheese."

Reluctantly he laid the knife back on the counter, touching its handle almost reverently. "Knife make pretties," he said wistfully.

"You don't need a knife. You'd started cutting yourself, so Grandma took it away. Here's your cheese." She slapped several slices onto a plate and shoved it in his direction.

"Got sody crackers?" He gave his bottom a vigorous scratch.

She sighed in pure exasperation. What had she done to deserve such a relative? "Here are some Ritz." She handed him the box.

"Like sody crackers better."

"But I don't have any. Now go back in there. I'm busy."

He shuffled away, already stuffing his mouth with crackers and leaving a trail for bugs to follow. Martha Sloan hastily swallowed a tranquilizer and began to gather ingredients for tuna salad.

Within half an hour he shuffled back into the kitchen.

"Done," he announced, going toward the door. "Take me home."

"I'm *busy*," she told him again. "Who brought you here?"

"Cline. Gone to the store." Uncle Billy didn't elaborate on which store. In his mind there was still only one, up at the crossroads, which sold everything from candy to buggy whips. He had shopped at the modern strip malls, of course, but with his head down, terrified to lift his eyes and fully contemplate so much richness.

"He'll come back for you." Martha Sloan was chopping onions, thinking she'd like to chop Uncle Cline for dumping Uncle Billy on her without warning. She didn't mind doing her duty, but she appreciated being asked first, preferred to do her uncle-sitting at Grandma Sims's rather than in her own lovely home.

As a small girl, Martha Sloan had loved Uncle Billy—and the incredible, delicate animals those gnarled fingers could whittle from pine. But one day when she was eight, she realized all her friends laughed at him. After that he embarrassed her, too, with his old straw hat and overalls.

Today she had no time to drive him home. He should have called before he came.

He fumbled in his pocket and brought out a small wooden mouse. "It's new," he said with pride.

She barely gave it a glance. "I thought Grandma said you weren't to use knives again."

His gaze slid to the window, then to the floor. "She give it back to me."

"She did not," Martha Sloan said confidently. "You sneaked it."

"Made a pretty," he said, as if that justified any disobedience. "Here, you keep it." He handed it to her.

She stroked the smooth back. "It is pretty," she admitted, setting it on the countertop.

He edged toward the counter, reached a tentative hand toward the television.

"Don't you change that channel," she said sharply. "You can go back to the den if your shows aren't over."

"It's lonesome," he pouted, his lower lip quivering.

"Well, it's my television in here. You have to choose between your cartoons or my company. You can't have both."

"Wanna hear a joke?" His lips curved in a guileless smile.

"You and your filthy jokes. I ought to wash out your mouth with soap."

"Mean!" His lower lip began to quiver. "Mean to Uncle Billy! You need a beating. Mean!" He picked up his hat and scuttled sideways toward the door.

"Where are you going?" she demanded.

"Home." He stomped out, slamming the door behind him.

She went to the screen and called after him. "You can't walk that far. Come eat lunch with me, and I'll take you when the brownies are done."

He paused. A spring breeze ruffled his hair and sent waves of gardenia across the yard from the bush by the garage. Uncle Billy reached out and fondled one bloom. "Pretty." He turned a shrewd eye toward his niece. "Brownies?" He headed back toward the house.

She waited until he was seated at the kitchen table before she said, "You get tuna salad and one brownie. The rest are for a meeting."

"Don't like tuna."

"Then you can starve." She began to spoon salad onto his plate.

He flung the plate onto the floor with one sweep of his arm. It shattered, slinging salad across her white vinyl floor.

"You filthy old man!" she raged, raising the hand holding the spoon.

He ducked his head and scuttled quickly to the door. "Ain't coming back!" he shouted. "Mean!" He hurried off up the long curve of the drive.

She ought to stop him. He was nearly eighty, had no business walking that far along what were still, for all their traffic, country roads. No sidewalks, fast cars, too many hills and curves, steep ditches on each side. She was about to get her keys when the buzzer sounded on the microwave. She turned back to the kitchen with a shrug. Uncle Billy had walked all over the county all his life. One more walk wouldn't kill him. And if it did...?

Her mouth curved in an unpleasant smile. That would increase everybody else's share of the pot.

Lost in dreams of what she would do with all that money, Martha Sloan spent a happy hour baking brownies. She was icing the last batch when she heard someone come in the back door. She turned—startled, but unafraid. It was afternoon in a safe suburban community. She knew most of the people who came to her back door.

She knew this one.

She waved the visitor toward a chair. "I'll be with you in a second. This icing is getting hard, and I can't stop right now."

She bent, intent on her work.

A moment later, a slight noise made her turn. Her eyes widened, more in surprise than fear. "Why, what . . . ?"

Those were the last words she ever spoke.

# SEVEN

ABOUT FIVE THAT AFTERNOON, Sheila reached into the backseat for her suitcases. "Come on, Lady, let's go look at our new kitchen," she encouraged her hesitant dog, "then we'll go for a long walk."

She arched her back and took a deep breath of the fresh spring air. How marvelous to breathe! How marvelous to feel you were going to live—and wanted to! She had slept all day Monday in Aunt Mary's dainty guest room, rousing only to drink the homemade chicken soup that Aunt Mary's housekeeper, Mildred, considered essential to any cure. Last evening she had browsed for an hour through her new book, been well enough to find it funny and informative. By today she had even felt like returning to work.

In the afternoon, Mr. Hashimoto had listened to her report of last week's meetings with grave courtesy, then surprised her with a sudden smile. "Go home early. You have earned it."

Now, after picking up Lady, she was—finally—coming home.

She climbed the steps to her front door with a sense of déjà vu. Sara Sims had come onto the breezeway.

"Hey! Want to eat with me? Kevin was coming, but he had to go to Savannah. He just called, and I'd already bought pots of food."

She probably had. Sara Sims's idea of a proper meal was almost as extensive as her Aunt Ruby's.

Sheila shook her head. "I haven't unpacked since last week, and I'm still getting over my cold. I'm just going to take Lady for a walk, settle in a bit, and go to bed early. Thanks anyway."

Modern construction had triumphed in its usual fashion. The new kitchen floor clashed with the countertops, the new carpet was gray-beige instead of gray-blue, and her sofa was still spotted and stained. Sheila regarded the changes sourly, then sneezed. She'd call the manager later. First she must get the remaining smoke out while she could still breathe. She moved about the apartment opening windows, expecting to step on an asphyxiated carpenter in a dark corner.

Finally she pulled on a pair of jeans and a cotton shirt, and stuffed a pocket with Kleenex as a precaution. "Come on, Lady!"

They hurried around the building and onto a woodland trail, cleverly routed so that no buildings could be seen. In early spring the trails meandered through a fairyland of lacy white dogwoods, pale pink redbuds, and blazing azaleas. Today the trees were deep green and full of robins, woodpeckers, and darting jays. The air felt moist and clean, smelled of damp earth and honeysuckle. Full of the buoyancy that rewards those who survive a bad cold, Sheila felt that nothing awful would ever happen again.

Then, just as she strode past high rhododendrons and around a curve, she collided with a young man in a gray sweatsuit.

Lady, startled, circled behind the man, jerking her leash. That jerked Sheila, who took an inadvertent step forward. The man took a step back, tripped over the leash, grabbed Sheila for support, and took her down with him as he fell. Her knee slid several inches along the gravel path. Her hand, still clutching the leash, was trapped beneath him as they sprawled in an awkward embrace. Lady, held by the lead, planted her feet firmly on Sheila's shoulder and voiced sharp disapproval in her ear.

"Get off! You're heavy!" The man struggled to rise.

"I would if I could figure out how," Sheila replied with asperity. "Hush, Lady! You, lift your back so I can free my hand."

"I can't lift my back. We're both lying on it." He wiggled his shoulders and she managed to unclench her fist and withdraw her hand without removing more than half its skin.

She pushed herself up and painfully climbed to her feet. The man remained where he was, groping with one hand. "Do you see my glasses?" He found them and, propping himself on one elbow, settled them on his nose and looked up at her with eyes more caramel than brown. "Thanks. I'm terribly sorry..."

Lady bent over and gave his chin a forgiving lick. He looked from the dog to her mistress. "Oh, no, not you!" He slapped one palm against his forehead. Lady tried to lick him again, but he pushed her away. "Not now, girl. Can't you see I'm in trouble?"

Baffled, Sheila gingerly rubbed her skinned palm and lifted her leg to shake out her sore knee. From the way it was burning, it was skinned, too. She glowered at the young man, who continued to lie on the path gazing up at her with cheerful dismay.

"I don't see anything funny in all this," she told him sourly.

"Nor do I. Give me a hand."

She put out her left (and unscathed) hand, and was surprised. He was shaped like a Teddy bear, but he had a grip of steel. Standing they were much the same height. She was probably one inch taller—and fifteen years older—than he.

He rubbed one hand through his brown hair in a way that destroyed whatever style it had had, and shuffled his feet like a little boy in the principal's office. "Are you hurt? I really am sorry. And a minute ago, I didn't mean..." He stopped, tried again. "I mean, when I said 'Oh, no,' I didn't mean..."

"You certainly did." She was both angry and amused. Did he always dance around babbling, or was he truly embarrassed? And why? It had been a legitimate accident. But her hand and knee were throbbing.

Lady nosed the toe of the man's running shoe as if it were an old friend. "Have you and Lady met?" Sheila demanded. "Have *we* met?"

He gave her a rueful smile. "We haven't, but I've met your dog, under equally embarrassing circumstances. I'd planned to show up tonight with wine and apologies—really bowl you over. Instead—"

"—you showed up on the path and bowled us *all* over, saving yourself some trouble."

He sighed. "Not hardly. You see, I'm Andrew Lee, the fellow downstairs. I burned up your kitchen. Lady and I met Sunday across a hole in your floor. I really do want to make amends. For a start, you can call me Torcher."

"Torture?" she repeated blankly. "Don't you mean torturer?"

"Not torture, Torcher." He spelled it, his face perfectly solemn. But his tawny eyes were twinkling.

She kept her face equally grave. "Oh. Of course. Well, Torcher, I'm glad to meet you, I think. Do you make a habit of burning places up and knocking people down?"

"Not often. You just seem to have that effect on me." He pushed his glasses up his nose with one forefinger and looked at her with frank admiration. "When I moved in and discovered I had two beautiful women overhead. I seem to have gone to pieces."

"Or up in smoke?" she suggested.

He grinned. "Yeah. Hey, did you suffer much fire damage?"

"I'll only need to sue you for new furniture, new clothes, and the dead loss of last Sunday afternoon, but poor Lady! Imagine wondering for the rest of your life if the floor under your feet is going up in flames. Not to mention the trauma of having to spend two days with my aunt."

"A perfect ogre?"

"To dogs. Instead of wine, maybe you'd better bring dog biscuits. Lady's the one recovering."

Lady busily nosed a poplar in search of small game.

"I see," he nodded. "Absolute shock. I'll have to see what I can do. But first I have five miles to run. Want to join me?"

Sheila shuddered. "No, thanks. We'll proceed decorously in the other direction."

"Very well. See you later." With that promise (or threat?) he jogged virtuously on his way. He was not a clumsy runner, she noted. Perhaps his collision had been her own fault? She continued her walk at a hobble, keeping well to the side of the path.

SHE SOON WALKED the stiffness out of her knee, but it was smarting when she turned Lady toward home. Limping but at peace with the world, she was wholly unprepared for two police officers standing in the breezeway with Sara Sims. She wondered if Sara Sims had forgotten to pay a speeding ticket.

Then she saw the tears streaming down her neighbor's face.

"Sheila! Oh, Sheila!" She choked out the words through sobs.

Sheila took the steps two at a time in spite of her sore knee. "What's the matter?"

The taller officer stepped forward to speak, but Sara Sims flung herself at Sheila, nearly knocking her down. "It's Mama. Mama!" Sara Sims clutched her so tightly they both staggered. Lady braced herself on the bottom step and loudly reproved the men who had upset her friend. The shorter officer hurried down to steady them, gently disengaged Sara Sims, and drew them up the stairs.

"Come in here." Sheila hurried to unlock her door.

Steered between the men, Sara Sims walked through the door like a woman both blind and drunk.

The taller and, now Sheila could see, younger officer drew back. "I smell smoke!"

"It's okay," she assured him. "I had a fire Sunday. It's fine now." She led the way to the living room. Sara Sims fell onto the couch, sobbing wildly.

Lady was such a nuisance, dancing around barking at the officers, that Sheila shoved her into the guest room. Then she hurried back to the living room. "What's happened to your mother?"

Sara Sims raised her blotched face. Tears glued wisps of hair to her cheeks and forehead. Her lashes stuck together in little stars. "She's . . . been . . . shot!"

Sheila felt as if all the air had left her own body. Her knees buckled, and she sat on the first thing she came to—the coffee table. "Where? How?"

The younger officer cleared his throat and stepped forward. "At home, ma'am. Early afternoon, we think."

On top of her horror, Sheila felt insulted. She was not old enough to merit that "ma'am"! She frowned in his direction, then turned back to her neighbor.

Sara Sims clutched her hand and shook her head in disbelief. "Somebody shot her in the kitchen! Right in her own kitchen! And nobody found her until Daddy got home from work." She put her head down on the edge of the couch and bawled.

Sheila turned to the second officer in disbelief. "She's dead?"

It wasn't really a question, but he nodded, eyes grave. "I'm afraid so." He jerked his head toward Sara Sims, now shaking uncontrollably. "Do you have a blanket handy?"

"Of course." She liked him better than the other. Not merely because he hadn't called her "ma'am," but also because his eyes reflected genuine concern.

She tucked Sara Sims into a fleecy plaid blanket. Eventually the young woman stopped shaking, but her breath still came in deep, ragged gasps. Sheila went for a washcloth and wiped her flushed face. "Let me get you something to drink."

"Very sweet hot tea would be best, ma'am," the first officer suggested. He really was insufferable. Did he think she had learned nothing in her many years? She had even learned to boil water—in a microwave, yet. In exactly a minute, she was back at Sara Sims's side with a steaming mug.

"Do you need to go to your parents' house? Would you like for me to drive you?" In her neighbor's place, Sheila would hate to arrive in a police car. Her instincts were sound. Sara Sims took a big swallow of tea, a bigger breath, and gave her a grateful nod.

IT COULD HAVE BEEN an hour's drive behind commuters returning home from Atlanta, parents driving children to and from practices, and teenagers heading to and from part-time jobs. Sheila usually made a point of being home before Gwinnett's late rush hour began.

But the young officer came to life in the driver's seat. Siren blaring, he cut a swath through startled traffic and roared onto I-85, Sheila close behind. When they left the expressway, they screamed along country roads at a speed that—even with a stunned young woman beside her and a sore knee to which her jeans were now stuck with her own blood—delighted her soul. It was the closest she would ever come to driving in the Monte Carlo.

Sara Sims was silent most of the way. Finally she said, in a small voice, "Mama and I didn't... We fought a lot. But now I wish..." She stopped.

This was when Sheila was supposed to murmur platitudes about mother love being greater than quarrels and reassure Sara Sims about her mother's eternal destiny. Since she was not convinced Martha Sloan had known what mother love was, and was unwilling to perjure herself about the woman's probable destiny, she merely gave Sara Sims a quick smile and concentrated on keeping the galvanized officer in view.

"It's the house on the left." Sara Sims needn't have spoken. The policeman had made a spectacular turn and kicked up gravel as he slid to a stop. Sheila followed only a shade more sedately down the curving drive.

Although Sara Sims's great-grandmother lived in a small white frame house with a tin roof and the next generation of her family in modest brick ranch homes, her parents' home was an enormous old white house with four fat columns. It sat surrounded by several acres of fenced, landscaped lawn with a pond at the bottom.

"Circle the house and park in back," Sara Sims directed. Then she gave a weak cry. "Oh!"

Sometimes it is the smallest things that bring reality crashing in. In this case, a fluttering strip of bright plastic, strung across the drive as a police barrier. Sara Sims covered her face and began to rock, sobbing helplessly.

The officers were no help. They had already leaped from their car and headed around the corner. Sheila went around the Maxima and took Sara Sims's arm. She climbed out like a person dreaming. They started for the front door, Sheila hobbling stiffly and painfully. This was no time for personal problems, but the movement was disengaging the cloth of her jeans from her wounded knee. It took all the willpower she could summon to walk toward Dudley.

On Sunday, Dudley had looked merely well-groomed—gray suit, red tie, white shirt, well-shined shoes. Today, he looked human as he came to meet them.

He was coatless, wearing a white shirt with cuffs rolled up. His arms were clasped across his midsection as if to hold himself from falling apart. His tie was crooked, his shirttail coming out on one side, and his eyes were red behind their round glasses. Several strands of limp hair hung in his face.

Sara Sims pushed the hair back with a gentle hand. They looked at each other for a long moment, then she went into his arms. "Oh, Daddy! I got here as fast as I could. I couldn't drive..."

"Of course not, honey. Of course not." He buried his face in her hair.

Sheila waited a short distance from them. Was there more help she could offer? She also had to admit she was curious. What exactly had happened here on this beautiful spring afternoon?

She limped a discreet distance from the huddled mourners and contemplated the house. Two stories with a high roof, it stood proudly among enormous oaks, hickories and magnolias, haughtily aloof from a distant subdivision which tried to accomplish the same graciousness on half-acre plots with new plantings.

Dudley's suddenly raised voice interrupted Sheila's thoughts. "...shot in the chest. I came home from work and went through to the kitchen. She was lying on the floor."

Sara Sims stroked his sleeve. "I want to see her, Daddy."

He shook his head. "Not like that, honey. Not like that." His voice broke. Sara Sims buried her face in his coat and he held her very close.

Sara Sims raised her eyes to Dudley's again. "I still want to see her. It has happened, Daddy, and if I don't, I'll always imagine it anyway—maybe worse than it really is. I have to," she repeated urgently.

"We'll ask the officers." He spoke in the "we'll see" tone that every child hates. But Sheila suspected Sara Sims would get her way in the end. She was as much her mother's child as her father's.

Dudley turned toward the house and pulled her with him.

They had forgotten Sheila, until she turned toward her car. Her feet grated on the gravel.

"Oh, Sheila, don't go. Not yet!" Sara Sims put out one hand to stop her.

Sheila looked a question at Dudley. He nodded. "If you just stay until somebody else arrives. Ruby, Cline..."

Somebody did.

With a whirl of gravel, a muddy red pickup truck slid to a stop. Roger swung from the cab. He pointed first to the police car, then at the fluttering barrier. "What are *they* doing *here?*"

"What are *you* doing here?" Sara Sims retorted.

"I was down this way and thought I'd stop and see Uncle Dudley about something. What's going on?" He turned to Dudley, dismissing the women as incapable of giving straight information.

"Martha Sloan has been murdered."

Dudley said it quietly enough, but Roger's jaw dropped, his eyes bulged, and he expelled one enormous breath. "No kidding."

Dudley shook his head. Sara Sims took an angry step toward her cousin, willing to pour out her fury on the first hateful person who came along. "Would he kid about something like that?"

"I guess not. What happened? How did they do it?"

To Sheila's ears, he sounded more curious than grieving. Dudley seemed to feel the same. "She was shot, Roger. And Sara Sims and I need to get inside." His arm still rested on his daughter's shoulder. He drew her toward the door. "The police will want to talk with us, and I'm afraid reporters will be here any minute." A smile lit his thin face. "I'm surprised they didn't follow Sheila in. It was a notable arrival."

She smiled back. "To say the least."

"Where is she?" Roger looked around as if expecting to see his aunt's body decorating the lawn.

"In the kitchen," Dudley said shortly. "Are you coming in, too? The police may have some questions for you."

"Me? Well, sure, I guess so. I don't know what I can tell them, but . . ." Roger sprinted onto the porch and held the door.

Sheila was about to say her farewells again now that Roger had arrived, but Dudley put out a persuasive hand. "Sheila, I hate to ask it, but *could* you stay, just until somebody comes?"

She agreed with his unspoken assessment: in an emergency, Roger wasn't a somebody who counted.

She nodded. "I can make calls for you, and fend off reporters until somebody else gets here."

As she moved to repark her car, however, she fervently hoped Ruby or Evelyn would arrive before the television cameras. Sheila herself might not mind appearing on television in jeans, but Aunt Mary and Mr. Hashimoto would be equally scandalized.

# EIGHT

INSIDE, the house was much as she had imagined it—a
square hall with a bent staircase along the left wall and back,
the living room through an arch to the left, the dining room
through an arch to the right. Behind the staircase was another room, then a swinging door to the back wing. All was
furnished in elegant mahogany, but the colors and fabrics
were bland, as if a decorator had feared to offend. Knowing Martha Sloan even slightly, Sheila understood.

Sara Sims and her father were seated side by side on the
couch. Roger sat in one chair by the fireplace and in the
other sat a broad man with a shock of white hair and ruddy
cheeks. He wore a rumpled gray suit, a blue shirt with cig-
arettes in the sagging breast pocket, and a navy striped tie
that was slightly askew.

"...and you can't think of any enemies Mrs. Tait might
have had?" He broke off when he saw Sheila. "Are you a
member of the family?"

Even in grief, Dudley retained impeccable manners. He
rose. "Sheila, this is Detective Alan Belk. Mr. Belk, Sheila
Travis, Sara Sims's neighbor. She drove Sara Sims over.
Come on in, Sheila."

From the kitchen they heard the rise and fall of voices.
Roger shifted uneasily in his chair, kept looking in that direction.

Sheila took a large wing chair and stretched out her sore
knee to ease it. As the others talked, she studied the detective. Closer to sixty than fifty, he was thick but not fat, with
nicotine-stained fingers and large teeth. His hair was long on
top, looked as strong as rope. The whole man gave the im-

pression of having been carved from a chunk of Stone Mountain granite.

When his blue eyes met hers, however, they were mild, the color of a June sky. They rested on her, then moved on, leaving her strangely reassured. This man, she felt, cared deeply about people whose grief he must probe.

"Now," he said to Sara Sims, "if you can tell me where you were this afternoon..."

"You suspect *me?*" Sara Sims clenched one fist, ready to strike.

"Oh, no," he soothed her. "This is just a formality. Just tell me where you were..."

"Well, I was at work, then I went to the grocery store, and I went home. Have you," her voice trembled, "found the gun?"

"Not yet, but we will."

"If it was me, I'd throw it in the pond."

"We'll look there first thing." He sounded like he meant it, wasn't just humoring a child. Sara Sims answered promptly when he continued, "Now you work where? And you shopped where?"

Gently he drew Sara Sims's afternoon in fine detail, then turned to Roger. "And you, sir?"

Roger's hands went up in immediate denial. "Me? I had nothing to do with this!"

The detective took out a cigarette, looked at it, and put it back in his pocket with obvious regret. "I'm not accusing you of anything, just asking where you were this afternoon."

"I was here and there. I'm a builder, with several houses under construction. I travel all over the county in a given day. Today I spent most of my time at our site near Dacula. My crews can verify that."

The detective interrupted. "Just give me your name and a number where we can reach you." That completed, Belk turned to Dudley. "And you, Mr. Tait?"

"I was down at the courthouse all morning, met friends for lunch, and went to my law office about one. The commission offices can vouch for the morning, several people can vouch for lunch, and my secretary can supply details about the afternoon. I assure you that I did not kill my wife." He gave a strangled little laugh. "She was worth a great deal to me."

He could, Sheila reflected, be speaking of affection or money. Either way, he had lost more than he had gained today.

She was distracted from the policeman's next remarks by an embarrassing rumble from her stomach, reminding her she had had no dinner. Heaven only knew when she would get something now. She wondered if Sara Sims had eaten before the police arrived. Dudley certainly hadn't, with Martha Sloan lying at his feet.

Belk rose. "We are checking for prints, of course, and for anyone who may have seen anything—maybe a neighbor. But—" he shrugged massive shoulders "—you don't have any near neighbors, and traffic on the road here goes so fast. I doubt that we'll get much there. Still, we'll leave no stone unturned." He went back to the kitchen.

The doorbell pealed. Roger went to answer it, but halfway across the room, his beeper sounded. He paused, disconcerted.

"I'll get the door," Sheila offered, trying to conceal her limp as she walked.

It was the first reporter. Turning him over to Dudley, she went, at Dudley's suggestion, to the den behind the stairs to call Ruby.

Roger was still on the phone, his back to the door.

The swinging door to the back squeaked open as a policeman hurried through to the hall. In an instant, Sheila saw a white floor, gleaming counters, and Martha Sloan. She lay on her back, one arm outstretched, face up. She could have been resting except for the red stain on her blouse.

Roger whirled, saw Sheila. "Listen, I've got to go. I'll come through. I swear it." He hung up. "Okay, I'm finished."

Sheila scarcely heard him. She had been thinking about what she had seen. Whoever had killed Martha Sloan had faced her to do it—and gotten very close. She was surprised to feel tears on her own cheeks, and anger within her. Nobody ought to die like that!

Roger strolled to the swinging door to the kitchen, started to push it open. She grabbed his arm and he stopped, a balky look on his face. "I was just going to see if they needed any help."

"They don't, and I do. I'm supposed to call your Aunt Ruby. Do you know the number?"

"Sure." He rattled it off, then returned to the living room, obviously disgruntled not to get at least a glimpse of the body.

Cline answered the phone. When Sheila identified herself, she could almost see him beam. "Why, hey, honey. Of co'se I remember you. What you want?"

"I'm over at Sara Sims's parents' home. Mr. Tait asked me to call. Mrs. Tait has…" She paused, wondering whether to blurt out the truth. He was, she remembered, well over seventy.

"What's the woman been up to now? I'd let you talk to Ruby, but she's plucking a chicken. Billy took a notion to chop off the head of her best layin' hen this afternoon. Now she's got to fix it for tomorrow's dinner. She's madder'n a wet hen herself."

Sheila decided to give him forthrightness equal to his own. "Mrs. Tait has been murdered, Mr. Shaw."

"Murdered? Did you say 'murdered'?"

"She was shot. Sometime after noon, I believe."

"Lord 'a mercy." There was a silence. She sensed he had sunk into a nearby chair. "Lord 'a mercy," he repeated in disbelief. "Just after noon, you say? Was there…" he paused "was there much blood?"

"I don't know," Sheila replied untruthfully. She felt that was something he ought to hear from the family—or the police.

He was already talking again. "Wait a minute. I'll get Ruby. That hen'll have to wait." He laid the receiver down with a loud clunk.

Ruby came to the phone as breathless as if she'd run a marathon. For several minutes Sheila could only agree that it *was* a terrible thing, that you *couldn't* tell what the world was coming to, and that we *do* have to remember that our lives are in God's hands. "Was there a lot of blood?" Ruby finally echoed Cline.

"I haven't been in there," Sheila said, truthful this time.

"And they don't have any idea who did it?"

"Not that I've heard."

Ruby didn't speak for a long moment, then wheezed, "Well, you tell Dudley we're on our way. Tell him to wait till I come and I'll call Bubba and Evelyn and Merle and Aubrey. And poor Bessie, of course. I declare, I just can't believe... Must have been a total stranger. Probably one of those homeless tramps."

Sheila stemmed the flow of words and suggested they come at once. "Nobody has eaten dinner," she added, inspired.

"I'll pack up a few things, then. I don't know what I can find, but something. Poor, poor Dudley!"

Sheila thought "poor Martha Sloan" might also be appropriate.

As they were about to hang up, she asked, "Will you tell your mother and brother, or shall I call them?"

"Oh, no!" Ruby spoke quickly, as if Sheila was already dialing. "It would just upset her, honey. Tomorrow I'll tell her Martha Sloan's been taken. That's all they ever need to know. They don't read papers, and their TV's broke. If we see Wart before we leave, I'll tell him, but he might not be back yet. He's been gone all day. They don't need the shock at her age." With that jumble of pronouns, Ruby hung up.

Only then did Sheila remember who "poor Bessie" was: Martha Sloan's mother. Strange that Ruby would wait to notify her. She lived next door. Why not just bring her? Sheila didn't have time to wonder. A slew of reporters were at the door.

She deftly confined the reporters to the front yard and fended questions until she was heartily relieved to see Ruby and Cline's green pickup growl up the drive.

Noting its "Made in America by Americans for Americans" sticker, she was glad her Nissan was out of sight behind a bush.

Ruby climbed from the pickup in a light blue double-knit pantsuit. She sailed toward the porch in a cloud of righteousness and Avon, leaving open-mouthed reporters in her wake. She had taken one bag from the back of the pickup and motioned for Cline to hand a second to Sheila. "Come he'p me," she grunted. She was out of breath, face flushed and perspiring. She paused to press a hand to her chest before bustling in the front door.

Sheila was torn between following Ruby and remaining with the reporters, but Cline drew the reporters to himself. "I'm Mrs. Tait's uncle. Can I help you folks?"

Today he wore cowboy boots, a tan Western-style shirt, baggy brown pants, and mirrored sunglasses. Bombarded by several questions at once, he drew himself up like an out-of-shape John Wayne and rasped, "Give me a minute, fellas. I'll try to get the story straight, then I'll tell you what we know. Wait on the porch a spell. I'll be right back." Actually, what he said was "rat back," but everybody understood.

Relieved of duty, Sheila followed Ruby into the dining room and helped her set out a feast: ham, biscuits, plain biscuits, jam, sliced tomatoes, homemade pickles and pimento cheese, cold green beans, a loaf of bread, mayonnaise, and a plastic carton of potato salad. Sheila couldn't help wondering what had happened to the half-plucked chicken? She did not ask.

Ruby opened the potato salad and set it diffidently behind the rest. "We had to stop at the Winn Dixie for that. I didn't have any made up. But it tastes almost as good as mine."

"It looks delicious," Sheila said truthfully. She could eat it carton and all. She found silver in the buffet and took Limoges plates from the china cabinet. Martha Sloan would probably not have used her ornate repoussé and Limoges for an informal buffet, but unfortunately, Martha Sloan was not coming.

"I didn't devil eggs," Ruby wheezed on. "I didn't like to take time to boil them. I wanted to buy bananas for sandwiches, too, but the ones at Winn Dixie were green. Have we got enough, do you think?"

It would be enough unless the entire Confederate Army showed up. As she reassured the old woman, however, Sheila eyed her curiously. Was Ruby fluttering and fussing because she was nervous—or afraid? Murder in the family was a legitimate cause for nerves. But why did Ruby keep nibbling her thumbnail and looking over her shoulder at the kitchen door, as if expecting Martha Sloan to make a personal appearance?

"You all come in and eat a bit now," Ruby called to Dudley, Sara Sims, and Roger. "You may not get another chance."

"I couldn't eat a bite," Sara Sims said, pressing one fist to her mouth.

Dudley started to shake his head, too, then put one arm around his daughter. "Aunt Ruby's gone to a lot of trouble," he said softly. "Let's eat a little something." They fell in behind Roger, whose plate was already piled with food.

As soon as she was satisfied that they wouldn't starve, Ruby headed for the den telephone. "You'll need to look up some numbers for me," she gasped over her shoulder to Sheila, who had just picked up a plate. "I can't keep all these numbers in my head, and my eyes aren't what they used to be."

In the door to the den, Ruby stopped and pointed to the kitchen. "Is that where it was?" When Sheila nodded, she gently pushed the door open a crack and peeped in. Her broad back concealed Martha Sloan from Sheila's view, but she was surprised to see Cline leaning against one counter talking with the detective.

After a long look, Ruby gently let the door swing closed, stood for a minute to steady both it and herself. Then, trembling and pale, she turned to her mournful task.

Sheila was astonished at how brief Ruby could be when she chose. "Bubba? I'm at Martha Sloan's. She's been killed, honey, and it's terrible. You 'n Evelyn'd better get on over here. Roger's here already." She dug into her pocket and found a tissue. Her fingers clenched and unclenched on it as she spoke.

"Aubrey... ?" She used the same script, with slight variations, for every call. In less than fifteen minutes she had notified the family. She had also called two pastors—Martha Sloan's, from First Baptist Church, and another.

"We was all raised Primitive Baptist," she explained to Sheila after the last call. Her three chins quivered. "Billy 'n Cline and me still go the Sundays they have services. It's just once a month, you know. Martha Sloan turned Missionary Baptist when she married." She conveyed that her niece had gone from true blue to slightly off-green.

She waddled to the dining room. Sheila felt her stomach quiver in anticipation of a sandwich and some of Ruby's spurned store-bought potato salad, but Ruby stopped at the door.

"Would you just see how Cline's getting on before you eat, honey? I'll make sure the others get enough. I couldn't eat a bite myself. I'm too upset." Sheila left her standing beside the table, absently munching a ham biscuit.

On the front lawn Cline spoke into a reporter's microphone. "A stranger probably looking for money. Didn't get much, either. A little cash she kept for emergencies and the kitchen TV. Thank goodness he missed her wedding rings—fine diamonds.''

Why a thief would kill a woman in an isolated house, then fail to rob the house of jewelry, a personal computer, and an expensive stereo system, Cline did not explain. Another microphone thrust its way past the first. "Do the police have any clues to who the killer might be?"

"Not yet, but it was a tramp!" Cline was so convincing that Sheila could almost see the man, in ragged jeans and a red cap. Cline started to step away, reconsidered. "She wasn't bothered. People need to know that. He didn't mess with her or anything." Cline would never use the word "rape" in mixed company.

Afterward, Sheila congratulated him on his publicity skills. "I used to do that for the railroad when we had an accident." He pulled something from his pocket, rubbed it between his fingers, thrust it back hastily. It was a small wooden mouse. A talisman of some sort, she supposed.

He went on, "Reporters are pretty decent folks if you treat them fair. I wish they'd go on home, now, though." Sheila did, too.

Apparently, however, nothing else of importance had happened in the metro area today. The entire front yard remained a maelstrom of journalists, photographers, and sound crews trampling the Bermuda grass and hoping that either the police would appear with the body bag, or hysterical family members would arrive to provide TV viewers a thrill with their bedtime snack.

Sheila herself, more acquainted with murder than she liked to admit, found herself watching each face, too, as it arrived. She was not looking for hysterics. She was looking for guilt.

# NINE

BUBBA'S CAR caused the first stir. Sheila recognized the model immediately—a black '53 Buick in mint condition. Her grandfather had owned one just like it when she was a child. It was the first car she had ever recognized by name.

"What on earth?" Cline pulled his earlobe in surprise. "Bubba *never* drives that car when he's under the weather! I hope he gets here without killing himself—or somebody else."

As the Buick weaved down the drive, reporters dodged onto the grass and hovered behind magnolias and oaks until Bubba brought it to a jerky stop. Not until he started to climb out did they swarm, thrusting microphones into his face. He swatted them like mosquitoes.

"Get them things out of here. Who killed m' sister? That's what I want to know!" Still shouting, he reeled toward the house.

Cline stepped forward to help him to the door. "Where's Evelyn?"

Bubba stuck out his lower lip. "Wouldn't come with me. She'd—sh-said she'd drive her own car." He lurched toward the door.

Evelyn arrived a few minutes later in a blue Ford. Her plump body was stuffed into jeans and a red T-shirt, and she made her way with obvious embarrassment through the reporters. "I don't know anything," she protested again and again. "I don't know a thing."

When she reached the porch, she clutched Sheila's elbow. "I came just like I was. This is awful!" She indicated the journalists.

Inside, she ran one hand down her hip. "I've always dressed up to come to Martha Sloan's. Feels funny, being here in jeans."

"Welcome to the club," Sheila agreed.

"But your kind of jeans go anywhere," Evelyn objected. "I look like what I am—straight from work at the hardware store." She looked up and saw Sara Sims carrying a stack of laundry toward the stairs. "Oh, honey, let me do that for you."

"I'll do it. I need to keep busy." Sara Sims clutched the clothes to her chest and hurried up the stairs.

She was very pale. Sheila suspected she had just finished viewing her mother's body. Had she grabbed up laundry as she passed the utility room? It wasn't surprising. As someone once said, "An abnormal reaction to an abnormal situation is normal behavior."

Evelyn seemed to understand. "Sure, honey," she called gently, "You take those on up. Could I make coffee?"

Sara Sims paused, shook her head, then changed her mind. "Coffee would be good. Aunt Ruby forgot to bring something to drink. See if the police will let you have the coffee maker and milk and sugar, and get a pot going in the dining room."

"Sure." Evelyn moved toward the back of the house, at ease now that she could be useful. Sheila returned to watch arrivals.

Aubrey came in a silver Chrysler. He was dressed in a green polo shirt and gray pants with a sharp crease. Sheila wondered if he'd taken time to change before he left, or had already been dressed for an evening out. He looked lean, tanned, and fit. Reporters crowded around him for a statement.

He gave the cameras a charming smile, turned his silver hair to catch the best light, and expressed his sympathy for the family. He was careful to point out, however, that the dead woman was his *late* wife's niece. Viewers might think he had not seen Martha Sloan for months, if not years.

As he joined Sheila on the porch, one female reporter exclaimed to another, "He's beautiful!" He was. He was also, Sheila discovered when he clutched her arm, trembling like an aspen. Was he nervous of reporters, or terrified by something else?

"I can only stay a minute," he whispered, his dentures clicking. "I just came by to tell Dudley how sorry I am. Can you tell me what happened, exactly?" She told him as exactly as she could, not being privy to any more than she had heard from Cline.

"And to think I was playing golf."

Roger joined them on the porch. "Hello, Uncle Aubrey."

"Why, hello, Roger!" Aubrey grasped him by the forearm and gave him a hug before hurrying inside. Viewers would think he hadn't seen Roger for months, either.

Roger spoke out of one side of his mouth, "I called and told Erika to stay home. I didn't think we should bring the kids over." Sheila, picturing the children cavorting among reporters or climbing over Martha Sloan's furniture, heartily agreed. "Sorry I tied up the phone earlier," he continued in a low voice. "I had to return a call." He probably hoped she'd say how much she had heard. She wasn't about to tell him. He shuffled his feet uneasily, then said, "There's still food in the dining room, if you're hungry."

She was. In a minute she would take a bite out of his forearm. She was also beginning to shiver in her light cotton shirt. Atlanta is, after all, in the foothills of the Blue Ridge Mountains. Hot days are almost always followed by cool nights. She turned to follow him in.

Aunt Mary, of course, would disapprove. Having eaten dinner in her own penthouse dining room, she would think Sheila should forgo food in order to sidle around back to search for clues. Sheila wasn't interested in clues. Detective Alan Belk exuded ability to handle this case.

She planned to eat a bite, tell Sara Sims good night, and go home.

Sara Sims was not there.

Everyone else was. Dudley and Ruby sat on either end of the couch. Cline slumped, fat legs wide and hands dangling between them, on a wing back chair by the fireplace. Aubrey sat, legs primly crossed, on a straight chair in one corner, distant from the others. Roger lounged about in the hall. Bubba roamed the living room, picking up objects and putting them down. Evelyn moved competently around the dining room.

Dirty plates scattered about showed that the family had taken advantage of Aunt Ruby's hospitality. Sheila stepped into the dining room, ready to fill a plate of her own. Roger was wrong. Only half a biscuit and a few lone pickles remained.

"Did you ever get anything to eat?" Evelyn asked, dismayed.

Sheila willed her stomach not to betray her. "It's okay. I'm just going to speak with Sara Sims and go."

Evelyn looked around, puzzled. "I don't know where she is. I haven't seen her since she went upstairs."

If Sara Sims preferred to grieve in her old room, Sheila understood. She would tiptoe out the front door and talk with her later.

But Roger had taken a position that blocked the archway between dining room and hall. Hands in pockets, he now cocked his ears toward the kitchen and remarked, "They're taking her out."

Immediately everyone became aware of the unmistakable bumps, thumps, and one raised voice. "Easy now!"

"Oh, God," Ruby breathed, covering her face. Cline pressed his fingers to his lips. Dudley closed his eyes as if in prayer.

Bubba looked around the room with an avid stare. "You got anything to drink, Dudley?"

"In the kitchen, Bubba, but I can't get it now."

Sheila wondered if he would have gotten it anyway.

"I got coffee made, hon, as soon as they bring me some milk and sugar," Evelyn told him.

Bubba perched on the front of a vacant chair with a mild oath.

"I wonder if they'll ever get the guy who killed her?" Roger asked, earning Sheila's Gauchest of the Year award. He automatically assumed it was a man, of course. In Roger's book, only a man would do anything important. This time, she hoped it was a man who had.

She wanted to leave, but not when every eye was focused on Roger at the dining room door.

Cline, from his chair near the fireplace, spluttered at his great-nephew. "Of all the half-assed questions!—pardon my French."

Dudley waved him aside. "It's okay, Cline. We have an excellent police force, Roger. I am certain they will do their best."

A police officer came in from the back. Everyone tensed.

It was the young officer who had been at Sara Sims's earlier. He carried a tray containing a cream pitcher and sugar bowl, and gave Sheila a smile of recognition across Roger's shoulder. "Just bringing in the other things you asked for, ma'am. The chief will be back with everybody a little later."

"Move, Roger," Evelyn ordered. "You're blocking the door." He backed up to lean against the buffet. "Now you're smack in front of the coffee pot! Honestly! Go sit somewhere." She gave him a light smack. He drifted away into the living room.

Meanwhile, the policeman handed Sheila the tray. "There you are, ma'am." Resigned both to staying and to his offensive form of address, she took it to the buffet and began to help Evelyn pour.

The coffee smelled so good it made her eyes water. She vowed she would make sure she got at least half a cup.

Evelyn called to the others. "I hope nobody needs Sweet 'n Low. They forgot it."

"We've got some in the china cabinet." Dudley rose, opened the glass door, and handed her several small packets stored in a lovely hand-painted bowl.

Roger, having joined Ruby on the couch, was now seeing the world from a lower perspective. "Is that blood you've got on your shirt, Uncle Dudley?"

Dudley looked down in surprise. As every eye in both rooms gazed in horror at several brown spots on his shirttail, he grimaced. "I suppose it is. When I found her, I lifted her head, hoping..." He stopped, folded his lips inward and tightened them. "Sorry."

"It's okay." Evelyn handed him a steaming cup. "Take this with you, and run upstairs to change."

Bless her, Sheila thought.

But Roger wasn't through. "Why did you get blood on your *shirt*, Uncle Dudley? When did you take off your coat?"

"If you are accusing my daddy of anything, Roger Sims, you can go home!" Sara Sims stood halfway down the stairs, eyes blazing.

"Oh no, I didn't mean..." Roger held up one hand as if to protect himself. Sheila understood how he felt. Sara Sims looked like a bantam hen ready to attack.

Dudley gave her a weak smile. "It's okay, honey. I always take my coat off to drive home, but Roger may not know that."

"Oh." Roger rose. "I'd better call Erika again. Any idea how long we'll be here, Uncle Dudley? The police won't want to talk to me again, will they?"

Aubrey rose, too. "I ought to be getting home, as well. I just wanted to see you, Dudley, for a minute and say how sorry I am."

Dudley shook his head wearily. "The police say we all have to be tested to see if we've fired a gun today."

"It's just a formality," Cline hastened to reassure them.

"Not me," Aubrey protested. "I'm not really family."

"Sure you are, Uncle Aubrey," Roger replied, "and you had as much reason to kill her as anybody. You always hated her guts."

Several people gasped. Evelyn took a quick step of protest. But it was Bubba who said, with unexpected authority, "Roger, apologize to you uncle!"

To Sheila's surprise, Roger turned red and obeyed.

Aubrey accepted the apology with icy dignity, then Roger headed for the den, to general relief.

Ruby, trying to smooth over the incident, spoke in short, breathy sentences. "Merle asked if she should come. I said no, but to call Amy. Faye's up in Roswell at some school game. Won't get home until late, and there's no way to call her."

Sara Sims's next sentence baffled Sheila. It sounded like "Did you call Dunkin' Bow?" She could not picture the family having an Indian friend intimate enough to merit a call.

Ruby was not at all baffled. "I didn't know how. You ought to do it, honey." She pressed a hand to her fat cheeks as if to cool them. "Who could have done such a terrible thing?"

Cline spoke at once. "Some tramp, sugarplum. Has to be."

Dudley, halfway up the stairs, passed a hand over his forehead. "I should be the one to call Dunkin' Bow."

"Get dressed and finish your coffee first," Evelyn called up to him, "and pull on a sweater. You look chilled clean to the bone."

Now that she'd said it, Sheila realized that was exactly how he looked—as if the blood had frozen in his veins. He nodded and continued up the stairs.

Sheila moved into the hall in time to hear Sara Sims moan, "Please, dear God, let him call before time for the news."

"Who's Dunkin' Bow?" Sheila whispered. When Sara Sims replied, she was glad thought-reading was not yet possible.

"My big brothers. Dunk works for our congressman up in Washington and Bo's in graduate school at the University of Georgia. They won't believe this has happened. I can't either! Sheila, tell me it's all a dream!" She clutched her friend's arm with a grip that threatened to cut off the circulation.

Sheila held her while the young woman sobbed into her shoulder. From the couch, sniffs and wheezes indicated Ruby was also weeping.

Cline tapped his boot on the carpet like the drip of a faucet, and kept his eyes fixed on his own toe except when he darted worried glances at Ruby. Evelyn moved silently about the dining room, picking up dishes and putting them down, uncertain what to do in the absence of a sink.

Finally Dudley came downstairs, wearing a clean plaid shirt, red pullover, slacks, and loafers. He seemed to have put back on some of his usual aplomb with fresh clothes.

As he entered the room, Aubrey spoke. His voice sounded very loud amid the silence. "Has anybody told Bessie? I could fetch her."

Everyone froze—except for their eyes. Gazes darted from face to face and around the ceiling. Then, to Sheila's astonishment, pandemonium broke out.

It was as if they used that one issue—whether Martha Sloan's mother should be told, and how—to vent all other feelings.

"... make a scene!"

"... can't keep her from ..."

"... loves evening news!"

"... knows what she'll say?"

They spoke loudly and simultaneously. Sheila couldn't even distinguish voices. Only Aubrey was silent. He wore the satisfied smile of a child who has let the cat in among the parakeets.

The heat of their argument brought the young officer from the kitchen. Sheila waved him back. "They're just discussing how to tell an older member of the family."

"Oh? I thought somebody else was being murdered." He backed into the kitchen with a puzzled frown. Sheila awarded him Second Gauchest of the Year.

At last Dudley held up one hand. The room fell silent. "She's sure to find out," he said in a resigned tone. "She always watches the news. So we'd better let Aubrey bring her over here now and get it over with."

Sheila thought than an extremely odd way to describe telling one's mother-in-law that her daughter was dead.

Until she saw Bessie.

FRAIL. That was the first word that came to mind.

Yet the woman was tall, with large bones.

She wore a caftan swirled in red, purple, yellow, and orange. Several strands of red beads dangled to her waist. Her feet were shod in youthful red pumps with flat heels. Her steel-gray hair was worn long and straight, curled under at the ends like a medieval page's, framing a still-beautiful face as unlined as a saint's.

A second look showed Sheila that her frailty was not of body, but of mind. Her wide-spaced blue eyes were lovely, but they had a terrible blankness behind them. And fear. This woman looked as if she lived her life in fear. After today, Sheila thought sadly, she might live in holy terror.

Sheila was sure none of the family had informed the reporters who Bessie was, but they had gotten the word somewhere. The woman was scarcely out of the car when they jostled about her.

"How did you hear about your daughter?" one asked, thrusting a mike into her face. Sheila wondered if he'd cut tact classes with Roger and the young policeman.

Aubrey took her elbow. "You don't have to talk with them now, Bessie. Come on inside."

"Oh, I don't mind." Bessie struggled visibly with her fear, then turned, gracious as royalty. "They have been so kind as to come." She turned to the reporter and smiled. "I'm visiting my daughter. I don't come very often, anymore. But I've come to see her tonight." She turned her eyes and caught the blaze of lights across the front of the house. "Oh!" She clapped her hands like a child. "She must be having a party!"

At that point, considerate reporters backed away. One diehard thrust a microphone into Bessie's face and motioned his camera crew to follow him. "You say you intend to see her?"

"I'm her mother. Of course I shall see her." She walked away, skirts swinging, beads clicking. She called back over her shoulder, "She doesn't say bad things to me. I'm not afraid of her."

He darted ahead, held the mike so close it impeded her walking. "How did you learn she had been murdered?"

Bessie gently pushed the mike away. Then she realized what he had said.

She stopped. One hand pressed her left cheek, and her terrible, blank eyes widened. "Murdered? Oh, dear!"

Her lids flickered uncertainly. She clutched Aubrey's elbow and swayed. Sheila hurried toward her from the porch.

Bessie was already recovering. "Oh, dear," she repeated, but now her tone was more dismayed than startled. Her hand left her cheek and extended toward heaven, one long forefinger pointing at the rising new moon. Her voice rose over the darkening lawn. "I told her. I told her again and again. But she just wouldn't listen."

Again she pressed her hand to her cheek, then, shaking her head, she shuffled toward the front door muttering audibly into the mike. "I was afraid of this. Oh dear, oh dear."

"You were afraid she'd be murdered?" A second reporter hurried up, willing to fling away good manners and consideration if a good story was finally breaking. "Who did you think would kill her?"

Bessie looked at him as if he were retarded. "Why, her husband, of course. The way she talked to him..."

"Mrs. Sims! Come inside!" Sheila took her other arm. Between them, she and Aubrey pulled Bessie up the steps.

The door opened. Dudley stood there, framed in light.

Bessie shook off her supporters and hurried across the porch, arms outstretched. "Poor Dudley!" she cried in a tone of pity every microphone would pick up and record. "I warned her, but she never listened. Oh, my poor, poor Dudley!"

# TEN

"Do you think he did it?"

The petite elderly woman set down her sherry and regarded her niece through eyes as brown as Sheila's own. Across the room, Porter Phillips held up a hand in protest.

"No fair, Miss Mary! Sheila can't solve it this quickly. That would spoil our chance to help!"

Sheila sipped coffee and regarded them both, then slid lower in the big, soft chair. Her knee, throbbing from Mildred's cleaning, rested on a huge ottoman. "Sheila isn't solving anything," she informed them. "Detective Belk is one of the most competent detectives I've ever met. By tomorrow the reporters will have Dudley's alibi and another suspect—and I have no idea who it will be. My preference, of course, would be Roger Sims, Martha Sloan's nephew. But that's only because he's so obnoxious."

"It's as good a reason as any," Porter assured her.

"Nonsense." Aunt Mary corrected him. "Obnoxious people take out their frustrations openly. It's the nice ones you have to watch out for."

"Then neither you nor I will ever commit murder," Sheila retorted. "Porter, now—after the kind way he forgave me for forgetting the High Museum tonight—he's probably seething with hidden frustrations!"

"Oh, my dear, I am! But I'm glad I thought to check here for you when you weren't at home. Miss Mary was a scintillating date, if a bit risqué in her comments on the paintings." He rolled his eyes.

"Don't try to leer, Porter," Aunt Mary chided him. "You look more like a slender Falstaff."

Sheila looked from one to the other. "A pun, Aunt Mary? What have you been drinking before you broke out the sherry? Let me remind you that I have just come from a house of—well, partial mourning, anyway, and I don't feel very giddy myself."

"Speaking of obnoxious..." Porter swirled his sherry and held it up to the light to admire the color. "I thought the media handling of the victim's mother was especially uncouth."

"It certainly was," Aunt Mary agreed. She enlightened Sheila. "Porter and I were watching my program at nine, and it was interrupted by a snippet of that interview."

Sheila wondered whether the greater offense in Aunt Mary's mind was what the reporters had done with poor Bessie, or that they had interrupted her program to do it.

Aunt Mary had gone smoothly on. "...a journalist's godsend. She," she concluded, emphasizing the pronoun, "was dressed." She eyed Sheila's jeans with distaste.

"I didn't have time to dress. I didn't even have time to take care of my knee! I'd just come from a walk."

"One *can* walk in dresses, dear. A woman of your position cannot afford to appear on television dressed like..."

To Sheila's astonishment, Porter interrupted Aunt Mary and got away with it. "What happened after you took Mrs. Sims inside? You stayed awhile, didn't you?"

"Yes, but only because I was determined to tell Sara Sims good-bye. Dudley and Aubrey took Bessie—Mrs. Sims—in and sat her on the sofa. She quivered, literally quivered as she looked around that room full of family. I was reminded of a bird dog Granddaddy had when I was little—Star Baby. Remember, Aunt Mary, how she would sit with her skin rippling all over?"

"That dog was too highly bred. I can sympathize with Mrs. Sims, however. That much family would give a *sane* woman shivers." Mary Beaufort considered one brother, one sister-in-law, and one niece sufficient for anybody.

Sheila smiled and savored her hot, strong coffee. She was glad she had come. She had not planned to drive all the way back to Aunt Mary's after she left the Tait home. She had intended to go straight home, eat soup, and finally unpack. Once in the car, however, she had headed automatically to the one person with whom she could discuss the murder—and to the hot supper Mildred would magically provide. She had also found Porter Phillips, drinking sherry and quite mellow about her forgetting their date.

Now, after supper, Sheila occupied her favorite chair while Porter lounged in its mate and Aunt Mary curled herself into one corner of her pink sofa, tiny feet tucked beneath her.

Mildred glided into the room to heat up Sheila's coffee. Sheila gave her a grateful smile and—mostly to challenge Aunt Mary's automatic "You drink too much coffee, dear"—took several sips before she spoke again.

"That could be Bessie's problem—being too highly bred. Sara Sims said that she comes from a First Family of Virginia. How and why she married a Georgia farm boy, I didn't like to ask, but the whole family treats her like porcelain. She almost is."

"What happened after she sat down, dear?"

"She took Dudley's hand and looked at him without saying a word. Tears filled her eyes and ran down her cheeks, and, like I said, she quivered. Finally she said the same thing she'd said to the reporter—'I told her, but she just wouldn't listen.' It was eerie, for her voice had no expression whatsoever."

"How did Mr. Tait respond?"

"Like the gentleman he is. He patted her hand and said, 'I didn't kill her, Nana. You needn't worry about that or anything else.' Then Bessie stood up, squeezed Dudley's hand, and said, 'I must go now. Thank you so much.' As if she'd been paying a brief social call! Dudley took her arm and escorted her to the door, exactly as if she *had* been paying a social call. Nobody else said a word. Then Aubrey drove her home."

Aunt Mary sipped sherry and thought that over. At last she pursed her lips. "Aubrey. That would be Mr. Wilson, the one who kept trying to leave?"

"Yes. I know you don't like to call strangers by first names, Aunt Mary, but it's a lot easier for me in this family."

"Very well, dear." Aunt Mary's tone conveyed that some people could use surnames *and* keep everyone straight.

Sheila ignored the tone and answered the original question. "Aubrey *did* leave, or at least didn't plan to return after he took Bessie home. He had already made it clear to both family and reporters that his connection with the family at this point is minimal. If I were Ruby, I'd never ask him to Sunday dinner again." She paused, realizing that Aubrey had managed to avoid being tested for gunpowder on his hands.

Aunt Mary tapped one shell-pink nail on her beige silk lap. "What did the others say after Mrs. Sims left?"

"Nothing. At least nothing about her. Wasn't that odd? I thought they'd say a great deal, but nobody referred to her at all. When I said good-bye to Sara Sims, I asked if her grandmother has Alzheimer's. With a look as blank as Bessie's own, she said, 'No, Nana's an artist'—as if that explained everything."

"Perhaps it does, dear. I've known some very vague artists."

"Bessie Sims isn't vague, she isn't *there.* I don't know how else to explain it. Anyway, when I left, they were all talking about funeral arrangements and arguing about which pastor to use. An outsider would have thought Martha Sloan died peacefully in her bed, properly mourned by her mother."

"You *were* an outsider," Aunt Mary reminded her. "They're talking about it now, you can be sure."

Porter sighed. "Don't you wish you could be a fly on the wall over there right now?"

"I would prefer for Sheila to have effaced herself and stayed a bit longer," Aunt Mary replied, tightening her lips.

Sheila frowned reproachfully. "You'd both like for it to be one of them, wouldn't you? You've had a dull winter. But while Martha Sloan may not have been liked very much, I suspect Cline is right and she was killed by somebody looking for a quick dollar. They had all lived with her for years, after all, and you don't kill a relative just because she's got a sharp tongue. At least," she added, "I haven't, so far."

Aunt Mary was a lady. She never heard unpleasant remarks. "Does anyone inherit money from her, dear?"

"I shouldn't think so. Now if old Mrs. Sims had died, Martha Sloan herself could have inherited quite a lot. In a book, it would be Grandma Sims who'd been murdered."

Porter stood. "Well, it isn't a book, and we aren't likely to solve anything tonight, so I'd better toddle on. I have to be at work bright and early tomorrow. I'll call you later in the week, Sheila?"

She nodded and started to rise. "I need to be going, too."

Aunt Mary gave her a quick look that for years had meant, "Hold your horses, dear." In the blink of an eye she had whisked her feet into tiny black pumps and accompanied Porter to the door. Sheila was too weary to mind Aunt Mary's monopolizing what should have been her date.

Aunt Mary returned with her mouth puckered like the opening of a drawstring purse. "Now we can talk, dear. Did you really forget your date tonight, or just not intend to go?"

"I forgot, Aunt Mary. I haven't abandoned all the precepts I learned at your ladylike knee. I hadn't remembered the date since Sunday, driving home from the airport. Since then I've been, as you know, in a cloud of pills and chicken soup. I honestly don't know if I would have remembered even if Martha Sloan Tait had *not* been murdered."

Aunt Mary tilted her head and considered her niece from beneath arched brows. "If you were really interested in Porter, dear, pills, chicken soup, and even murder wouldn't keep you from thinking about him."

"True." Sheila drained the last dregs of her coffee and set the cup with a click on its saucer. "So now you know. I am not really interested in Porter. He's a nice man, and pleasant enough, but when I look at him, I don't feel a thing."

Aunt Mary pursed her lips again. "I wonder what it would take to tear down that wall. Don't look at me like that, Sheila. You know what I am talking about, and it is understandable enough, heaven knows. Anybody who lived with Tyler Travis for fifteen years would need a wall. That man walked over feelings with hobnail boots." She held up a small hand to wave away Sheila's automatic protest. "You needn't pretend to me he didn't. When I think of the way he missed your birthday dinner that time I was visiting, to attend some boring function . . ."

"Tyler put his work first, Aunt Mary," Sheila said in what she hoped was an icy tone. She just wished her voice hadn't trembled as she said it. "That was the way he was. It made him a good diplomat. And if it made him a less-than-perfect husband, that was my problem, not yours."

"Well," Aunt Mary said briskly, "it is nobody's problem now. Tyler's gone. You can take down the wall, dear. Let somebody else in. Have a little fun."

"I will," Sheila assured her, "just as soon as I find somebody to have fun with."

Aunt Mary nodded, satisfied. "Very well, dear." It was the same tone that she used in a board meeting when one agenda item was taken care of and they could move on to the next. "I'd still like to know for sure what the Tait woman had to leave and to whom. Perhaps Charlie . . ."

"Poor old Charlie."

Charles Davidson, one of Atlanta's leading financiers, was Aunt Mary's personal investment counselor—and more. How much more, and why, nobody had ever been able to find out.

Sheila tried again tonight. "How on earth do you stir him out of staid respectability? Even his wife calls him Charles. But I honestly think he'd go to jail for you! Want to tell me why?"

"We go a long way back, dear." Aunt Mary settled herself with a discreet, reminiscent smile. "I'll just ask him to check on Martha Sloan Tait's estate, shall I? And the financial situations of the rest of the family."

Sheila stood and stretched. "Sure, why not? If you both get arrested, I'll bring brownies to jail. Now I really must get home. Lady will be starved!"

"She'll be all right until morning. Stay the night, dear. You can get a good night's sleep, and Mildred will bake pecan muffins for breakfast."

Sheila gave her a quick hug. "You temptress. Secretly you hope my poor dog will starve to death. Admit it." Aunt Mary did not deign to reply.

"It's funny," Sheila mused. "I don't remember you disliking Granddaddy's bird dogs."

Aunt Mary's lips curled. "Those dogs worked for their keep."

"Lady works—she guards my house like a tiger." Sheila remembered how valiantly the little dog had attacked an intruder last fall. Aunt Mary may have been remembering, too, for as Sheila dropped a kiss on her dry old cheek, she touched her niece's cheek in swift and unusual tenderness.

"I'll call you tomorrow," Sheila started to the door.

"Not until after three, dear. I'm going..."

"I know, you're going to lunch at your club and stay for bridge with friends. You always do on Wednesdays."

"Why no, dear. I'm going out to lunch at that new place up in Buckhead."

Sheila eyed her warily. "Alone?"

Aunt Mary trotted over and adjusted blinds that needed no adjusting. "Well, not exactly, dear. I'm meeting someone."

"A male someone, Aunt Mary? A single man about the same age as your poor niece who doesn't have enough men in her life?"

"Why, Sheila!" Aunt Mary sounded so genuinely shocked that Sheila might have been misled had the brown eyes not been so wide with innocence.

"Admit it, Aunt Mary. You are trying to make another match. I can see it now. First an appetizer, then the subject of Sheila. Don't you know by now that you are so charming that any other woman fades away into the sunset?"

"Nonsense, dear." Aunt Mary permitted herself one small pat of her perfect silver curls. "I am merely having lunch with a friend."

"Fine. Just don't try to make a new friend for your lonely niece. Understood?"

"Of course, dear," said Aunt Mary. "Call Mildred and leave a message if anything more happens on this case."

"That goes without saying. I know you like a little excitement in your life." Sheila left with a smile.

Thirty minutes later, however, as she let herself into her own apartment, she gave Sara Sims's door a somber look. No matter how you got along with your mother, you didn't want to see her dead.

She was greeted with yips of welcome and the sound of rustling paper. Lady proffered a note, ripped by her sharp little teeth.

Lady and I are feeling very mistreated. Hope she isn't catatonic before you return. I probably shall be. Look beneath the stairs outside your door. A.L.

She fumbled beneath the stairs and drew out a parcel wrapped in gold foil and tied with red ribbon. It contained four homemade chocolate chip cookies and a package of the best dog biscuits money could buy.

# ELEVEN

*Interlude*

SHEILA TAPED a brief note on the downstairs door before she left for work the next morning, but received no reply. Nor did she see him again all week. "Sorry," she said to Lady with a shrug. "I seem to have blown your beautiful friendship." She was sorry if Andrew Lee could be offended so easily. He had seemed more resilient.

Meanwhile, as she had predicted, Dudley's media reputation was soon safe again, buttressed on one side by his secretary's assertion that "Mr. Tait was too busy Tuesday to kill anybody," and on the other by the general consensus that his mother-in-law was "a bit peculiar"—a genteel Southern phrase covering anything from homicidal maniacs to political liberals.

Alan Belk was interviewed daily. He reported "progress is being made" without being specific about what that progress was. By Friday, he had still made no arrest.

Sheila left work early Friday to attend the funeral. It was held in the elegant sanctuary of First Baptist Church, where a full choir anthemed Martha Sloan to her heavenly (or otherwise) reward. Having been privy to Ruby's zeal in the matter, Sheila was amused to see how much care had been taken to include pastors from both Baptist persuasions, and how uncomfortable both pastors were with that decision.

In the crowd, she could barely see Dudley. He was surrounded by Sara Sims and two tall young men she assumed were Dunk and Bo. Kevin was there, too, next to Sara Sims in spite of her brothers' obvious efforts to shoulder him out.

Sara Sims did not return to her apartment all week. She did call on Saturday to ask Sheila to please water her plants, and "do something" with the chicken she had left on the table when the police came. After four days of hot spring weather, there was only one thing Sheila could do with it.

# TWELVE

SUNDAY EVENING Sheila was making sweet and sour beef stew when Sara Sims and Kevin appeared at her door. Sara Sims thrust out not one, but two bunches of daisies. "One from me and one from Daddy. He told me to shower my beautiful friend with thanks. I…I hope you like these." She seemed strangely tongue-tied.

Sheila took them with a smile. "I love daisies, and have just the vase for them."

Sara Sims gave her a quick hug. "I really am grateful. We couldn't have made it through last week without you."

Sheila, now also embarrassed, returned her hug. As she went to find her vase, she called over her shoulder, "Want to stay for dinner? There's plenty."

Kevin shook his head. "We're going out."

"We can stay a minute," Sara Sims coaxed. "I want to catch Sheila up and tell her the awful things the police are saying." She gave Kevin a smile so adoring that Sheila felt a stab of fear. Was she already so serious about this man?

Sara Sims settled herself on the sofa and patted the seat beside her. Kevin sat. Sheila produced white wine.

"What's happened, and what awful things are the police saying?"

The young woman set down her wine and clutched her hands together in her lap. Sheila saw they were trembling. "They found the gun—in the pond, like I suggested. The kitchen TV, too. But what's worse, they found Uncle Bily's fingerprints on a knife lying on our kitchen counter. They think he shot Mama!"

Sheila was astonished. "Why?"

Sara Sims shrugged. "They didn't say. I picked up the phone last night to make a call and Daddy was on the line with them. I wasn't about to hang up when I heard what they were talking about. They said they have Uncle Billy's prints on file because he once wandered off and got picked up for..." she paused, blushed, explained hastily, "...well, he went wee-wee in a gutter on the courthouse square. Anyway, they say his fingerprints were on the kitchen table and the knife."

"But couldn't he have left those prints anytime?"

Sara Sims shook her head. "He almost never went to our house, because Mama didn't..." She stopped and gave a slight shrug. Sheila appreciated her reluctance to criticize her mother now.

Kevin ignored them, sipping his wine and thumbing through a magazine he had found on Sheila's coffee table.

"What did your father say?" Sheila asked.

"He flat-out lied. Said Uncle Billy used to come over every now and then to visit Mama during the day, especially if he could get a ride with somebody. Then Daddy told them he didn't think Uncle Billy was a very likely suspect, but he'd talk to him, and they could question him if they liked."

"Did they?"

Sara Sims shook her head. "Not by the time we left Aunt Ruby's this afternoon. Daddy went up to the lake house today for some time alone, so he hasn't talked to him, either, that I know of. The terrible thing, Sheila, is that I don't know where Uncle Billy *was* that day. Nobody was home. Grandma Sims and Aunt Ruby went to get Grandma's hair washed, then they ate lunch at Ivey's Barbecue. Grandma and Grandpa Sims used to eat there a lot when he was alive, and she still likes to go now and then. But she's so slow about everything that it takes ages. That day she and Aunt Ruby left in the morning and didn't get back until nearly two. Then Aunt Ruby helped Grandma Sims into bed for her nap and went to take her own nap. Neither one of them saw Billy until later in the day."

"What about your Uncle Cline or Wart?"

"Uncle Cline went shopping in the morning for some garden supplies, then he went over to their church and worked on a new building that afternoon—they go to the Primitive Baptist, you know, and the men are putting up the new part themselves. And Wart won't say where he was, but he wasn't at home."

He had still been gone when she called Ruby, Sheila remembered.

Sara Sims hadn't paused for breath. "Sheila, would they really arrest Uncle Billy?"

"If they had conclusive evidence that he did it, they would have to arrest him, Sara Sims. What does your Uncle Billy say?"

"He won't say anything. When I tried to ask him if he was there, he got all upset and pitched a fit. He's been odd all week—odder than usual, I mean. Normally he follows Uncle Cline like a puppy dog, and Aunt Ruby is constantly trying to get him out from under her feet. But this week Aunt Ruby asked every minute or two, 'Where's Billy?' She and Uncle Cline won't let him leave the property, and it made him so furious he won't stay in the same room with Uncle Cline. I guess he's just upset about Mama, like the rest of us."

"Well, I wouldn't borrow trouble. If they had enough to convict Uncle Billy, they would have already arrested him. Something must be holding them up." She refilled their glasses automatically, her thoughts far away. Would Billy Sims know how to fire a gun? Where would he get one? And after a lifetime of Martha Sloan, what could anger him enough to kill her at this point if he hadn't earlier?

Meanwhile, Sara Sims had prattled off onto another subject. "You wouldn't believe how sweet Kevin's been all week, Sheila. He's fetched and carried for the whole family, haven't you, honey? He took Faye to get a dress for Aunt Merle, and it was so pretty she says she wants to be buried in it. Poor thing. She probably will. And he took Wart to buy suits for himself and Uncle Billy, too. Uncle Billy looked so sweet at the funeral!"

Sheila agreed. It was amazing what a difference a suit made on a man you had only seen in overalls. Instead of simple, Billy had looked vague and bothered—not unlike tycoons she had known.

Picturing Billy at the funeral reminded her of something else. Cline, at the funeral, trying to keep close to Uncle Billy, and Billy sidling away at every opportunity.

Sara Sims drained her glass and set it down. "Well, I guess we'd better be going." Then she proceeded to talk for another five minutes—mostly about Kevin's extraordinary helpfulness to her family. "... suggested he and Faye and I wash dishes for Aunt Ruby and Aunt Evelyn today, to give them a rest. Wasn't that sweet?"

Right now he wasn't sweet. He was beginning to seethe. Sara Sims was too engrossed in her own conversation to notice.

Sheila finally took pity on him. "I think you really do need to take your date out and feed him, Sara Sims. Sounds like he's worked himself to death this week. How do you keep the family straight, Kevin?"

Sara Sims answered for him. "I made it easy. Show her, honey."

With a grunt, Kevin fished a piece of paper out of his hip pocket and handed it to Sheila. "My guide to the family funeral. Nobody should be without one." It was a rough family tree:

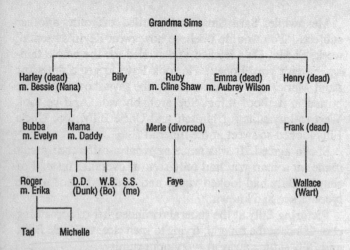

"See?" Sara Sims asked. "It's simple. Dunk is Dudley David Tait, Jr., but he couldn't say Dudley, so he named himself 'Dunk-Dunk.' It stuck. Bo was named William Bradford, after Grandpa Sims who died just before he was born, but he was so pretty that Nana kept calling him 'Beau.' Finally, when everybody was doing it, Mama insisted it be spelled B-O."

Privately, Sheila thought the men should have outgrown baby names. She knew, however, that in many Southern families it is a badge of real belonging for a grown man to be known as Billy, Tommy, or, as in a former president, Jimmy.

Kevin stood up. "It's a lot of family. I didn't even know she had brothers until we had to go to the airport to pick up Dunk. Nice guy, though. I liked him better than Bo. Bo's a radical."

Before Sara Sims could fly to Bo's defense, he pulled her up by one arm. "We need to go, Sara Sims. We've got a reservation."

"Your poor Grandma Sims has lost a lot of people," Sheila murmured, handing the list back to Kevin. She wouldn't need it again, she hoped. He might.

"Yeah." Sara Sims was being towed toward the door, but she wasn't about to forgo a lingering farewell. "You heard that Daddy was almost accused, didn't you? Oh, yeah, I forgot—you were there when Nana came. Wasn't she ridiculous? Lisa, Daddy's secretary, didn't help any. From what she told reporters, you'd have thought Daddy had plenty of time to kill people any day last week but Tuesday. But at least he's been cleared. Poor Daddy."

Kevin jerked her arm and she jerked back. "I'm *coming*, Kevin. Just let me say thanks to Sheila, for making me feel better about Uncle Billy. After all, why pick on him? Other people in the family could have killed her, too. The only ones who absolutely couldn't are me, Faye, Aunt Merle, Aunt Evelyn, and Daddy—we're the only ones who go to work. Not that I think any of the others did it, but it would have been easier for most of them than for Uncle Billy. I tell you..."

Kevin jerked her arm again, and less gently. "You've *been* telling her, Sara Sims. Come on! They're going to give our table to somebody else."

"We have to go?" she pleaded. "Whatever Sheila's cooking smells heavenly."

"We have to go." He pulled her out the door. She went laughing, heady with infatuation, thinking it all part of the game of love.

Sheila looked after them thoughtfully. She wasn't so sure. Was something beginning to turn sweet old Kevin sour?

# THIRTEEN

AFTER THEY LEFT, Sheila thought about what Sara Sims had said at the end. It was certainly true. Ruby could have gone to Martha Sloan's after settling her mother down for a nap. Cline could have gone instead of going straight to work on the church. Roger had admitted to the police that he drove all over the county that day. From what she had picked up, Aubrey spent his retirement shuttling between his church and the golf course. She didn't know how Bubba spent his days, but probably alone and unaccounted for much of the time. Wart could be presumed to be out in a field when he was really in Martha Sloan's kitchen.

Now that she thought about it, almost any person who did not work in an office or schoolroom all day could drop by an isolated house, shoot somebody, and return home without anyone being the wiser. It was a shivery thought.

Her shivers were interrupted by a barrage of knocks. Lady barked a frenzied welcome.

Sheila opened the door to find Andrew Lee, looking distinguished in a navy suit and paisley tie. "For you." He held out a bunch of daisies. His gaze went past her to the vase already adorning her coffee table. "Uh-oh. Somebody else passed the same corner."

"Sara Sims, from across the hall. There are two bunches, one from her and one from her father."

"Her father? Why would an old man be sending you flowers? Especially cheap flowers. And his wife barely cold!"

"In the first place, he's not that old." Sheila suspected Dudley was approximately as much older than she as Andy was younger, but she didn't say that. She had her pride. "In the second place, he was being grateful for my bringing Sara Sims home on Tuesday. That's all.''

"Well, you'll have to put mine in your bedroom and dream of me."

"Or in the study and work around you," she retorted. "From your grasp of Sara Sims's predicament, I assume you got my note Wednesday morning?"

"Sure, but you'd gone to work before I got up, then I had to go out of town that afternoon. I just got back. I'm sorry about your neighbor's mom. Is she home?"

Presumably he meant Sara Sims, not Martha Sloan. "No, she's out to dinner. I'll introduce you another day."

It had just occurred to her that Andy and Sara Sims deserved each other. Both could talk your ear off, and having been married to a talker, Sheila felt talkers should stay together and leave the rest of the world in peace and quiet.

Suddenly Andy demanded, "Are you listening? I just asked what smells so good!" When had he eased past her and into her kitchen?

"It's one of my favorite recipes—sweet and sour stew."

"Umm." He peered into the pot. "Who's the lucky guy?"

"You, I suppose. I was cooking ahead for next week, but what the heck?"

He replaced another lid. "I see you use a rice cooker. Very wise. You never know how long rice may have to sit after it's done."

"Especially tonight," she agreed wryly. "It's been done nearly an hour. Sara Sims and Kevin dropped by."

"Kevin?"

"Her boyfriend, or man friend, or significant other. I'm not up on terminology."

"Oh." Andy shed his coat and tie, draped them over a dining room chair. "This is great. I owe you a dinner for ruining your kitchen, which I see they repaired by using what should have been my floor. I have what should have been yours. Figures, doesn't it? At least it gives me a good reason to come often. A man should stay in touch with his own floor. Now, to pay my debts." He rolled up his sleeves, peered into the refrigerator, and gathered items into his arms like a mother gathering children.

"You owe *me* the dinner," Sheila pointed out.

"Right. I'm making the salad." He washed and tore lettuce with dedicated competence.

"You like to cook?" she asked, wondering where she had another vase to hold daisies.

"No, I like to eat. Living alone, what's my alternative? I can't impose on you every night of the week. Can I?" he added hopefully.

"Certainly not."

"When I leave tonight I'll know how to make what you've got in that pot. One night I'll invite you down and make it even better."

He shoved his glasses up his nose with one hand and sliced a tomato with the other. She watched, fascinated. "You've never seen anybody slice a tomato single-handed? You ought to see me shave while I shower. By appointment only." He deftly added tomato to lettuce and began sorting green onions. "Some of these are a tad old, did you know?" He mournfully held up a withered specimen.

"It goes with living alone—don't *you* know?" she retorted, reaching a blue pitcher down from the top shelf.

He regarded her with a disapproving look. "I could have gotten that, if you'd asked. I'm not *that* much shorter than you."

"I know. I frankly didn't think. It's another thing that comes with living alone."

"Not thinking? I've never had that problem."

"No, not asking for help when you don't need it." She filled the pitcher with water and started breaking daisy stems to create a table centerpiece she could see over. "Does it bother you to be shorter than some women?"

"Not at all, because I know that when I get to heaven, I'll be at least ten feet tall. I have a large soul."

"And a big mouth," she teased, but gently. Andy was more fun than anything else that had happened this week. Carrying the flowers to the table, she put on place mats and napkins.

With a flourish he sprinkled Parmesan and bacon bits over the salad. "Voilà, madame. Compleat. With an *e, a.*"

"Are you ever serious?" she asked as they seated themselves.

"Heavens, no. It's a serious world. I try to do my bit to leaven it a bit." He patted his solid middle. "Just a lump of leaven in the bread of life, that's me."

After dinner, however, when they carried wine into the living room, he turned mellow. "Ah—' he was thumbing through her records "—let's have Pachelbel's *Canon in D,* Smetana's *Moldau,* and Bach's *Well-Tempered Clavier.* Have you ever wondered if he also wrote one for the ill-tempered clavier? His family probably burned it."

He started the canon and sank onto the couch, glass in hand. He could, she was pleased to discover, listen to music without talking. After the Smetana, he sighed. "I always feel I've been on that boat all the way down the river." Then he grinned. "Okay, so I can be serious. Don't let the word get out."

"I wouldn't think..." she began, when they heard laughter outside the door.

"Your grieving neighbor?" He cocked an eyebrow.

"She deserves to laugh a bit." Sheila felt oddly defensive. Sara Sims was making a terrible first impression. She must have drunk too much, for she was giggling like a little girl.

"May she get her just deserts." Andy held his glass aloft and stood. "Speaking of dessert, I don't suppose there is any?"

"Wine, woman, and music are enough for some people," she pointed out. "You got stew and salad as well."

"But nothing for my sweet tooth. Did you eat all my cookies?"

"Every crumb. They were delicious. Unless you want a dog biscuit, I really have nothing more to offer you."

"I could think of one thing." His attempt at a leer was more ludicrous than lecherous.

She stood, held out her hand. "Good night, Andrew."

"I don't suppose you are lonely, or frightened of the dark?"

Actually, she was both. Being on her own had recently begun to lose its novelty. The first year of widowhood had been both frightening and exhilarating—making decisions without worrying about how Tyler would receive them, eating when, what, and where she liked, reading until she fell asleep. But lately she had begun to feel a little hollow at the core. Beyond Aunt Mary, Porter, and a smattering of high school friends with whom she had little in common, she had almost no social life. Maybe that was why she had so much time to spend with Sara Sims. One day she had surprised herself in the shower, whispering fiercely, "I wish I had *somebody!*" She also had an irrational but very real terror of the dark. But this was no time to admit to either.

"I have Lady and a night-light, thank you." She walked toward the door. "But it has been fun. I'm glad you came."

"And my salad was delicious?" He moved closer. Outside, a car engine roared.

Part of her wanted to laugh. Did Andy not realize he was nearly fifteen years younger than she and looked like a hopeful little boy? What astonished her, however, was that another part of her found him very attractive, and her starved body was starting to tingle. She was just wondering what she was about to get herself into when someone knocked on her door.

Sara Sims's voice accompanied the knock. "Sheila? Sheila! If you're still up, I need to talk!"

"Damn the child," Andy muttered, moving away.

"Temper, temper," Sheila rebuked him. The knock had instantly clarified her own feelings. All she had felt was relief.

"Come on in," Andy greeted Sara Sims. "The more the merrier."

"Who are you?" she demanded, belligerent and slightly flushed.

"Sheila's secret passion. They call me Superman, but underneath, I'm just a mild-mannered reporter."

Recognition dawned. "You're the man who burned up Sheila's kitchen! The new floor doesn't match, either."

"We know. We have swapped floors as a sign of our undying affection." Andy slapped the general region of his heart.

Sara Sims laughed and flapped one hand at him. "Get real!"

Sheila was stung. It was one thing to know she had no intention of getting involved with Andy. It was entirely different for Sara Sims to assume such a relationship was ludicrous.

Sara Sims, however, was full of her own problems. She lurched to the couch and sank upon it, chin on one palm. "I need some advice, Sheila, when he leaves. Go home, boy."

Andy lifted his own chin. "See if I ever burn up *her* floor!"

"He was just leaving," Sheila said, giving him a look she'd learned from Aunt Mary.

Perhaps she hadn't learned it well enough. Or perhaps he would be impervious to Aunt Mary, too. In any case, he joined Sara Sims on the couch.

"Three heads are always better than two. Pour forth, drunk but fair damsel, and we'll solve all your problems. Tell Uncle Andy."

"I'm not drunk," Sara Sims said, chin in air. "Well, maybe a little. But I have a reason." She swayed toward him, then regained her balance. "It's this guy I've been dating. We're kind of serious, you know?"

"No, I do not know," Andy informed her, "but I am learning. Pray continue."

"You talk weird." She wrinkled her brow in a frown, turned so that she addressed only Sheila. "You know Kevin?" Sheila nodded. "Well, last week he was talking about getting married. Hinting, at least. I said I thought we ought to wait awhile first, because I hoped—" she hiccupped, "—I hoped Mama would learn to like him. Now...now..."

"Now there is little chance of that," Andy concluded. "So?"

"You are gross!" She flounced around so her back was to him. "When I mentioned it tonight, Sheila, he said he thought maybe we were too precipitous." Her tongue tangled on the last word, and she sank against the couch, sniffling.

"Precipitous?" Andy repeated. "I am impressed with your young man. How many people of our generation even know that word?"

Sara Sims blew loudly into a tissue Sheila handed her and spoke over her shoulder to Andy. "He's not your generation, he's grown up. He says his feelings haven't changed, Sheila, but we ought to cool things down for a little while, really get to know one another. Have I done something wrong?" Her voice rose. "I've scarcely seen him all week, except with other people, and I love him so much..." Her voice trailed off and she began to sniff again.

Andy rose and brought her the whole box of tissues. "Sheila, not being male, has no wisdom to offer. I can tell you precisely what the man means."

"What?" Sara Sims blew her nose like a trumpet.

Andy drew back from the blast. "Why, what he says, of course! The week your mother dies is not the week to discuss getting married, no matter how modern you are."

"You think that's what it is?" She was eager to believe it.

Sheila gave Andy a warning look, but he was full speed into his counsel. "Of course that's all there is to it. I heard him laughing just now. Was that the laugh of a man about to spurn your love?"

Sara Sims sniffed again, a hopeful sniff. "I guess not. We did have fun. We went to..."

He held up one hand. "Spare me the details of what you had for dessert. Sheila has failed to produce one." He stood. "And now, having solved your problems, I take myself off to my lonely bed—Sheila offering me no better alternative. Oh, about that recipe. Is this it?" He rattled off a list of ingredients.

Sheila stared. "Exactly. How did you do that?"

"I told you, I like to eat. You ladies get to bed at a decent hour, now, and don't keep the neighbors awake."

He juggled three apples from a bowl on the counter, returned two, and chomped the third as he left.

# FOURTEEN

*Monday*

SHEILA AWOKE SHIVERING in one of the moist cool mornings that flit across Atlanta in late spring. She pulled up an extra blanket and permitted herself a ten-minute doze before Lady and the demands of Hosokawa International dragged her from her bed. Then she took her morning coffee, as she almost always did, to the balcony off her living room, to sit in a wicker chair and watch the mist rise from the small pond down the hill.

"Shape your spirit to the shape of the day and its Maker," an old Japanese fisherman had urged her as a child. She had found it good advice.

Today, her spirit refused to be shaped. Futile concern for Sara Sims jostled fruitless questions about Martha Sloan's murder. Was she really killed by a tramp—or by someone with reason to hate her? Was that someone her Uncle Billy? Who benefited from her death? No one, so far as Sheila knew. Had Kevin's hints of marriage been real—or figments of Sara Sims's hopeful mind? As she swallowed the last of her coffee and tended her trident maple bonsai tree, Sheila wished the whole Tait family on a distant galaxy.

She and Sara Sims came out their doors at the same time. She did not envy the young woman this first day back at work since her mother's death. She knew well how new condolences can reopen old wounds. But she personally would not have returned to work dressed to remind everyone she was mourning.

If Sara Sims had asked her advice on clothes instead of on boyfriends, Sheila would have discarded that black-and-white checked jacket entirely and bought one in spring green to enliven the young woman's pale skin. She would have replaced the white blouse and big black bow under Sara Sims's round chin with a blouse in jewel colors and some long beads. Mentally exchanging the too tight black skirt for a taupe one with a flare, Sheila was embarrassed to hear Sara Sims asking, "What's the matter? Do I have dirt on my skirt?"

"Oh, no. Sorry. Are you feeling better?"

"Yes." Sara Sims raised her chin with new dignity. "I've decided to give Kevin some space and time. If it's really love, it can't hurt, and if it isn't, I don't want him. Oh—Daddy called while I was dressing. He said there's a man in Alabama who shot a woman yesterday. They're checking to see if he killed Mama, too."

Someone, Sheila reflected as she started the ten-minute drive to her office, had taken her wish for a prayer. Between Sara Sims's new resolve and Gwinnett County's excellent police department, she might be finished with Tait family problems.

She thought too soon.

SHE ARRIVED HOME from work to find Sara Sims, clad in jeans and an oversize pink shirt, kicking the tires of her white Geo with the ferocity of a thwarted child.

"Got a problem?" Sheila asked unnecessarily.

"It won't start." Sara Sims kicked it again, then headed to the steps. "It was making a funny noise on the way home, and when I tried to start it just now, it didn't do a thing. I guess I'll have to see if I can find Bo."

Sheila had every intention of spending this evening trying recipes from *Armchair Gourmet*. So why, she would demand of herself later, did she ask, "Do you need me to run you somewhere?"

Sara Sims's face lit with acceptance. "Oh, Sheila, would you mind? I've baked an angel food cake for Grandma Sims. It's the only kind she can eat, and she loves it. It won't take long, and I did want to get it over there for her dinner. Thanks!''

In the time it took Sara Sims to fetch the cake from her car and get into Sheila's, Sheila had thought three things. First, she really did mind. If she hadn't been sitting down, she would have kicked herself harder than Sara Sims had kicked her tires.

Second, it *would* take long. Gwinnett was just gearing up for the afternoon maelstrom and it was twenty miles each way.

Third, if Sara Sims had had time to bake a cake, she'd come home plenty early enough to stop by a mechanic's and get her car fixed on the way. That wouldn't have occurred to Sara Sims, of course.

But, Sheila admitted, taking a deep sniff, the child certainly could bake. She hoped Sara Sims had made a second cake to share with good Samaritans.

It wasn't the drive that she minded most, even with stop-and-go traffic at major intersections and having to wait for a train with a hundred and twelve cars. What she minded most was Sara Sims's incessant chatter on one monotonous subject.

"Do you think it's okay for a woman to call a man, Sheila? Do they like that, or do they feel like they're being chased?"

She prattled on without giving Sheila time to reply. "It feels good, though, to have an evening to myself for once— you know? Time to wash my hair and read a book or something."

A few minutes later, revealingly, "I tried to call him this morning, but he didn't answer. He called about four, though, from Macon. He won't get home until tomorrow."

Sheila feigned an interest she did not feel. "What does he do out of town so much? I thought he managed a sporting goods store."

"He does. But the owner has other stores, too, and since Kevin played semipro football, he gets sent down to advise them and stuff." Her voice was full of pride. "Someday he hopes to own his own place."

Still later, "He was so sweet on Sunday, helping with dishes. He was good with Uncle Billy, too. Uncle Billy kept coming in the kitchen bothering us. I think he just wanted to get away from Uncle Cline. When I asked him if he'd been over at Mama's the day she died, he pitched such a fit that even Faye got annoyed, and she's got the patience of a saint. But Kevin knew just what to do. He handed him a dish towel and said, 'Here, Uncle Billy, dry a few plates,' and he *did* it! Uncle Billy never dried a dish in his life. He likes Kevin." She heaved a tremendous sigh. "I like Kevin, too. I just hope Kevin still likes me."

Sheila rested one hand on the foil wrapping the cake. "If you keep pinching pieces off, there won't be any cake left."

Sara Sims tightened the foil with a guilty blush. "I always eat when I'm upset. Just like Aunt Ruby." She remained quiet, however, and the cake remained unpinched until Sheila pulled into Grandma Sims's rutted drive.

At the near corner of the house, an enormous dog was chained to the back fender of the derelict Chevy. Black with tan patches on his hindquarters and chest, he lunged and roared a warning to anyone within a mile's radius. "Who's that?" Sheila asked, resolved not to put a foot outside the car. Determination and power could probably snap that chain, and this dog had plenty of both.

Sara Sims climbed out, undisturbed. "That's Bull, Wart's dog. He doesn't bother people he knows. Want to come in?"

"Not on your life. Bull and I haven't been introduced. I'll just wait for you here."

"I'll only be a minute." Sara Sims hurried in with the cake. In a few minutes Bull stopped barking, but he crouched on the long grass and kept a warning eye on the strange car.

Sheila rolled down a window and reached into the back-seat for the *Gwinnett Daily News* she had bought on her way home from work. Her attention could not be held long by new changes in the former Soviet Union, plans for a civil rights march in Forsyth County, or plans for a neo-Nazi counter-march. She scanned details of the county commission's latest scandal, but Dudley Tait was not mentioned. Soon she let her head drop against the back of the seat. Dark would not come for nearly an hour, but an early evening breeze had sprung up, filling the air with the scent of honeysuckle and the soft twitter of birds preparing for sleep. Sheila closed her eyes and enjoyed a few minutes of uninterrupted serenity. Very few.

Sara Sims returned with a pucker between her eyes. "Grandma Sims wants me to look for Uncle Billy. She doesn't know where he is. Normally he comes in from the barn long before this for his dinner. Wart's gone somewhere, too—probably took his dirt bike down by the railroad tracks."

Just then, in the distance, a train whistled for a crossing. Sheila seldom noticed the trains, which crossed Gwinnett day and night. This evening, however, the whistle made her shiver. Later she would wonder if she'd had a premonition of what lay ahead. Now she eyed Bull, who looked tensed to spring, and said, "I'll just wait here."

"Bull can't hurt you," Sara Sims said impatiently—and obviously untruthfully. "He's chained. Would you mind coming? I know it's silly, but I've always hated poking around out back by myself. Especially at dusk. Snakes are more active then, and I'm always scared one will bite me."

Sheila climbed obediently, if reluctantly, from the car, wondering exactly what she was supposed to do if one did. Bull growled deep in his throat, but did not rise as they passed.

"Maybe we ought to check Aunt Ruby's first," Sara Sims suggested. "Sometimes Uncle Billy goes over there to watch cartoons. His television's broken."

The path was worn from years of use, but the spring crop of brambles had not yet been cut down. They tugged at

Sheila's new panty hose. She wished she had taken time to dress like Sara Sims, in jeans and sneakers. But, she reminded herself, she had not planned to rove through briers!

The old couple were eating supper—bowls of homemade vegetable soup and cornbread—and Ruby was watching the evening news while Cline methodically mixed peanut butter and sorghum molasses on a small plate. Rags sat patiently and expectantly at Cline's knee.

"I haven't seen him all day," Ruby said, wiping her mouth on a flowered paper napkin and starting to rise. "Have you, Cline?"

Cline didn't hear. "Have you seen Billy?" she shouted at him.

He reached onto the counter and placed a hearing device in his ear. "What did you say? What about Billy?"

"He hasn't come to supper, and Mama's worried about him. You haven't seen him, have you?"

Cline spread a wedge of cornbread with the tawny mixture as he replied. "I ain't seen hide nor hair of him since this morning, but he knows not to leave the property. Let me just finish up here and I'll help you look. He could be in the barn. The cat's had her kittens, and he's mighty taken with a little yellow one." He took a gargantuan bite and wiped his chin. "You ladies want a mite to eat?" He waved a generous hand over the sparse table.

Ruby pressed her napkin to her mouth again, flushed at having so little to offer. "We've started eating our main meal in the middle of the day. It's supposed to be better for you, and our cholesterol was up last month. But we've got lots of soup, if you'd care for some."

Sheila, not keen on traipsing a snaky track, would have liked to stay. She hadn't eaten peanut butter-and-molasses since she was ten. It was Sara Sims, surprisingly, who turned them down.

"No, I promised Grandma Sims I'd find him. Thanks."
She whirled and departed, leaving Sheila to make their
farewells.

Sheila caught up with Sara Sims at the far end of the path.
"What's your rush?"

"I'm afraid he's taken a notion to wander off. Once he
followed a stray dog almost to the Yellow River, and one
night years ago they found him sitting on the railroad tracks
waiting for the next train, because he thought Uncle Cline
might be driving and he wanted to ask him a question." She
licked her lips and shook her head. "I know they've told
him to stay home, but he's been so funny since Mama
died—I guess that's what's really got me worried." She
turned left, toward the unpainted barn at the end of a well-
worn tractor trail.

Sheila understood her hesitation about going there alone
at dusk. Even in overalls and boots it wouldn't be inviting.
In heels it was almost impossible—parallel ruts, still muddy
from Saturday's rain, bordered by a morass of stickers, tall
grass, and suspicious-looking holes. She chose the mud.

Were snakes really most active at night? She didn't know,
but found herself acting as if she believed it. When a tus-
sock jerked to life at her ankle, she jumped back, terrified.
An equally terrified cricket leaped to safety at the side of the
path.

Perhaps she should have laughed with relief at her own
foolishness. Instead, she silently cursed Wart for failing to
mow his tractor path. Picking her way gingerly behind Sara
Sims, she also vowed never again to ask anyone if they
needed help.

The barn was weathered and small, just one story with an
abbreviated loft. Grandpa Sims had probably put it up years
ago to store tools and winter feed. Few Georgia nights would
be severe enough to have made him pen his cattle.

Sara Sims tugged the double door, which swung easily.
Sheila felt grudging respect for Wart. Her respect increased
when she saw the condition of the tractor, which filled most

of the barn. Her own father, a retired professor of agriculture, preached and practiced good care of equipment. His daughter had to admit that oiling barn hinges and maintaining a tractor were more important than mowing grass and brambles where few people ever walked.

Little of the now-failing light came into the barn through its one dirt-crusted window. The air was damp and chilly, smelling of hay, manure, and years of use. A rustle behind the tractor made them step back.

"Mew!" A large striped cat with sagging teats glided around a huge tire and glared at them. Her eyes glowed in the gloom. "Meow!" She expanded her rebuke to a snarl. "Meow!"

"Uncle Billy?" Sara Sims's voice was muffled by dust and bales of hay. "Uncle Billy, are you in here?"

Sheila saw a slight movement in the corner nearest the dirty window. She moved slowly toward something swinging in the shadows.

Then she saw what it was.

"Oh!" Sheila couldn't move. It was a horrible sight.

In an instant Sara Sims was beside her—breathing hard and pressing a fist against her mouth. She didn't speak, but each time she breathed, she whimpered.

Uncle Billy hung from a noose swung over a rafter. An old chair lay on its side just beyond his dangling feet. Even in this poor light, they could see that his face was purple, his tongue swollen out of his mouth.

With his eyes bulging in their sockets, he looked as horrified as Sheila felt.

# FIFTEEN

GO CALL THE POLICE! Tell them to send Detective Belk, if possible.''

Sheila's voice was intentionally sharp. Unless Sara Sims could be gotten to move quickly, she would have hysterics. Sheila—who had seen a few corpses in her time—felt close to hysterics herself.

"But we can't leave him! Get him down!" With a shriek, Sara Sims darted toward the grisly figure.

Sheila caught her roughly by the shoulder. "Call the police," she repeated, "and tell your aunt and uncle. I'll stay here until someone comes." She gave the shoulder a shake for emphasis.

Sara Sims's face was pale in the dimness. Her eyes darted from the thing in the corner to Sheila, and back. Then she swallowed hard. "Okay." She whirled and ran from the barn.

As soon as she had gone, Sheila fumbled in her shoulder bag for the flashlight she had begun to carry after being locked in a deserted Charleston motel one night. Careful not to move her feet at all, she swung the circle of light all around her for a good look at the floor.

Satisfied that there were no visible footprints to disturb, she moved slowly toward the dangling figure.

He hung from a barn rope thrown over a rafter fuzzy with dust. Bits of dust had drifted like pepper onto his white hair. Wrinkling her nose at the smell of his excrement, she looked at the ground around the chair. The straw was disturbed as you would expect when Billy kicked over the chair. Otherwise, she could see no marks.

Prowling, she began to commit the scene to memory. Once the police or Cline Shaw arrived, it was unlikely she would get another chance to investigate.

"Ghoul," she chided herself, "leave this to the police."

But she had been too involved in—and too lucky at unraveling—several deaths in the past two years to merely go outside the barn and wait for the police to arrive.

Knowing that Cline might arrive at any moment, she looked quickly again at Billy himself. A tiny corner of white paper stuck out of his overall chest pocket.

Using a tissue from her purse, she pulled out a note, written in large, poorly formed capitals:

I WS AT MRTA SLONS TUSDY.

Cline's arrival was heralded by the gasps of a man unaccustomed to running and sounds like an ox stumbling through uneven grass. Sheila had time to shove the note back into Billy's pocket, still the stiff body, and scurry across the barn. When Cline arrived, Rags panting at his ankles, she was demurely shielded by a tractor tire from view of the corpse.

"I got here fast as I could." He flipped a switch and one single bulb made a feeble attempt to light the semi-darkness. For an instant Cline leaned against one tire to catch his breath. "Where's Billy?"

Sheila pointed mutely. Rags saw the old man first. He immediately sat down on his haunches, threw up his nose, and howled. Sheila stepped back to give Cline a clear view and put out a hand as if she needed support. Actually she wanted to feel his response when he saw the body. She needn't have bothered. He was not the least bit subtle.

"Great God Almighty!" It was a prayer. He took one step forward, swayed, sagged toward the huge tire, slid to his knees, and toppled to the ground. Rags stopped howling and bent to lick his master, worried eyes appealing to the lady for help.

Sheila checked Cline's pulse and loosened his collar, then wasted no time worrying about whether to stay or go for help. She hared up the rough track heedless of hose, expensive shoes, or ferocious dogs. Bull growled as she passed, but remained crouched.

She ran breathlessly into the house. Grandma Sims was eating cake at her kitchen table. "Where's the phone?" Sheila gasped. The old woman pointed with her fork.

Sheila dialed 911 and spoke crisply into the telephone. "Possible heart attack. Come at once." She expected the woman on the other end to argue that she had already received an emergency call, but the woman merely took the address and directions and said that help would soon arrive. Sheila hung up, blessing whoever had thought of a universal, simple help number.

"Is it Billy?" Grandma Sims's eyes pinned Sheila to the spot.

Mostly to give herself time to think, Sheila pulled out a chair and sat down, deciding to leave Cline out of her story for now. "Mrs. Sims, I have some bad news."

It wasn't her place to tell the old woman her son was dead, but somebody must before sirens screamed into the drive. Neither Ruby nor Sara Sims was hurrying over.

Grandma Sims made it easy. "Billy's dead, ain't he." It was not a question.

Sheila nodded anyway. "I'm afraid so. He died in the barn."

The old woman twisted a heavy gold band on a finger that was little more than bone and knuckles. At last, as if dredged up from habit long forgotten, tears squeezed out of one dark eye and drizzled down the cobwebbed cheek.

"He was my fav'rite." She tugged up her apron and used one corner to dab her eyes. "You ain't s'posed to have fav'rites, but he needed me most, and he never left home." Her lips trembled. She put out one hand and stroked Sheila's forearm. "I do thank you for coming to tell me," she said with ancient dignity. She added, as one old enough to be privileged to ask, "Get me some water, please."

Sheila filled a jelly glass at the old white sink. Grandma Sims's hand shook so much that Sheila had to guide the glass to her lips.

When she had drained the glass, the old woman shoved back her chair and struggled to her feet. "Call Ruby to he'p me. She's all I got left." Her voice trailed away like her family, disappearing into the darkness.

Sheila offered her arm. "Ruby is busy. Let me help you."

She more carried than led the old woman into the back bedroom, stale with years of occupation. She helped her onto the bed and removed her worn slippers, took the proffered dentures and tried not to retch as she dropped them into a nearby glass of water. She had just pulled a quilt over the bent shoulders and tiptoed from the bedroom when the quiet was shattered by sirens.

It was the ambulance, arriving ahead of the police. She hurried onto the porch. Two paramedics leaped down. Bull strained his chain and thundered.

"In the barn." She pointed. "Lying by the tractor. Don't touch the other one. The police are coming, I hope."

"Other one?" The driver checked her clipboard.

"Just deal with the man by the tractor," Sheila urged them. "The police will be here any minute."

She spoke from assumption, not knowledge. Where was Sara Sims all this time? Had she even called the police?

She left the front door open while she looked fruitlessly for a phone directory. Finally she asked information for Ruby's number. The phone rang and rang. Nobody answered.

"Sheila? Sheila!" Sara Sims's nose was pressed against the screen door. "Aunt Ruby's had a fit or something! She seemed fine when Uncle Cline left, started putting dishes in the sink getting ready to go to Grandma Sims's while I called the police. Then all of a sudden her face got red as fire and she toppled over. I can't get her up!"

Sara Sims's own face was flushed, her eyes wild. Sheila dragged her inside and pushed her toward a chair. "Your grandmother is resting. You stay here, and I'll get help for Ruby. Did you call the police?" she asked over her shoulder at the door.

Sara Sims nodded. "Yeah. But I don't know if they are coming. Aunt Ruby fell while we were talking, and I hung up."

Sheila ran toward the barn, twisting her ankles in the mud and cursing herself for ever believing that well-dressed women wear heels. The paramedics were kneeling by Cline. His eyes were open, and he was struggling to sit up.

Sheila motioned the ambulance driver outside so Cline couldn't hear. "His wife needs you in the house next door. She collapsed and can't get up."

The paramedic went to the barn door. "I need to go up to the house for a minute. I'll be back." Sheila appreciated her calm, and envied her flat, lace-up shoes.

She wasn't as calm as she pretended, though. She thought Sheila couldn't hear her in the van. On the phone, her voice rose in incredulity. "All hell's broken loose over here, Lou! Get another unit over right away. We're working with one man, there's another one down, and what sounds like a bad heart next door."

"Man down?" Sheila asked. "Don't you mean dead?"

"That's our lingo for dead," the paramedic snapped. Sheila couldn't help but think that "man up" would have been more accurate in this case.

The woman jerked her head toward Ruby's. "Let's see what you have next door."

"*I* don't have anything," Sheila felt like protesting, following her through the brambles.

They heard Ruby before they reached the door—deep, sonorous gasps. She was crumpled on the kitchen floor, unconscious. While the paramedic examined her, Sheila scanned a list Ruby had posted by the wall phone.

She tried Merle. No answer.

Dudley was out, as well.

With a sense of unreality, she dialed Bubba's number. He answered, only half sober. As soon as Sheila heard that Evelyn was still at work, she hung up on his ramblings and dialed the hardware store number on Ruby's list.

At the familiar voice, she wished she could use the paramedic's line, "All hell's broken loose over here." Her own "There's trouble over at Grandma Sims's" seemed feeble for the facts.

Evelyn, however, responded with her usual efficient calm.

"It'll take me nearly an hour to get there. I'll have to close up here and stop by for Bubba. Meanwhile, tell them to take Ruby and Cline to Humana Hospital in Snellville. Faye can meet them there to sign them in. Tell them Ruby has pills by her bed. She'll need them. Before I come, I'll try Dudley's beeper. You call his house and leave a message on the machine in case I miss him. Keep trying Faye and Merle. They go out to dinner a lot, but they should be back soon." She paused, considered her arrangements. "And tell them to take out Ruby's bridge, too. She could swallow it."

Sheila hung up considerably relieved. At least one family member was capable of handling an emergency.

SHE HAD SCARCELY gotten back to Grandma Sims's when a police car screamed into the yard. Sara Sims motioned Sheila to the door. "I can't talk to them, I just can't."

There were two—a tall, dark officer in his midtwenties and a short blond one whose fuzzy pink cheeks made him look about fifteen. He was clearly terrified of the now frantic Bull.

"Hush!" Sheila shouted, unable to stand another bark. To her astonishment, the big dog subsided and lay down, chin on paws.

"We got a person-down report," the taller one said. "In the barn, I believe?" She nodded. "Need help, or do the paramedics have it under control?"

Sheila stepped off the porch. "We need help. Is Detective Belk also coming?"

"You know Belk?" His tone made it clear he thought she was a personal friend of Belk's trying to bypass the appropriate officer—himself.

"The man who is dead is the uncle of Martha Sloan Tait, who was murdered last week."

The younger officer's blue eyes grew wide. "No kidding? Rotten luck for the family." He was still keeping well away from Bull.

The tall officer stepped back and motioned her with his flashlight. "I'll need to see the scene to decide whether Detective Belk is needed or not. Show us where, ma'am."

Slipping down the muddy track toward the poorly lit barn for what she hoped was the last time that night, Sheila faced a painful truth. She *was* old enough for grown men to "ma'am."

It did nothing to improve her temper, however, so when he turned at the door to dismiss her, she replied sharply. "I found the body. Will you have any questions?"

He hesitated, clearly nonplussed. A lady should want to put as much distance as possible between herself and unpleasantness.

He jerked a hand at his minion. "Starkey, take her statement. I'll examine the body." He swaggered into the barn on the more important task.

Sheila described finding Billy, and Starkey struggled with his pencil. In only a few minutes the tall officer returned. "Looks like a clear case of suicide, ma'am. No need for Detective Belk here. We'll call the coroner's office."

She did not like to mention that Billy might be a suspect for Martha Sloan's murder. Her information for that, after all, was Sara Sims's report from eavesdropping and her own surreptitious reading of Billy's note. But she was deter-

mined to make sure Alan Belk arrived before she faded into
the sunset or the body was removed.

"But you will notify Detective Belk?" she demanded.

"Probably not, ma'am. We don't...suicide isn't really..." He stopped. Surely he hadn't been about to say
"important enough for us to bother about"!

Sheila gave him her most quelling look. "This may be
connected with his case. I am certain he would want to know
about this death as soon as possible."

"Mebbe so." He wrote a few words—probably "inter-
fering female." She said nothing more. It would be simpler
to return to the house and call Belk herself.

To her relief, he was pulling into the drive as they reached
the house. Once again Bull sounded the alarm, once again
he obeyed her order and crouched, silent but watchful, at
the end of his chain.

Detective Belk climbed out of his car. He looked more like
a chunk of Stone Mountain granite than ever against the
twilit sky. The dark officer went to meet him in the driveway. "Sorry you bothered, sir. Routine suicide." Sheila
wanted to kick him.

Belk grunted. "Long as I'm here, I might as well have a
look." He saw Sheila, and wrinkled his brow. "Let's see,
now, you aren't Mrs. Tait's daughter..."

"I live across the hall from her daughter. I drove her to
her mother's last week, and stayed awhile to help out. Tonight I brought her over to her grandmother's and we found
the body."

He shook his head. "If I was you, I'd give up chauffeur-
ing, ma'am. Looks like it complicates your life." He turned
and lumbered down the track. "I'll just have a look, Jack.
Didn't leave a note by any chance, did he?"

The other officer's voice faded out as they moved away.
"In his pocket. Doesn't say much..."

As she turned to go back into the house, Sheila reflected
that it felt good when Detective Belk called her ma'am. He

would have used it whether she was eight or eighty, and meant nothing but respect.

WITHIN A VERY FEW MINUTES, two ambulances shrieked off into the night with Ruby and Cline. Sara Sims reached Merle, who agreed to meet them at the emergency room. Leaving Sara Sims trying to find her father and listening with one ear in case Grandma Sims needed her, Sheila went back to Ruby's to clean up from dinner.

Rags was sitting dejectedly on the back stoop. "Come on in, boy, and let's get us both something to eat." He went straight to a rug near the freezer and lay down, head on paws. If huge tears had oozed from his dark eyes, she would not have been surprised.

He might not be hungry, but she was ravenous. Quickly she mixed molasses with peanut butter and spread it thickly on a slice of bread. It was as good as she had remembered—and, with a glass of milk from the fridge, made a quasi-balanced snack.

She was scrubbing stubborn globs from Cline's plate when Rags raised his head and gave a low "woof!" Dudley appeared in midapology. "…as soon as I could." He looked drained tonight, almost gray. When he saw Sheila he stopped, bewildered.

"It's me," she said ungrammatically. "Sara Sims is waiting for Evelyn next door, and Mr. and Mrs. Shaw have been taken to Humana."

She had been around this family too long. She had almost said "Aunt Ruby and Uncle Cline."

"What happened to *them?* Evelyn said Uncle Billy's dead."

She explained, concluding, "Detective Belk is down at the barn. He may want to talk to you."

Before they could say more, wheels skidded to a stop outside. Kevin, in a black turtleneck and slacks, filled the door. "What's going on? Why are the police next door?"

Dudley pulled no punches. "Uncle Billy has hanged himself."

Kevin took a step back and put up both hands as if to ward off a bad joke. "That sweet old man? Why would he do a thing like that?"

Sheila tried to meet his eye, but he did not look her way. "Sara Sims and I found him in the barn," she said, to get his attention.

They both swiveled toward her, astonished, and spoke together. "You and Sara Sims?"

"Not Wart?" Kevin added.

Sheila shook her head. "We haven't seen Wart. He doesn't even know yet." She ran the last plate under hot water and stacked it in the drainer.

"Where is Sara Sims?" Kevin demanded.

"Next door. She thought you were out of town."

"I was, but I got home early. When she wasn't at her place, I thought I'd try her here."

"What was she doing over here anyway?" Dudley demanded. "She told me she was going to spend the evening with a book."

"She made her Grandma Sims an angel food cake. Her car was acting up, so I drove her over."

He gave her a lopsided smile. "Sara Sims seems to be making a habit of dragging you into our family problems, Sheila. I'm sorry."

She smiled back. He looked drawn and very weary. "Do you feel up to going to the barn?"

"I'll go right down," he promised.

He did not, though. Instead he tugged his cuffs down, adjusted his tie, ran a hand across his hair. She didn't say, "You don't have to groom yourself to see a body." After finding his wife a week ago he had a right to be squeamish, and what he had waiting for him was not pretty.

"How'd you come to find him?" Kevin asked her. "What were you doing down at the barn in the first place?"

"Looking for him. His mother got worried when he didn't come to dinner, and asked Sara Sims to look. Mr. Shaw said he might be in the barn with new kittens."

"I wish Cline had gone himself, instead of sending you all," Dudley said with a frown.

"Or Wart," Kevin added.

Sheila gave them both a sour smile. "Me, too. You'd better be getting down to the barn," she told Dudley. She knew she probably sounded like Martha Sloan, but she might scream if he didn't show signs of heading in that direction. When he still didn't move, she understood, a bit, why the woman had become a shrew.

"Don't nag," Kevin rebuked her. "He'll go in a minute."

"Nagging is telling somebody the second time to do what they didn't do when you told them the first time." She didn't say it, but only because she was being polite.

Dudley took a deep breath of resolve. "She's right. I do need to go on down. Would you tell Evelyn and the others I'm here? I'll try to keep everybody from bothering Grandma Sims."

"I'll tell them." Kevin turned and plunged into the darkness. Dudley followed him at a slow lope. Bull's challenge once more filled the night.

Sheila wiped the counters and considered what to do next. What she did *not* want to do was what good manners required: go home.

"I'm surprised at you!" she told herself sternly. "Usually you are kicking and screaming *not* to get involved with death. Why are you so keen on sticking around all of a sudden?"

She knew the anwer. She minded this old man's death far more than she had Martha Sloan's—more than she would mind if the rest of the family died simultaneously. Maybe Billy killed Martha Sloan and hanged himself in remorse. Or maybe he knew who had done it, and could not live with the knowledge. Whatever, he reminded her of an ancient promise: "A dimly burning wick He will not quench." Billy Sims had been a dimly burning wick. Something had quenched him. Sheila wanted to know what it was.

The phone startled her. The man on the other end began speaking as soon as she answered. "Is Mr. Shaw there? I've been out of town, and just got his message."

"I'm sorry, he's not here now," she replied cautiously.

"Well, tell him Hank Warren called about those stocks he's wanting to talk about. He can call me back tomorrow morning. I'll be here all day."

Sheila took the number. She doubted, however, that Cline would be thinking about investments on Tuesday.

# SIXTEEN

PREPARING TO LEAVE, she paused at the kitchen door. Should she turn out the lights and lock up? Her purse and flashlight were next door, beyond an infinity of yard, garden, a stretch of overgrown bushes, and Bull. Right now, Ruby's lights and Grandma Sims's anchored the path at both ends, like a rope bridge stretched across a dark ravine. Sheila knew her limitations. It would take more courage than she possessed to flip Ruby's switch.

"Besides," she assured herself, "somebody will need to come back to pack suitcases for the hospital and do something about Rags."

Thus is weakness rationalized into virtue.

She walked slowly, ears pricked and body tensed to bolt at the slightest rustle. All she heard was an occasional voice from the barn and Bull whining uneasily on his chain.

By now the yard was almost full of cars. She recognized Evelyn's Ford and Aubrey's Chrysler. Just as she was crossing Grandma Sims's yard, a battered blue Mustang squealed into the drive and screeched to a stop just before her legs merged with a bumper sticker reading "Hugs Are Better than Drugs." Bull jumped up, blaring a challenge.

Sheila had time to read "Honor Your Mother—Earth" and "Have You Thanked a Tree Today?" before a tall young man climbed from the driver's seat. "Shut up, Bull!" He used the same tone with Sheila. "Who are you, and what the hell's going on?"

"I'm Sheila Travis, a friend of Sara Sims's—and I was almost your new bumper. Are you Bo, or Dunk?"

"Bo. Sorry about the entrance. Dad's answering machine said come as quick as we could." The bare porch bulb

showed her a man probably forgiven often and much because of spectacular good looks. Dark hair curled just below his ears. His teeth gleamed white in a tanned face. His
eyes were large and dark, his jeans fashionably ripped and
tight enough to outline muscular thighs. He interrupted her
survey to demand again, "What's going on?"

Before she could reply, Sara Sims ran outside and flung
herself against him. "Oh, Bo! It's terrible! Just terrible,
Bo!"

Only their eyes were alike. Did she resent not getting the
genes that made him tall, lean as a greyhound, attractive as
a model? If so, she gave no sign. She went as naturally into
his arms as if she'd been comforted there all her life.

"What's the matter, Sis?" He pushed her back to look
down into her tear-stained face. "Is it Grandma Sims?"

She shook her head, sniffed, and gulped. "No, it's Uncle
Billy. He's hung himself. In the barn."

He shook her by both shoulders. "Are you putting me
on?"

"No. Sheila and I found him. He looks awful!"

Bo froze, then he shoved her away and started down the
track at a dead run. "No way! No way he did that!" The
last they heard was a long drawn-out cry of anguish that
trailed behind him through the barn door.

Kevin stood behind Sara Sims, massaging her shoulders
where Bo had gripped them. "He seems more upset than
you are."

Sara Sims leaned against him, spoke in a stricken whisper. "Bo loved Uncle Billy more than the rest of us. They
played together, even after Bo grew up."

Kevin nodded. "Yeah. I saw them outside yesterday
playing with water pistols."

"Cowboys and Indians," Sara Sims sniffed. "They do it
a lot."

Echoing her remorse, a giant sob rolled from the porch.
Beneath the swinging bulb, Bubba sat in an old metal chair.
He again wore his khaki jumpsuit and baseball cap, but in

deference to the evening's chill had added a red windbreaker. It wasn't the chill that had flushed his cheeks and
nose, nor was it the tears that coursed down his cheeks as he
gently bounced in his chair.

"Poor Bo. Poor Unca Billy," he mumbled. "Poor
Grandma, inside wish..." He stopped, shook his head to
clear his diction. "...ins-s-side *with* her ter...ter...terri-
ble—" he finally got his tongue shaped around the word
"—her *terrible* grief." He weaved so in the chair that Sheila
feared he'd fall on his face.

Sara Sims, ready to vent self-reproach on anyone else,
flew up the steps and shook him by the shoulder. "What are
you doing here dead drunk? Go tell Aunt Evelyn to make
you some coffee. Or go home. Get off this porch! I don't
want people seeing you here."

"Wha' people?" he protested, waving at the dark empty
yard.

"Reporters." She swiped her nose with her sleeve. "They
may start coming soon, like they did for Mama. Come on,
Uncle Bubba, get inside. Right now!"

Sheila doubted that reporters would cover the suicide of
an elderly retarded farmer—unless they heard that his death
might solve Martha Sloan's. She wondered how long it
would take for them to make the connection.

In any case, she agreed that Bubba needed to go inside.
The night air was getting chillier, and damp. She offered him
her arm.

He drew back, clutched the chair as if he expected her to
pry him loose. "I b'long here. B'long more'n you. *My*
grandma. *My* Unca Billy!" He glared fiercely up at them all.

"Tell his wife to deal with him," Kevin advised, steering
Sara Sims toward the door. "She's used to him."

Sara Sims spoke over her shoulder to Sheila. "Let's go on
in, Sheila. After she gets coffee poured down him, maybe
you can take him over to Aunt Ruby's to sleep it off."

Inside, the small rooms were bright and close. Sheila felt
assaulted by the odor of old meals, old age, and an un-

pleasantness she couldn't identify until she saw they had lit a small kerosene heater in the fireplace. She also smelled an odor she associated with illness, even death.

For a moment she paused, reluctant to shut the door, but the woman huddled near the heat looked too ill to stand the night air. She was talking as they entered. "...but praise God, Faye got home in time to go. Mama and Daddy aren't in rooms yet. I couldn't stand to sit around the hospital and wait. I just couldn't."

She must be Merle, this once stout woman reduced to loose skin draped over bones. A family portrait of Ruby, Cline, and a very small girl with bright red hair smiled down from the mantelpiece. Only a faint resemblance to that child lingered now in Merle's dark eyes and the red wig she wore to hide the effects of chemotherapy. Her green two-piece dress was stylish, but Sheila wished there were more of Merle to fill it.

She had been addressing Roger, propped on the other end of the mantelpiece, and Aubrey, who sat on one end of the sagging sofa protected by a faded sheet. Tonight Aubrey wore a yellow sport coat, dark green tie, brown slacks, and polished brown wing tips. Again Sheila wondered if he had planned to go out, or had stopped to dress for the occasion. He gave her a wide smile that seemed dreadful in that place. "Why, hello, Mrs. Travis. I didn't expect to see you here tonight."

"Me neither," she agreed, sinking into a straight chair near the kitchen door without further explanation.

Evelyn was wiping the kitchen table, and the rooms were so small she could easily take part in the living room conversation. "She drove Sara Sims over to bring Grandma a cake."

"Is any of it left?" Roger asked. "We didn't have dessert."

"*We* didn't have dinner," Sara Sims said scornfully. "Sheila and I came over here before we'd eaten." Sheila didn't waste sympathy on her. That crumb-stained plate on the table hadn't been there when Sheila left for Ruby's.

Sara Sims continued in a snarl. "And your daddy's stinking drunk on the porch, Roger. A fine sight if reporters start arriving."

Evelyn waved one hand toward the door. "Go get him, honey."

"Let him rot," Roger retorted. Evelyn went out and guided Bubba to a chair in the kitchen. Roger trailed after them, hitched out a chair and commanded, "Get me some of that cake, Mama, and a glass of milk."

Evelyn moved to the cupboard for plate and glass without a word. Bubba leaned his head against the kitchen wall and dozed with his mouth open.

While Evelyn cut Roger's cake and the others talked monotonously about the need for rain, Sheila rose and went to the bathroom. She was on her way back when she heard Roger. He was speaking softly, but his voice was audible in the tiny hall that led to the bathroom and three small bedrooms. "I will continue to do what I can, Mama. You know that."

Sheila couldn't hear Evelyn's reply, but when Roger spoke again, his voice was elated. "Maybe so, but in the long run, it's one less way to slice the pie."

Outside a powerful engine shifted down, turned in the driveway, and roared past the house toward the barn. "Wart's home." Roger announced unnecessarily.

Sara Sims joined Aubrey on the couch and motioned for Kevin to join her. He shook his head. "I need a breath of fresh air."

"Me too," Roger seconded him. He hastily finished his milk and they left together.

Sheila, facing one of the room's two windows, saw soon what she expected to see—the flare of a match, the glow of one cigarette, and two men headed toward the barn.

Sara Sims looked so forlorn after Kevin left that Sheila sought a subject to distract her. "Does your whole family collect those small wooden figures?'' She nodded toward a row of tiny animals marching across Grandma Sims's mantelpiece. ''I saw you had some in your living room.''

To her dismay, Sara Sims's eyes filled with tears and sobs again shook her body. Aubrey said to Sheila, ''Billy carved those. It was amazing what he could do with a scrap of wood.''

''I can't understand what made him kill himself,'' Merle sobbed, dabbing her eyes with a tissue.

''We'll probably never know,'' Aubrey said. If he meant it for comfort, he ruined it by adding, in a distressed tone, ''I just hope he hasn't gone to hell for taking his own life.''

''He ain't going to hell,'' Bubba growled, scraping the kitchen floor with his chair.

''We've got enough on our hands without worrying about that,'' Evelyn agreed. ''Let's leave Uncle Billy to the mercy of God. But I think you need to call Amy, Merle. See if she can't come home early. With both Ruby and Cline at Humana, you and Faye are going to have your hands full.''

Merle sighed. ''Amy wouldn't be any help—you know that. She has her mind on a party or her nose in a book. Faye says I should have sent her to a Baptist college, but when she got that scholarship to Yale, I didn't have the heart to refuse her. I tell you, though, that child gets more like her daddy every day. Can charm the stripes off a coon, but she does what she wants to, and nothing else. Faye begged me not to marry that man. Practically went down on her hands and knees. But I was in love.'' She dragged out the last word in wry self-reproach.

Sara Sims picked up a glass of tea from the coffee table and said with the callousness of youth, ''Faye wouldn't know love if it bit her.''

''Oh, I don't know about that.'' Merle gave a high little laugh.

''I'll tell you one thing,'' Evelyn added. ''You can count on Faye.''

Merle nodded. "Everybody does. Too much, if you ask me. Last week now, she stayed home from school with a sick headache. Could not lift her head when I left for work, but when I got home, there was a note that she'd gone to watch the girls' swim meet in Roswell. Didn't get home until after ten, and her headache got so much worse she had to stay home the next day, too. When I asked her why she'd pushed herself, she said what she always says, 'I promised my kids I'd be there.'"

"That's Faye all over," Evelyn agreed.

Their litany of praise was interrupted by shouts, then barks from a frenzied Bull. Sheila and Sara Sims dashed onto the porch, followed by Aubrey and Evelyn.

In the front yard, Bo and Wart stood at the edge of the darkness, jaw to jaw and fist to fist.

"I know what I know!" Bo shouted.

"*How* do you know?" Wart jeered. He limped one step back. "You ain't been around enough in the last few years to know anything!"

Bo didn't give an inch. "I'm right, and I'm gonna prove it."

"You ain't proving nothing, except you've got a big mouth. Now get off my land!"

"Your land? Why, you..." Bo swung and caught Wart on the jaw. Wart's fist smashed Bo's nose with a crack that made Sheila's stomach turn.

Sara Sims cried out in alarm.

With a roar of anguish, Bo hurled himself onto his cousin. Bull nearly snapped his chain trying to rescue his master.

In an instant, all Sheila could see was a mass of arms and legs, first upright and then rolling over and over in the tall grass. One minute Wart held Bo by the hair and pounded his head against his own car's tires. The next, Bo managed to free himself and pinned Wart to the ground, pounding his chest.

Sheila felt something poke her own ribs.

"Whack 'em!" Grandma Sims commanded, giving Sheila's ribs another poke. "Take this and whack 'em both good. Make 'em stop. You hear me? Make 'em stop it!"

Sheila hadn't known the old woman was even up. Now she stood, wrapped in a quilt, clutching Evelyn for support and shoving her cane at whoever stood nearest.

Gingerly, Sheila took the cane and waded toward the battling cousins. Before she reached them, Sara Sims snatched the cane and ran straight into the fray.

"Stop it, stop it!" She beat their backs indiscriminately. For the first time, Sheila saw how much she resembled Grandma Sims.

While Bo and Wart both dodged her furious blows, Kevin and Roger finally stepped in. Each took a challenger by the arms and lifted him out of swinging range. They panted, glaring at one another.

"That ain't no way to act in my front yard," Grandma Sims quavered at them. "And your Uncle Billy laying dead in the barn! Pull yourselves together and act right!" She took back her cane and shuffled into the house without another word.

Wart rubbed one forearm across his sweaty forehead. Bo wiped a flood of blood from his upper lip and moved stiffly toward his car.

Before he got in, he uttered his final challenge. "I know what I know, and I'm going to prove it. Uncle Billy never tied that knot. He wouldn't have known how! Somebody else killed him, and I'm gonna find out who!"

# SEVENTEEN

AN HOUR LATER Sheila received Mildred's steaming mushroom omelet, crisp spinach salad, and black coffee with a grateful smile. "Once again, you may have saved my life."

"We aim to please." Mildred smiled and rested her hand lightly on Sheila's shoulder before returning to Aunt Mary's kitchen. They had been friends and conspirators for years.

Aunt Mary removed the tortoiseshell half-glasses that made her look like a fluffy owl and lightly drummed her nails on the tablecloth. "As much as I dislike discussing business with meals, Sheila, the lateness of the hour makes it imperative. Do you think there's anything *to* what that young man said?"

Sheila, engrossed in eating omelet, had to swallow before she could reply. "I don't know. The others said that Wart has been teaching Billy many things lately, including how to write. But the knot did look professional. I couldn't have tied one that well."

"Pshaw." No one could put as much disparagement into a "pshaw" as Aunt Mary.

Sheila was stung. "Do you mean 'Pshaw, of course you could, dear,' or 'Pshaw, you are such a klutz that *anybody* else could tie a better knot'?"

"I meant 'Pshaw, I wish I had seen that knot for myself.'" Aunt Mary heaved the deep sigh of one surrounded by incompetents.

"Oh, I do, too," Sheila agreed with relish. "I would love to have seen you wading through briers, skipping over snakes, and tiptoeing past the tractor. Not to mention mastering the mastiff."

Aunt Mary raised one hand to stop her. "What mastiff?"

"He's not really a mastiff, he's a blend of all the nastiest dogs in the world. He belongs to Wart."

"Then if someone else did hang that poor man, perhaps the dog barked. Did you ask?"

"Whom would I have asked? Mr. and Mrs. Shaw had gone to the hospital, and old Mrs. Sims had gone to bed."

"What about the young man you keep referring to as 'Wart'?" Aunt Mary shuddered delicately. "Doesn't he live there?"

"I keep referring to him as 'Wart,' Aunt Mary, because that's his name. And he wasn't home most of today. I probably shouldn't admit this, but after the fight, when people were milling around making coffee and trying to act like nothing had happened, I did ask some questions and listen in on a few conversations. Wart told Kevin he'd been up to Alpharetta to look at a motorcycle that Kevin had apparently told him about. Later Sara Sims asked him where he was all afternoon, and Wart wouldn't tell her—just said he'd been off the farm. It wouldn't have taken all afternoon and most of the evening to get to Alpharetta and back, so that could be important."

"Hmmm." Aunt Mary had produced her pad and pencil and was taking notes.

Sheila continued, feeling rather like she was giving dictation to an unlikely secretary. "Cline apparently napped part of the afternoon, then went up to his church to work on the building. Aubrey was at the golf course, as usual. Ruby had a meeting of some sort, and was gone from two until five. But if anybody did kill Billy, Roger would be my favorite candidate. By his own admission he is all over the county every day, and he remains the most obnoxious member of the family except for Wart."

Aunt Mary shook her head in dismay. "Such restless people."

"Not at all. It's just that things are spread out in Gwinnett. It's five miles from Grandma Sims's to the nearest grocery store, twenty miles to the only mall. People can easily drive fifty miles a day doing errands. Dudley and Bubba were actually on the property, though."

As Sheila had expected, Aunt Mary's ears perked up—at least figuratively. Aunt Mary was too well bred to let them visibly perk.

Sheila hated to let her down, but it had to be done. "Dudley went to Bessie's, next door to Ruby's, about three to discuss business. Bubba arrived with some groceries, and they left together. That's as close to an alibi as anybody has—except for Merle, Faye, Evelyn, and Sara Sims. They were all at work, surrounded by people."

"I wonder what business Dudley Tait had with Mrs. Harley Sims?" Aunt Mary mused. "He already has her power of attorney, so there is very little about which he would need to consult her. Is she competent to do business?"

"She's not competent to do anything." Sheila interrupted herself to thank Mildred for peach cobbler and a refill on coffee, then asked, "How do you know all this, Aunt Mary?"

"Charlie, dear." Aunt Mary rose, returned to the table with a familiar brown envelope, and drew out some papers. "According to these, Martha Sloan Tait had a modest life insurance policy naming her husband as beneficiary. No other personal assets. Bessie Sims has an inheritance from her father, her husband's social security, and a fixed income from a hardware store owned formerly by her husband and now by her son. The terms of inheritance, by the way—that his mother receive a fixed income for life—must be a hardship on her son and his wife these days. Their business is slowly failing."

"Oh!" Sheila was truly sorry. It seemed unfair that Evelyn should have that worry, in addition to all her others.

Aunt Mary was still reporting. "The land under all three houses is still part of the Sims farm. Papers were drawn up years ago to deed it over to Ruby and her brother Harley, but the old woman decided at the last minute, apparently, that she didn't want to divide up the farm." She handed Sheila a three-page report accompanied by copies of property deeds, bank statements, and other legal documents.

Sheila shook her head fondly at her aunt. "I hope I'm not here when the police come to take you and dear Charlie away. I also hope you never decide to have him investigate me. This is amazing. I don't see, however, that it advances us at all."

"You never can tell, dear. I was particularly interested in some of the financial statements. Harley Junior, for instance. The man you call 'Bubba.' He inherited a prosperous hardware store from his father, but it has gone downhill for several years. Didn't you say he drinks?" She took Sheila's nod for a complete answer. "It would be good to know whether the drinking harmed his business, or business failure started him drinking." She stopped and put a small check beside an item on a list beside her. "And Roger, his son. A builder, but not always a reliable one. Currently he has three unsettled claims against him for poor construction. In one, an entire staircase fell. Fortunately no one was hurt, or he could have been liable for injuries. He also has two houses unsold. They cost him thousands of dollars in interest monthly. Yet he just started another three houses in a higher price range."

Sheila whistled.

Aunt Mary nodded. "He is pouring money down drains. He also owes a considerable amount on his own new house, has his children in a private school, and just bought an expensive car for his wife. Unless he sells a house in this next month, or secures another loan, he may declare bankruptcy."

"Aubrey Wilson, now." She made a third check on her list. "He is dating Gussie Mae Curtis, widow of the drugstore man. I've known her for years. Rich, but foolish. Spends a fortune on travel and doodads."

Sheila smiled. Aunt Mary considered anybody foolish who spent money rather than investing it.

"Mr. Wilson's teaching pension won't keep her happy for long," Aunt Mary continued, almost to herself. "That woman runs through money like gossip through a small town, and she expects her men friends to at least pay their own way. We need to know if he has any other sources of income."

She tucked the papers neatly back into their envelope. "As I believe you said last week, Mrs. Sims the elder could be in danger from several sources, but none of this gives us a financial motive for the deaths of either her son or her granddaughter."

Sheila understood her downcast tone. In Aunt Mary's book, what other good motive could there be besides a financial one?

"I took a call for Cline tonight from his broker that interested me. For one thing, why would he call after working hours?"

"Mine does all the time," Aunt Mary said, unimpressed.

"Yes, because yours is working with sizable investments in markets around the world. I wonder how much Cline told him he had to invest."

Aunt Mary poised her pencil. "Did you remember his name, dear, and the name of his firm?"

"No, but give me a telephone book and I think I can find him." Sheila found the broker's number, then remembered something else. "I wonder... On the day Martha Sloan was murdered, Billy killed Ruby's best laying hen. She was plucking it when I called them. Both she and Cline asked, as soon as they'd heard about the murder, 'Was there a lot of blood?' I wonder if Billy already had blood on his overalls, and killed a chicken to account for it?"

Aunt Mary's brown eyes looked very far away. "Would he have been that clever, dear?"

Sheila shrugged. "I really don't know."

"Didn't you say Mr. Shaw may be able to come home tomorrow?"

"That's what Faye said when she called."

"Then you must go back over there. Ask Mr. Shaw about the overalls. Ask Mrs. Sims whether she heard the dog barking, or saw any of the family around yesterday afternoon. Have a look at..."

"No, Aunt Mary." Sheila stood to carry her dishes to the kitchen. "Detective Belk is handling this case. Very effectively, too. There is no reason for us to get involved."

"You are involved," Aunt Mary said in the tone of one being reasonable with a six-year-old who is refusing to wear a raincoat in a downpour. "And Alan Belk won't mind a little help. His aunt Karen and I have gone to the same hairdresser for years."

Sheila paused in the kitchen door, astonished. "Is that the result of more of Charlie's detection?"

"Oh no, dear, I spoke with him myself. As a friend of Mrs. Tait, I wanted to know what progress he is making on the case."

"A *friend* of Martha Sloan? Had you even met the woman?"

"Oh yes. I attended the Arts Council ball last year, and she was there. But don't try to change the subject, dear. We were discussing the questions you need to ask Mr. Shaw and Mrs. Sims."

Sheila shook her head. "I know the Southern old-girl network is strong, Aunt Mary, but I don't think a hairdresser connection entitles you to move in on this case. And even if I wanted to ask questions—which I don't say I do— I can't just barge in and start asking. I would like to know about the overalls—I'll admit it. But I can't butt into these people's lives uninvited."

"Then get yourself invited," was Aunt Mary's crisp reply.

# EIGHTEEN

*Tuesday*

IT PROVED EASIER than Sheila had expected.

On her way home from work Tuesday afternoon, she stopped by Sims's Hardware. She had needed shelves above her apartment desk for six months. Tonight was as good a night as any to get them up, and Sims's as good as any store to buy the necessary hardware from. At least that's what she told herself. It would never do to admit she was obeying Aunt Mary's dictum.

The store, a scant sixteen miles out of her way home, was a long gray cinder-block building surrounded by a gravel parking lot and shaded by an elderly oak. Located on a main road leading out of Lawrenceville, it had been built for both local trade and tourists. The interstate had lured both kinds of trade away. Today its very windows seemed sad.

Sheila pushed open the glass door to a jangle of bells. An elderly man shuffled forward. "How may I help you?"

When she explained what she wanted, his rheumy eyes lit with pleasure. "Right this way."

He led her past a glass and oak counter that was probably there before either of them was born, and into the dim recesses of the building. Watching his head precede his chest by several inches, Sheila could picture him with a shell on his back.

The shelves were neatly ordered—almost concealing how little merchandise they offered. He led her unerringly, if slowly, to the right place. "You're going to want to attach them firmly to studs, now. Do you have a stud finder?"

Sheila thought of several replies—none suitable for her present company. She shook her head.

He shuffled to another shelf and brought back a slender tool. "I always rely on tapping the wall myself," he confided in his habitual whisper, "but this is better if you aren't used to finding studs. Most ladies aren't." He was so sincere that Sheila was ashamed of her own thoughts. She wondered if Evelyn had considered putting him in television ads. Her business might improve.

They were discussing the holding properties of Molly bolts versus toggle bolts—at least, he was discoursing on the subject and Sheila was putting in an occasional "I see"—when Evelyn spoke behind her.

"I thought I recognized that voice. Hello, Sheila."

"Would you like to handle this sale?" the old man asked, shuffling a humble two steps back.

Evelyn waved a disclaimer. "No, you go ahead, Art. Bring her to the back for a Coke when you are done."

"His heart would have been broken if I'd messed up his sale," she confided later in the small partitioned area that served her as an office. She waved Sheila to a ladderback chair and offered her a choice between Diet Coke and "the real thing." Then she opened a Diet Coke for herself, propped her short legs on an upturned plastic bucket, and began to talk as if she had waited years for a female confidante.

First, with an indulgent smile, "You'd think Art worked on commission, the way he guards his customers. But I think half our customers come in to see Art, anyway." She shoved her hand through her thick, unruly hair. "Gracious I need a perm! Is your hair naturally curly?" When Sheila nodded, she sighed enviously. "I wish mine were. I never seem to find time to get it cut, much less curled. And these last two weeks..." She shook her head in dismay. "We don't always have a death a week in the family."

"You carry a lot of it, don't you?" Sheila didn't have to try to sound sympathetic. She pitied this woman more than she could say.

Evelyn pitied herself far less. "If I don't who will? Aunt Ruby can't do everything. And since my mama died, she and Uncle Cline are all the family I've got. But maybe you don't know that Uncle Cline's my real uncle—Mama's only brother. I always think if the hair doesn't tell people, the green eyes and freckles will. Merle is both my first cousin and Bubba's, and we all grew up together. Sometimes I feel like I married my brother!" She paused only long enough for a swig of Diet Coke. "Until two years ago, Grandma Sims could run circles around you and me. Ran the whole family, except for Martha Sloan. But Grandma's pretty limited now, even if she won't admit it. Makes it hard on Aunt Ruby, who nearly kills herself keeping her mama from doing too much." She sighed. "And Grandma Sims treats her like dirt. It makes me furious!"

Sheila slid down in the chair in a fruitless attempt to match her vertebrae to its rungs. "Have you heard from them today?"

"Yes, Faye called about nine. Aunt Ruby had a heart attack. Thank God. I was afraid it was a stroke, and she'd be crippled. She'll be home in a few days. Uncle Cline just fainted—they've already sent him home. I hope Aunt Ruby gets to come to Uncle Billy's funeral Thursday. It's at two-thirty," she added in a tone of invitation.

Sheila spoke with regret. "I have to be out of town all day Thursday. When did you get away last night?"

Evelyn gave her an impish grin. "Right after you did. I told Wart he could stay home to take care of Grandma Sims, and I hauled Bubba out of there. He didn't need any more strain. He's—" she paused, decided to maintain the myth "—he's not well. Can't even come down to the store most days anymore."

"Did I hear this used to be his father's store?"

Evelyn laughed. "And my grandpa's store before that. Aren't we a close-knit family? Grandpa sold out to Harley, Bubba's dad, when Uncle Cline decided to go with the railroad. I was six then, and I remember giving Bubba a piece of bubble gum up front at the old cash register to seal the bargain. Didn't expect to marry him, though." She looked about her ruefully. "I've spent my life here."

Sheila wondered whether Evelyn was glad or sorry, and tried to think of an appropriate response. But today Evelyn only needed a listener.

"It used to be a good business, but Home Depot has just about ruined us little people. We get by, because some of our customers are loyal and other people come in for a quick errand, like you did today, when they don't want to hassle an enormous layout for a few nails, but these last few years have taken the heart plumb out of Bubba. He used to be the friendliest, healthiest man, real active at First Baptist. Now..." Her voice trembled. She took a quick sip of Diet Coke before she continued. "They say all this growth is good for the county, but it's mostly good for newcomers. They get what they want, and we pay for it."

Sheila finished her own Coke. "Have you considered selling out?"

Evelyn laughed. "Who'd buy an old building that needs a roof? The best we can hope for is that somebody will want the land and pay enough to make it worth our while. Meanwhile, I come down and count the screws each day, and think about how it used to be."

She stood and stretched to a high shelf, fetched down a picture of a younger—and happier—Bubba and Evelyn standing with an older couple. Sheila recognized Bessie, very beautiful. "Wasn't Bubba handsome in those days?" Evelyn touched his face lightly. "Still is, on the rare occasions when he dresses up. And Harley Sims was the best-looking man I ever saw in real life. Bo's a lot like him. Roger, now, he's more like my family." She set the picture back on the shelf and again took her seat with her feet propped up.

"When Roger grew up, I told him, "You get into some other line of work, son. This store's days are numbered." So he chose building, since he could get materials at a good price here. But again, big developers eat the little ones alive. They have ins with the county commission, you see. You'd think, having Dudley in the family, Roger would have an in, too, but Dudley's too sweet. He tries to please everybody, and doesn't like to make a fuss. So the commission votes the big guys ordinance variations, and makes little guys like Roger toe the line. The big guys have more margin for error, too. They can afford to let a house sit vacant several months. Builders like Roger can't."

She sighed, shoved her stubby fingers through her hair until it stood up like a short red bush. "He and Erika want what every young couple wants—a bigger house for themselves and the kids, new cars, all the nice things other people have. But he's really pinched right n—"

She broke off the last word, and flushed. "I shouldn't go on like this, Sheila. You hardly know us!"

"Sometimes it's easier to talk to a virtual stranger, and I really don't mind." She didn't. Sixteen years of living with Tyler and moving in embassy circles had made her a good listener, and Evelyn deserved a listener. Besides, Evelyn was providing food for thought.

If it had been Grandma Sims who was murdered, Sheila would be considering each member of this branch of the family tree very carefully. But Martha Sloan had been part of this branch. Surely this was a case in which the wrong woman had been killed.

There was one other family member who remained a mystery. Evelyn in this chatty mood might shed some light on her. When she paused, Sheila asked, "Do you have responsibility for your husband's mother, too?"

Evelyn crushed her Coke can. Sheila was amazed at the strength in her small hands. "No, she's got a woman living with her, Lillie, who does what she needs. We take her groceries each week, and Bubba mows her lawn if Uncle Cline goes on a railroad junket. Nana doesn't want or need much, though, except paints and china. All day long she sits and paints. She's got a houseful of stuff she's done—won't give anything away—but she never stops. China plates, china bowls, china dogs and cats. Don't you dare tell anybody I said this, Sheila, but my greatest fear for years has been that she's going to die and leave it all to me!''

Her chuckle was infectious. Sheila grinned. "Maybe she'll turn out to be famous, and make you rich. Otherwise, have the world's largest garage sale. Some people will collect anything.''

Evelyn shook her head and pulled down her T-shirt. "Bubba and Roger would never permit that. They are both crazy about that woman, and no wonder. She spoiled them both rotten, and wouldn't let me make Roger do a lick of work. Of course, she never did a day's work in her life, either. Never showed her face in this store, unless she needed money. Are you married?''

Startled at this sudden shift, Sheila hesitated before she replied. "Widowed.''

Evelyn took the hesitation for grief. "Oh, dear, I'm sorry. I thought you were one of the undiscovered jewels of the world, like Faye. I hope you won't take offense at what I was going to say.'' Without waiting for Sheila to even try to reply to that, she prattled on. "If you ever plan to remarry, check out your future mother-in-law. If she's beautiful and lazy, think again. Those women simply ruin their sons. Nana did. Martha Sloan did, too. Her sons are about as useful around the house as sloths. Dunk didn't even look for a job after college until she made Dudley wangle him one, and when Bo will ever finish college is anybody's guess. He's got one master's already, and is working on a second. He and Martha Sloan fought like cats and dogs about that, but she made sure he never went hungry up in Athens. Take my advice, Sheila. I know what I'm talking about.''

Sheila chuckled. "I have an aunt like that. One in any family is plenty.'' She was aware, however, that she had been on the receiving end of a good bit of Aunt Mary's tart spoiling.

The bell up front jangled. Evelyn automatically shifted in her seat, then sank back with a grunt. "Art will get it. I'm pretty much taking a day off today."

"You deserve it." Sheila would have said more, but the door opened and grace wafted in.

At least, that's what it felt like. Actually it was Faye, talking softly and sweetly to Art over her shoulder, then turning to Evelyn with a smile. "Hello, Aunt Evelyn. Don't get excited. This isn't a present for you."

She held up a Wal-Mart bag.

"What is it?" Evelyn asked.

Faye's laugh was low and musical. "Underwear for Uncle Billy to be buried in. Grandma Sims told me to pick up some after I saw Mammaw, and to ask you to bring it over after work."

"Uncle Billy never wore..." Evelyn started to protest.

Faye leaned over and laid a finger on her lips. "We are not to say a word. That's what Mammaw said. Grandma Sims is absolutely adamant that poor Uncle Billy can't be buried without underpants." She turned, saw Sheila for the first time, and covered her mouth. "Oh, I'm sorry! You must think we're awful."

Evelyn lifted a pile of catalogues off the only vacant chair and waved Faye toward it. "Don't be silly, Faye. Sheila's seen men's shorts before. And anybody who's been around the family even one day won't expect us to be too sorry poor Uncle Billy is finally at peace. Sit down and have a Coke and tell us how Ruby's doing."

Faye took a long, grateful swallow before she began. "Much better. They may let her come home tomorrow. But it was a warning, the doctor says. She's got to take care of herself from now on. I'm just glad we got a warning, and didn't lose her."

"But she won't take care of herself," Evelyn said practically. "You know that."

"We'll have to make her. Sit on her, if necessary." Faye laughed. "Can't you just see us doing that? It would take both of us!"

Sheila was interested. Not in what Faye was saying, but at the change in the woman. The first time they'd met, Faye had looked like a deer—quiet, gentle, nervous about offending. Today she was relaxed and gently sarcastic, her eyes sparkling and her body almost sensuous as she stretched arms above her head. Only her hair was the same, limp and long, pulled back today with a navy bow that looked dull and lifeless.

Sheila had seen in the past how unmarried women at family gatherings could slip into little-girl ways among those they had known as children. She found Faye far more attractive away from her grandparents.

Evelyn opened another Diet Coke and handed a second Coke to Sheila. "How's Grandma Sims?"

Faye shrugged. "Up and down. This morning she was pretty low. Kept saying you expect to lose your parents, but you never expect to outlive your children. Then Pawpaw came bumbling in telling her that now that Uncle Billy's dead she needs to call Dudley and arrange to sell the farm. 'Merle and the girls need to know you'll provide for them,' he told her. She got perfectly furious. Waved her cane and nearly hit him! He's right of course, but she wouldn't discuss it. Finally I told them we'd hire a hall and give them both boxing gloves. That sort of embarrassed them, and poor Pawpaw slunk back home to feed Rags. Aunt Evelyn, do you think there's really a chance that somebody might buy the farm? Wouldn't it be wonderful to have more money than we knew how to spend?"

Evelyn sighed. "I don't know, honey, and I'm not sure it *would* be wonderful. I know it sounds like the answer to a lot of prayers, but that kind of answer can turn on you." Again she shoved her fingers through her hair.

Faye finished her Coke and stood up. "I can't stand to look at your hair one more minute. Do you mind if I give it a good brushing and try to style it a little?"

Evelyn reached into a desk drawer and handed her a brush. "I thought you'd never ask," she said with a grin.

"Who cuts your hair, Sheila?" Faye asked. When Sheila told her, she patted Evelyn on the cheek. "You ought to go to him, Aunt Evelyn. Let him make you beautiful, too!"

As Faye started to brush and style the sadly neglected hair, Evelyn said to Sheila, "This child takes good care of me. She's like her grandma—the salt of the earth."

Faye twisted her mouth into a moue. "You know what Grandma Sims would say to that? That sometimes a body can get powerful tired of too much salt." She coaxed the unruly hair into a semblance of order. When a curl had formed on Evelyn's freckled forehead, she stood back to admire her work. "There. Now you look decent."

Evelyn patted her hair, then pressed one hand to her cheek. "I just remembered, Faye, I can't get out to Grandma's tonight. I have a Sweet Adeline's practice. I wouldn't go, but I missed last week because of Martha Sloan—doesn't that seem like more than a week ago?—and we have a big concert coming up Memorial Day weekend. I'll drop it off tomorrow."

Faye shook her head. "The man from the funeral home is coming by to get it tonight, when he picks up Uncle Billy's new suit." She chewed her lower lip, much as her cousin Martha Sloan used to. "And I can't. We have orchestra rehearsal."

"Faye and Dudley represent the family in the new community orchestra. He plays oboe and she plays cello." Evelyn sounded as proud as if she spoke of her own daughter. "But whatever are we going to do?"

They regarded one another in helpless silence.

Sheila set the second Coke unopened on the desk. "Could I drop it by? I don't have any other commitments this evening, and I really wouldn't mind."

Five minutes later she headed the Maxima in the opposite direction from her own apartment, dinner, and an evening with the *Armchair Gourmet*. She was in high spirits, however. She could hardly wait to tell Aunt Mary that her "invitation" to the Simses had come in the form of Billy Sims's eternal underpants.

# NINETEEN

SHE TURNED into Grandma Sims's with some sadness. Yesterday at this same time she and Sara Sims had come with the cake. Today the very porch on the little white house drooped with sadness.

Bull was not on his chain. Sheila decided to sit in her car for a moment to be sure he didn't barrel around a corner, unchained and eager for guest meat. He did not appear.

"Hey! You need something?" Cline waved from his own yard.

She was glad to make her way gingerly along the narrow path toward Cline, hoeing his garden next door. "Hello!" She could still not bring herself to use "hey" as a mere greeting. "I brought something to Mrs. Sims." She held up the small bag.

He pressed a hand to the small of his back to dispel stiffness from too much stooping, and tramped along a furrow of tomatoes to meet her, removing a straw hat with one hand and bringing the hoe in the other. Rags waddled after him, uttering short gruff welcomes. "Weeds have nearly taken over this past week," Cline said gruffly. "Thought I'd get a start on them—give Ruby one less thing to fuss about when she gets home."

"Hello, Rags." She bent and scratched the old cocker around each ear. He sat down heavily on her feet.

"That dog sure cottons to you," Cline said with admiration. "He don't take to many women. Ruby, now. She feeds him, doctors him when he's sick, but he won't have a thing to do with her. Nearly breaks her heart."

She smiled. "He probably smells my own dog, and thinks I'm her. Are you really up to gardening today?"

"Oh, I'm fine. Just fainted, apparently, from the shock of seeing poor Billy. Sorry I conked out on you, though." He wiped his forehead with one sleeve. Today's shirt was green, with silver fasteners and an embroidered yoke. For gardening he had exchanged boots for homely brown shoes run down at the sides. "Poor old Billy. I guess things just got to be too much for him."

Sheila didn't know what she was supposed to say, but she knew what she wanted to find out: whether Cline Shaw thought Billy had killed himself because he'd murdered Martha Sloan. She tried a direct question. "Did somebody say he'd left a note about being at Mrs. Tait's last week?"

He drew bushy eyebrows together in a frown. "I didn't hear anything about a note. Where'd you hear that?"

Too late she remembered a cardinal rule about communicating in the rural South: Giving information precedes getting any. "Sara Sims or someone said Mr. Sims had been over at her mother's the day she died. That he went over sometimes to watch television since his set is broken. I wondered if maybe he had been upset about her dying so soon after he saw her."

"He was pretty upset by her death," Cline allowed, "And yeah, he was there early in the day. I took him myself. But I didn't hear about any note, and don't go thinking he killed her!" His voice rose, and his eyes began to get pink around the green irises.

Sheila wondered what tack to take next. She wondered why he hadn't said before that Billy had been at the Taits' last Tuesday. Had he told Detective Belk? "Did you bring him back?"

"No, I planned to, but I had to come by the house for something and he was already here. I guess Martha Sloan ran him back, or he walked. Billy was a great one for walking."

That was possible. It was also possible that Cline had stopped by Martha Sloan's, found Billy gone, and shot her himself.

"Did Billy know how to use a gun?"

"Co'se he did. In our day, every boy in America knew how to use a gun. Billy was a crackerjack shot at getting squirrels." Then he seemed to catch the drift of her questions. "But don't you go thinking he shot Martha Sloan, now. He wouldn't harm a fly."

She bit her lip to keep from retorting, "Just squirrels."

He took a step closer and fanned himself with his hat. "You ain't a reporter, are you? You said last Sunday you work for Japs."

"I work for Hosokawa International, and no, I'm not a reporter. I'm just a friend of Sara Sims's who's concerned for all of you."

His eyes were still narrowed with suspicion. "Why'd you say you've come over today?"

She held up the Wal-Mart bag again. "To bring something to Mrs. Sims. Evelyn sent it." She didn't bother to explain where she'd seen Evelyn, and he did not ask.

She turned to go, then turned back as if she had just thought of the question. "When I called to tell you about Mrs. Tait's murder, Mr. Shaw, you asked whether there had been a lot of blood. Did Billy have blood on his overalls that afternoon?"

He shoved his sunglasses up his forehead to look at her closely and took a step forward. "You *sure* you ain't one of them reporters?" She shook her head. "Then I suggest you just do your errand, little lady, and get your butt off this property. Billy had chicken blood on his overalls. Nothing else. You've no call to come making insinuations about a poor harmless old man who ain't alive to defend himself!"

Did Cline believe Billy had killed Martha Sloan? Did Ruby believe it, too? That could explain why they both were so jumpy at Dudley's last week. Had they agreed to protect the old man, watch him carefully, perhaps, but never let on, even to the rest of the family? If they had conspired to that extent, to what lengths would they go to protect Uncle Billy's memory now if they thought he had killed himself in remorse?

Her silence seemed to make Cline nervous. He took another step toward her and his breath came in a short, angry hiss. "Mebbe I'd better walk you over and make sure you get back to your car all right. No telling where Bull might be, and he's mean. Just as soon eat you as look at you, old Bull would. You don't want to come wandering around here by yourself again."

Muscles stood out in his thick neck. His fists were clenched on the hoe so tightly she marveled that it didn't break. As she looked into his red face, she wasn't certain she wanted to stay even long enough to deliver Uncle Billy's shorts.

He followed her all the way. Sheila disengaged blackberry briers from today's panty hose and reflected that she had no more desire to come back than Cline had to see her. Her lingerie budget couldn't take much more of the Simses.

Grandma Sims was now sitting on her porch, walker planted firmly before her. She wore a sweater even though the day was hot, and a full white apron over her gray flowered dress.

"Hello, Mrs. Sims, I was—"

"I'm out here looking at the lilies," the old woman quavered. "Them Easter lilies never do bloom in time for Easter. Memorial Day lilies would be a more fittin' name, I've always thought. But the day lilies have made nice this year, ain't they?"

Sheila duly admired the orange and yellow lilies that had spread for many years to now fill one side of the yard. She was again about to proffer her parcel when Grandma Sims asked, "You bring the things for Billy? Evelyn called and said you was on your way."

Sheila handed her the bag. "The underwear," Billy's mother told Cline, taking it out and holding it up with several nods of approval. "Put it with his suit, Cline. It's laid out on his bed."

He went inside on the errand. Sheila sank into the chair beside the old woman. She had very little time before Cline would return.

"Mrs. Sims, do you remember if Bull barked yesterday afternoon? At a stranger, or somebody coming to the house?"

The old woman didn't seem to hear her at first, then she shook her head. "He don't bark, 'cepting for strangers or fights, like last night. He didn't bark yestidday till after supper, when you come with Sara Sims."

She sank again into silence, then she turned, and her eyes were so full of anger that Sheila automatically leaned away, as if struck. "You tol' me Billy had a heart attack."

"No..." Sheila started to explain, but was given no time.

"'Tweren't his heart. He was hanged." Her mouth worked fiercely and the old gnarled hands held on to the ends of the chair's arm supports until her knuckles were white. She rocked rapidly, and the sound of wooden runners on the uneven porch floor sounded to Sheila like a hammer driving nails into an old wooden coffin. At last the old woman turned back to her. "Bo thinks somebody killed Billy and hung him there."

She leaned over and smacked Sheila's leg with an old, dry hand. "Billy never kilt himself. He wouldn'ta known how. Bo says he's gonna prove somebody else did it." She smacked Sheila's lap again. "You he'p him, you hear me? You give him all the he'p you can."

# TWENTY

*Friday*

THREE DAYS LATER, Sheila was still trying to figure out how to obey Grandma Sims's odd command. Since a trip to Chicago prevented her from attending Billy's funeral Thursday afternoon, she had seen Sara Sims only briefly and the rest of the family not at all.

Friday afternoon she was strolling through Atlanta's luxurious Phipps Plaza when she saw a familiar, but unexpected, face.

"Faye?"

The woman froze as if caught in a crime. Perhaps in her circles it *was* a crime to walk through an expensive mall carrying a large bag from Lord & Taylor and new shoes from Saks.

"I like what you have done with your hair," Sheila told her.

Faye's dark eyes lit with pleasure. "Thanks. I went to your man. He's wonderful!"

He was. Faye's face was now framed in soft layers of waves. She'd shaped her eyebrows, too, and applied toner, blush, and mascara. She was also dressed in one of Saks's latest models. Sheila saw several men turn back for a second look.

"Do you have time for a cup of coffee?" Sheila asked impulsively. "I want to hear how your grandmother is doing."

Faye checked her watch. "A quick one. I have a date at seven." It was half past five, but Sheila—who could shower and dress in fifteen minutes—suspected that that casual sentence was new in Faye's vocabulary and entailed at least a bubble bath.

They settled in a corner booth, where Sheila got reports on Ruby, Cline, and Merle, and an abbreviated version of Billy's funeral. He'd been buried in the cemetery next to the Primitive Baptist Church his family had attended all his life. Faye also mentioned, briefly, her high school English and drama classes, then asked about Sheila's own job. At last she checked her watch again and pushed back her cup in a quick, nervous gesture. "I really do have to run, Sheila. You probably think I'm awful to be going out so soon after everything that's happened, but..."

"I think it's very sane," Sheila replied. "Is this man somebody special?"

Faye's cheeks grew pink. "Very." She sighed. "But it's not fair for me to be so happy with...everything, and with Mammaw and Mama so sick. Don't mention it yet, even to Sara Sims. Please?"

"Of course not," Sheila promised. In Faye's place, she doubted she could be so reticent. Faye's romance was the family's only pleasant mystery.

Secondhand romance, however, left her with a distinct desire to pamper herself. "Shrimp are almost as good as being in love," she told her reflection in the Maxima's rearview mirror. "I'll make tempura!" Even a steady hard drizzle didn't deter her. She arrived home soaked, with frizzy hair, but full of anticipation. It had been a while since she'd eaten a pound of shrimp all by herself.

She put on a colorful caftan and soft slippers and, because it reminded her of last week's festive meal, started Pachelbel's *Canon*. She was peeling and deveining shrimp when Sara Sims knocked.

"Oh, you're fixing dinner." Sara Sims poised hesitantly on the doorstep. Lady trotted over for a pat, got only a small one.

"Want to join me?" Sheila asked, automatically, before she thought.

"I might as well. Beth flew out this morning."

Sheila regretted her invitation. Sara Sims was clearly not going to appreciate her sacrifice. Maybe, she comforted herself, a true sacrifice has to be unappreciated.

Sara Sims drifted into the living room. "Where's your couch?"

"Gone to get re-covered, compliments of the management—after only three calls. You look pretty down."

"Yeah." She settled into a chair. "Ah, Pachelbel!"

In spite of the violin case she'd seen on Mother's Day, Sheila was surprised. "You like classical music?" she asked, pouring some nuts into a bowl and handing out a cold Coke.

"Yeah. We play on Sundays—Bach and Mozart, mostly. I'm just mediocre, but Faye and Daddy are good and Aunt Merle was a piano major in college. She hasn't felt up to playing lately, though." Sheila, remembering her dread of an afternoon of poorly rendered gospel music, was humbled. Sara Sims reached for the snacks and munched nuts and sipped Coke. "Isn't life a bitch?"

"A normal reaction to the funeral?" Sheila inquired.

Sara Sims shook her head. "That wasn't sad, not really. Who would have taken care of Uncle Billy once Grandma Sims is gone?" She picked up a small glass paperweight and peered into its depths. She set it down and groaned. "Men are so confusing." She heaved an enormous sigh.

"Kevin?" Sheila presumed she didn't mean the men in her family.

"Yeah. He's been so busy, I've only seen him once this week. He said he has to go out of town for the weekend. Then at the end, he up and said he'll maybe see me tomorrow. What should I believe?"

Sheila, slicing sweet potato, tried to think of a reply to save her hours of listening. "He's going out of town today and coming back tomorrow. Or maybe he forgot he wouldn't be here."

"Maybe." Sara Sims picked up a magazine, put it down again. "What are you making?"

"Tempura. Do you like it?"

"I don't know. What is it? I don't like sweet potatoes much."

Sheila repressed a sigh. Preparing tempura for her solitary pleasure had been pampering. Going to that much trouble for an unappreciative guest was drudgery. As she started to cut broccoli, Sara Sims came and leaned against the counter, watching. "You know what Wart has done? Asked Grandma Sims to give him the farm! He actually wants to farm it, like Grandpa Sims used to. Roger is livid, and Uncle Cline is furious. What's weirder, Aunt Ruby agrees with Wart. She and Uncle Cline almost aren't speaking! At Uncle Billy's funeral, she put Grandma Sims between them, and afterwards, she rode home with Daddy."

"Is Ruby especially fond of Wart?"

"None of us can stand him. He isn't..." She stopped and wrinkled her nose. "Those awful clothes, and that jacked-up truck with a shotgun in the window, and Bull, and his war games—Bo hates him. Of course, Bo's into saving the planet. As far as he's concerned, Wart is pure pollution."

What Bo thought about Wart had been evident Monday night. What Ruby thought was far more interesting. "What about Ruby?"

"She liked him fine when he was a well-scrubbed little kid. He didn't get strange until he hurt his leg and couldn't be a marine anymore. I think he started doing drugs in the hospital. He was *so* different when he came home. Aunt Ruby hates to be around him. That's why it's weird that suddenly she's his greatest champion. She doesn't want the farm sold, of course."

Sheila could wave a flag about paving over good farmland herself, but not when she was mixing ice water into rice flour.

Sara Sims suddenly giggled. "You should have seen her Wednesday night. We were over helping Grandma Sims choose what to wear to the funeral, and our preacher came by. Aunt Ruby thought he'd come about Uncle Billy, and tried to explain that Uncle Billy's own preacher was doing the service. Finally he told her he'd come to talk to Grandma Sims about willing money to build an education building in memory of Aunt Emma. Uncle Aubrey had sent him. Aunt Ruby got so upset, I honestly thought she'd hit him!''

Sheila grinned. ''Hitting people seems to run in the female line of your family. You did a pretty good job with Grandma Sims's cane Monday night.''

Sara Sims smiled at the memory. ''Yeah, I did, didn't I? Poor old Bo...'' She stopped and sighed again. ''He's been home all this time, and we haven't gone a single place together. I thought maybe tonight we could eat together, but he was going out. Wouldn't say where. Probably to see some girl.'' Her voice was gloomy.

Her gloom lightened once she had tasted the tempura. It lifted completely when Andy Lee showed up, suggesting that they all go out to the Scarlet Cockerel, a new club near the mall. ''It's fantastic,'' he assured them.

Fantastic at twenty-five and fantastic at forty are two different things. ''It's pouring rain,'' Sheila objected. ''You all go, and leave me to music and my book.''

''It's stopped raining. Come on, Sheila, it's you I came to invite. This pipsqueak is just coming along for the ride.''

As Sara Sims opened her mouth to protest, Sheila yielded. ''Who could refuse an invitation like that?''

The Scarlet Cockerel was, as she had expected, dark, hot, and noisy. She sat and sipped her drink, listening to Sara Sims and Andy bicker and wondering why, in a free country, she couldn't choose to spend an evening reading. But at least Sara Sims was no longer groaning about Kevin.

After two trips to the bar, Andy turned to the women with a flourish. ''Time for equal rights. Somebody else can make her way through the crush this time.''

Nose in air, Sara Sims rose and did just that. She returned elated. ''Look who I found!''

Behind her stood Wart, wearing slacks, a sport shirt, and vestiges of a black eye, and Bo, still bruised across the bridge of his nose. His arm was draped over Wart, but Sheila's initial impression that he was choking his cousin was eventually corrected.

They dragged chairs to the table and began to snicker over stories from their childhood. For a time Sara Sims preened like a queen with three consorts, noting the open envy of several tables of single women. Sheila sipped her drink and tried not to look like a middle-aged duenna.

Eventually Sara Sims tired of stories that left her out. "Are you really trying to make Grandma Sims give you the farm?" she asked Wart.

He shrugged. "Sure. Who else would farm it? Now that Uncle Billy's out of the way, I could make it pay in a couple of years."

"What a horrid thing to say!"

"Face it, Simsy, Uncle Billy has been a drag for years. You didn't have to live with him, or change his wet bed, or put up with his whining over every little improvement you made."

"Did Uncle Billy make anybody mad lately, Wart?" Bo kept his voice light, but his fists clenched beneath the table. "Madder than usual, I mean? Did he make *you* mad?"

Wart downed half his drink in one swallow and wiped his mouth with one wrist. "Uncle Billy killed himself, Bo. Leave it alone!"

Sara Sims picked up her drink in a way that made Sheila think she might throw it at her cousin. Apparently Andy thought so, too, for he put his hand over hers and observed mildly, "It's hard to make a small farm pay anymore."

"I can do it," Wart insisted. "With a little capital, I'm going to switch to pick-your-own. There's not a pick-your-own operation that size closer than Walton County. People'll flock in."

Once again Sheila gave him grudging respect. She herself would pick fresh vegetables that close to home.

"Great idea," Andy agreed. "When your tomatoes come in, give me a call. I'll send Sheila right over to pick me some."

"But the farm belongs to all of us," Sara Sims objected.

"It belongs to Grandma Sims," he retorted. "And she doesn't want it paved over." More than half drunk, he pointed a threatening finger. "Don't you try to talk Grandma Sims out of doing what's right, Sara Sims! It's my farm! While you were at college partying, and you—" he switched the pointing finger to Bo "—were reading books about saving the earth, I've been working my butt off doing it. I've *earned* that farm."

"Where were you Monday afternoon, Wart—plowing a field?" Bo asked.

Wart belched hugely, grinned at the expression on Sara Sims's face. "Nope. I told you, I was up in Alpharetta looking at a Harley Davidson by the time Uncle Billy strung himself up. Before that I was with some friends of mine, mapping strategy. Yessir, we got ourselves a strategy." He waved his glass over his head. "Supremacy for the supreme!"

"Hush!" Sara Sims ordered him.

"How do you know when Uncle Billy died?" Bo persisted.

Wart drained his glass. "Whenever it happened!" He looked at his watch, pushed back his chair with a screech, and jumped to his feet. "I gotta get home. This man's got things to do." He stumbled toward the door.

Bo stood, tossed a tip onto the table. "Not very subtle, was I?"

"Not very," his sister agreed. She flopped back in her chair in disgust.

"Ah, sisterly love," Andy murmured as Bo made his way to the door. "Where would any of us be without it?"

"Brothers are far worse than sisters."

"Oh, no, my dear. Take my own sisters, now. They..."

Sheila sipped her drink and let them wrangle unchallenged. She couldn't help remembering, however, that as recently as last Sunday night, Andy had been an only child.

# TWENTY-ONE

*Saturday*

LADY WAS WHINING. A pile driver was pounding. Sheila turned over, pulled the covers over her ears, and snuggled deeper into her pillows, but the dull, insistent thud continued. She sat up, suddenly alert. Who on earth was knocking this early on Saturday?

She checked the clock. Half past seven. Lady would have been tugging the covers with her teeth in a few minutes anyway.

She peered through her peephole just as Sara Sims opened her own door, clad in a huge faded University of Georgia T-shirt. Her voice carried as she stifled a yawn. "What are you doing here at this hour?"

"It's Wart!" Bo's voice was rough with disbelief. "He's..." Sheila missed the rest, for Sara Sims jerked him inside and slammed the door.

Sheila went to her kitchen and put on coffee. She had scarcely run a comb through her hair and pulled on a robe when, as she had expected, they knocked. "Sheila? Sheila!"

Sara Sims had pulled on navy sweatpants with the red T-shirt, but had not bothered to brush her tangled hair or wash mascara streaks from beneath her eyes. Bo, in contrast, was immaculate in a dazzling "Save the Panda" T-shirt, jeans, and deck shoes. Only their eyes were identical: chocolate brown and scared.

"Sheila?" Sara Sims said in a shocked whisper. "You won't believe what's happened now! Wart's dead!"

"Dead?" She struggled to believe it. "When? How?"

Bo poured mugs of coffee without asking permission. His hand shook as he lifted his to his lips.

"Grandma Sims found him this morning, and called Uncle Cline. He called me—or rather, Dad. Dad isn't home, so I went over. The paramedics think he's been dead almost all night." He spoke in a flat, even voice, but his mug trembled even when held with both hands. He gulped more coffee and winced as it burned him.

"How?" Sheila repeated. They could have gone to the dining room table, but instead they huddled in her tiny galley kitchen.

Bo shrugged. "They don't know yet. The man from the coroner's office said they might know by tomorrow or Monday, or it could take six to eight weeks to find out. Maybe he overdosed on drugs—but I didn't expect him to be dumb enough to use them on top of booze."

"If he did, they're going to think..."

He waved his sister to silence. "He must have used something after we got home. Maybe it was more than he realized. Or," he added, "maybe it was bad. There's a lot of that going around."

"They're..."

Again he waved Sara Sims to silence, but this time she refused to obey. "They are going to think you gave it to him! Or that you were doing drugs together. What else can they possibly think?"

"I don't do drugs!" Bo's eyes flashed indignantly.

"Sara Sims has a point, anyway," Sheila told him. "You were probably the last person to see Wart alive."

"Why'd you go out with him in the first place?" Sara Sims demanded. "You never liked him."

"I still think he killed Uncle Billy. I hoped I could get him to confess. But you heard him—he kept insisting that Uncle Billy committed suicide." He chewed his knuckles and looked very young.

"What motive could he have had for killing your uncle?" Sheila asked.

Sara Sims answered. "What he said last night—that Uncle Billy was a pain to live with. Besides, any way you slice it Wart's share of the pie went from a fourth to a third when Uncle Billy died."

"And," Bo added, "the only way Grandma Sims would ever leave Wart the whole farm would be if he'd promised to take care of Uncle Billy. Uncle Billy might have lived as long as Grandma Sims. I'm sure as Christmas he killed him, but we'll never prove it now. He was probably celebrating when he got home last night, and took too many pills on top of the booze."

Sheila found it a plausible theory. "Did he say anything on the way home to indicate he planned to use drugs after you'd gone?"

Bo tugged at one earlobe, considering. "I don't know. He was pretty loaded. Mostly he sang dirty songs, shouted out the window at blacks in other cars when we stopped for lights. I was trying to pretend I didn't know him, if you want the truth. He was more than halfway to la-la land. At one point he said, "We'll blow those suckers sky high, Bo!" Another time he said, "All I need is a sign." Maybe he was talking about drugs then. I don't know. I didn't pay much attention. After that he started to snore. I had to almost carry him out of the car and push him through the window."

"The window?" Sheila repeated, startled.

"Grandma Sims bolts her front and back doors," Sara Sims explained. "But Wart sleeps...slept in the front, so he used his porch window as a door."

Poor Grandma Sims, sleeping confident that she was safe when in fact anybody could have entered her house. Once more Sheila was amazed that it was not Grandma Sims who was dead. She studied Bo closely as she mused, "If Wart died within the next hour or two, you could easily have been involved."

Bo was furious. "I wasn't!"

"*We* know that," Sara Sims nodded, "but if the police find out you were together last night..."

"What does your father say?" Sheila trusted Dudley's considered opinion above either of these two volatile ones.

Bo shook his head. "I can't get him. He's gone up to our house on Lake Lanier for the weekend to check the ski boat and get food ready for Monday. He must have taken the phone off the hook. He wanted to do it alone, said he needs a little privacy. Privacy? We could all use some of that these days!" He rubbed his eyes almost into his skull. "I came to take you to Grandma's, Sara Sims. Uncle Cline can't be away from Aunt Ruby very long."

She pulled back. "What about you? Or Faye? Or Aunt Evelyn? Or Roger? Why does it always have to be me?"

"Uncle Cline said Faye's at a convention all day and Aunt Evelyn is having her Memorial Day sale. Erika said Roger's at a site and left his beeper at home. And we can't trust Uncle Bubba—you know that. Now come on!" He used the tone reserved for big brothers.

Before Sara Sims could respond, Lady gave a sharp bark. The next second, someone knocked at the door across the hall.

"You go," Sara Sims whispered to Sheila in exactly the same tone she had used at Grandma Sims's Monday night. The cases were certainly similar. Sheila opened the door to see the backs of the same tall dark policeman and his short blond partner, Starkey. The taller one gave no sign of recognizing her.

Starkey started to say something, but the other cut him off. "We are looking for William Bradford Tait, ma'am. Known as Bo. Does his sister live here?" He jerked a thumb toward Sara Sims's door.

Bo pushed Sheila aside and went onto the breezeway. "I'm Bo Tait. What do you want?"

"We want to ask you some questions about the death of Wallace Henry Sims. I believe you were with him last night?"

Bo took a step back toward Sheila's open door. "I'm not talking with you unless my dad's present. He's a lawyer."

"We'll call him," the policeman said, "from the station."

SARA SIMS SLUMPED in a chair, stunned. Lady pranced to go out, but Sheila hated to leave. "They'll just ask him some questions."

Sara Sims shook her head. "They think he killed Wart. Maybe, even, he did."

Before Sheila could reply to that astonishing statement, Andy Lee was at the door in his jogging suit. Sheila tried to motion him away, but Sara Sims saw him. "Wart's died, and the police think Bo killed him! They... they took him away!"

"Understandably." Andy took a mug from Sheila's rack, poured coffee, helped himself to milk from the fridge. "The police have a reputation to uphold, after all, and your family is providing more than your share of unsolved cases this month. They won't keep Bo."

"Careful," Sheila warned him, but Sara Sims was encouraged.

"You think so?"

"I'm sure so."

"You'd better get going to the farm," Sheila suggested.

"I guess so." Sara Sims shoved her fingers through her snarled hair. Her bare toes clenched and unclenched at the carpet.

Andy strolled over and looked hopefully in the cold oven. "Haven't had time to bake yet this morning?"

"Not yet," Sheila agreed, refilling her own cup. "Nor to walk poor Lady, either. I'll give you a toasted bagel with cream cheese and strawberry jam if you'll take her out."

"Sure, while the witch changes out of her rags. You are not," he said to Sara Sims, "the most ravishing thing I've ever seen first thing in the morning."

Sara Sims looked as if she might fly at him with claws extended. "Go," Sheila told him, giving him a push. "Earn your bagel."

As soon as he had gone, Sara Sims heaved a sigh of obvious reluctance. "I guess I ought to get dressed." On the way out, she paused to look at her reflection in the mirror over Sheila's small hall table. "I do look a bit like a witch," she admitted.

She returned in a few minutes with face fixed, hair smooth, and wearing jeans and a tan shirt that enhanced her creamy skin and tawny coloring. Sheila smiled approval. "Feel better?"

Sara Sims shrugged. "Presentable, at least. I tried to call Kevin, but he's still out of town. No wonder he wants space. Who'd want to get close to this family?"

Andy returned with Lady (too quickly to have taken her all the way to the designated area) and greeted Sara Sims's new look with a thumbs-up. "That's better. Now cheer up, old girl. Sheila will probably solve this case before you get home. Won't you, Sheila?"

Sheila, trying to pry open a frozen bagel, said nothing. Sara Sims looked from one to the other, mystified.

"She's a sleuth," he explained. "She found out who killed Dean Anderson last fall. She's solved lots of other mysteries, too." Catching Sheila's eye, he shrugged. "I have spies around town."

Sheila popped the bagel into the toaster, trying to decide whether to kill him now or wait for Sara Sims to ask the question that was forming in her eyes.

By the time Sara Sims opened her mouth, the question had become several. "Is it true, Sheila? Are you really a detective? Can you find out how Wart died, or Uncle Billy? Even who killed Mama?"

Sheila toasted the bagel, motioned Andy to cream cheese and a jar of jam on the counter.

"Not the good china?" he complained. "Or a bowl for the jam?"

"You get a knife. You're lucky it isn't through your heart."

"Temper, temper," he said cheerfully. He spread the bagel liberally with cream cheese and jam, reached a plate down from the cabinet, then handed the whole thing to Sara Sims with a small bow. "For you, milady. Sheila thought I was being piggy."

She reached for a second bagel and gave him a reluctant smile. "You get the next one. You can't talk while chewing bagel."

Sara Sims ate by the door, giving at least the impression that she planned to leave in the near future. As she chewed her own bagel, Sheila enjoyed the silence and considered whether she could be of any use to the Sims family.

"Say no!" her common sense commanded. "Leave this to the police, or a professional private eye." Only the memory of Billy Sims, dangling from a well-tied rope, made her hesitate.

She had come to no decision when Sara Sims swallowed and asked, "Are you really a detective, Sheila?"

"I've worked on a few cases."

"Would you take ours? I know Daddy would pay you."

Sheila shook her head. "I don't work for pay. But why don't you suggest to him that he call in a professional?"

Sara Sims's eyes widened in horror. "Not a stranger!"

It is no wonder, Sheila reflected, that people in the South try so hard to establish connections with every new person they meet. A Southerner fears nobody so much as a "stranger."

She asked what to her was a critical question. "Do you have any guesses about who killed your mother?"

Sara Sims's eyes filled with tears. "No, but somebody's gone crazy if it's anybody I know. Right now I'm scared this will go on until every one of us is dead!"

"We'll protect *you*," Andy assured her. "And you, at least, have an alibi for most of last night."

Sheila raised her eyebrows at that. She had bid them good night at her own door a little after twelve.

"We were talking," Sara Sims explained hastily.

"Alas," he mourned. "It's too bad you sent me home. I could have alibied you for the whole night."

Sara Sims set her plate on the counter. "If you're going to start talking dirty, I'm leaving."

She walked to the door with her nose in the air. Just before she stepped through it, however, she threw him a smile.

"Wait!" Andy called her back. "I have an idea. Have all your family members been notified about Wart's death?"

Sara Sims shook her head. "Sounds like Uncle Cline called Bo and they're leaving the rest of the calling up to me."

Andy went to Sheila's phone and ripped a page from her message pad. "Don't call anybody. Give us the names and addresses, and Sheila and I will visit each of them. Maybe they will give something away."

"You're going to spy on my family?" she demanded, indignant.

"Not at all," he assured her with dignity. "We are going to console them on the death of their beloved nephew and cousin."

She gave a snort of disdain. "Right. See if any one of them sheds a tear." She took the pad and wrote rapidly.

Sheila had opened her mouth to say she had other plans for the morning, and that that wasn't the way the best detectives did things. She shut it with a snap. What did she know about how the best detectives did things? And after the past two weeks it was good to see Sara Sims's eyes sparkle with something besides tears.

# TWENTY-TWO

TWO HOURS LATER she was not certain they knew any more about the Sims family deaths than they had known before. But they certainly knew a great deal more about the family.

Erika had sent them to Roger's newest building site, currently a morass of red clay and a skeleton of two-by-fours in a subdivision of two-hundred-thousand-dollar homes. He was deep in conversation with a man in khaki pants and navy blazer.

"Not your usual Saturday Yuppie wear for new-home inspection," Andy murmured as they made a treacherous way up a muddy hill that left great gobs of clay stuck to their shoes.

"... just a little more time! One more week is all I need! One week, man!" Roger's voice floated clearly. The other man shook his head, looked about him, and said something they couldn't hear. Then he turned and proceeded down the hill, his nose pinched with distaste at the mud.

Roger turned and started up the staircase, shouting to a man hammering on second-floor subflooring. "You might as well knock off, Jake. You heard what the man said. We're finished for now. Kaput. They won't give me an extension."

Sheila and Andy clambered up the makeshift outside stairs and Sheila called his name. He turned, puzzled, then remembered who she was. "Looking for a house? Looks like this one is going cheap." He was breathing rapidly, his jaw clenched. He received their news with no visible change of expression. "Wart, huh?" He paused, a gleam in his eye. "Well, I'll go by when I get cleaned up. Too bad for Grandma Sims."

"Too bad for Wart, too," Sheila pointed out.

Roger shrugged. "He won't be missed. Now if you'll excuse me, I have things to do." He clumped up the remaining stairs without a further word.

AUBREY CAME TO his door in a white monogrammed robe over maroon silk pajamas. His hair was neatly combed, his dentures gleaming. He did not invite them in, but spoke through the screen door. Like Roger, his sympathies were all with Grandma Sims.

What he said was banal. Sheila was far more intrigued by the way he kept looking back over his shoulder. She understood when, just for an instant, she saw a plump woman in a ruffled peignoir flit across the back hall. Gussie Mae, she presumed.

"Did you see the brochures?" Andy asked as they returned to the car.

"No," Sheila admitted. "What brochures?"

"For a three-week trip to India—lying on the coffee table. I peeked through the window while you were talking to him. Looks like our man is planning an extended vacation."

Probably planning to use Emma's inheritance to finance Gussie Mae's tastes, Sheila agreed—but privately. She had been too well brought up to gossip aloud with anyone except Aunt Mary herself.

BUBBA, to their surprise, was neither drunk nor alone. He was sitting under a sweet gum tree playing a hose on two small figures in bright red bathings suits. "Erika let me have them for the morning," he explained, giving the hose a flick of his wrist that sent the water spiraling and made the children shriek with laughter.

When Sheila told him Wart was dead, he immediately pulled himself up from his chair and headed for the faucet. "Got to cut it short, kids. We need to get you dressed and over to your other grandmother's. I've got to go see Grandma Sims."

"He may be a lush," Andy murmured as they drove away, "but for my money, he's the most human member of the family we've seen today."

Sheila heartily agreed.

THEY DECIDED TO CALL Evelyn and leave a message at the register, and to let Cline call his daughter himself. At noon, therefore, they parted—Sheila to make herself lunch, and Andy to sulk because she wouldn't feed him, too.

"I haven't adopted you to raise," she pointed out.

"You could," he replied. "Besides, I want to sit and watch your little gray cells at work."

"My little cells are pink, and they are planning to take an hour's nap," she informed him. "Alone."

Sara Sims returned about two and sank into Sheila's chair as if she planned to stay. "Boy, am I tired! Grandma Sims is pitiful. Sits at the table and stares into space—won't eat, won't sleep, won't even talk. I didn't know what to do!"

"You didn't leave her alone, did you?"

Sara Sims stretched her arms high overhead. "Oh, no. There are lots of people there. I came home to rest, and I'll go back later."

Sheila hoped she didn't plan to do all her resting in Sheila's own chair. "Would you like a Coke?" When, she wondered, had she begun to automatically offer this Atlanta panacea for distress? Perhaps she should consider investing in Coca-Cola stock.

Sara Sims drank in long, deep swallows before she asked, "Have you figured out who killed Mama?"

"No, but I have a few questions. First, what happened with Bo?"

"The police asked him about last night, then let him go. But not until noon. Dad kept his phone off the hook, and Bo refused to talk until he got there. Finally they sent somebody from the Buford police to the lake house to tell him to call them.''

"So is Bo cleared of all suspicion?" Sheila had been remembering Sara Sims's "Maybe he did" all morning.

Sara Sims shrugged. "I guess so. All the grown-ups seem to think Wart died from a bad heart we didn't know about. His daddy did, when he was thirty-five. I still think it was an accidental overdose." She traced a design in the frost on her glass.

"Sara Sims, do you have any reason to think Bo might have had something to do with Wart's death—besides the fact that they didn't like each other?"

Sara Sims went to the window. For some time she watched ducks on the pond. Finally she said, without turning, "If you are going to solve this, you have to know everything, don't you?"

"Yes."

"Well, maybe Wart knew something Bo isn't telling. When Mama was killed, Bo said he was at school all day. But I'd gone over Monday to do laundry. On Tuesday when I went in to look at Mama, there were clothes on the drier she'd washed since I was there. They were Bo's. They weren't there Monday night!"

Sheila remembered meeting her near the stairs. "The clothes you carried upstairs to put away?"

Sara Sims nodded, miserable. "Bo often comes home for a morning if he doesn't have classes. It's only a forty-minute drive. Mama did his wash to save him spending money at a Laundromat. Sheila?" she wailed, "Do you think Bo could have killed Mama?"

"What motive could he have?"

Sara Sims sniffed. "They fought all the time. Mama wanted to choose his friends, his major, his whole life. At Easter he told her he wanted to go into the Peace Corps. She was livid! They were still fighting about it when..."

Sheila had a hard time believing anybody would kill to get into the Peace Corps. It sounded like a contradiction in terms. But she remembered how obstinate Martha Sloan Tait could be. "Have you mentioned finding his clothes to Bo?"

Sara Sims shook her head. "I...I was scared to."

For once, Lady missed a cue. A volley of knocks sounded on the door before she began to bark. Kevin swaggered on the threshold.

"Is Sara Sims over here, Sheila? I saw her car..."

Sara Sims flew across the room and hurled herself against him. "Oh, Kevin, another awful thing has happened!"

He pulled her onto the breezeway, closing the door behind them.

Only a few minutes later Sara Sims returned, eyes damp but shining. "He has to go by the store for a few hours, but he'll come over to Grandma Sims's at seven. And look!" She held out her wrist to display a dainty gold bracelet. "He bought it for me in Macon!"

Sara Sims had scarcely picked up her Coke and admired her bracelet again when Andy arrived. "Do I see that our mutual neighbor has returned?"

Feeling like the girl's social secretary, Sheila poured him a Coke and pulled a straight chair over to form a circle.

Sara Sims set down her drink with a deep sigh. "What else do you want to know, Sheila?"

If Sara Sims didn't mind discussing the case before Andy, why should Sheila? "For one, do you think Bo would have killed your Uncle Billy if Billy saw him kill your mother? You said they were very close. Would Billy have killed himself if he saw Bo do it? Or even to draw attention away from Bo?"

Sara Sims groaned with exasperation. "Who knows what Uncle Billy would do? He never did what you thought he would."

"Bo hasn't killed anybody." Andy spoke with conviction. "Bo's no killer. And the way you told me about it last night, Bo is the only one who thinks Uncle Billy was murdered."

He used the kinship name automatically. Soon, Sheila thought wryly, I probably will, too.

Sara Sims had an answer ready. "Bo's also the only Eagle Scout in the family. He can tie every knot in the book."

Andy drew himself to his full seated height. "I, too, am an Eagle Scout, but we didn't learn knots in order to hang poor old men. You obviously know nothing of the Scout code."

"Be prepared."

"And always be helpful. There is nothing helpful about hanging a man. Put Bo out of your mind, woman. He is as innocent as I am."

Sheila went to her desk for paper and a pen. "Draw me a family tree again, Sara Sims." When Sara Sims finished, Sheila looked it over. "Doesn't Faye have a sister?"

"Oh, yeah, Amy." Sara Sims took the list and added the name. "She's a half sister, really. Aunt Merle was married twice. I didn't put her on because she's up at Yale and not involved in any of this."

"Did you leave off anybody else?"

"Nobody but Wart's mother and grandmother. They're both dead."

Sheila studied the list again with a frown. "Billy's death and Wart's benefit everybody," she said finally. "They cut Mrs. Sims's principal heirs in half. But I can't see how anybody benefited from your mother's murder."

Sara Sims shook her head. "*We* certainly didn't. Poor Daddy, rattling around in that big old house all by himself—it nearly breaks my heart, but we can't do much about it. Bo is taking classes all summer, and I'm too busy to get over there very often." She admired her new bracelet—naively revealing her thoughts.

Andy looked at the bracelet sourly. "I'll bet it's your boyfriend doing all these murders. Trying to narrow down the heirs to you and you alone."

"Don't be ridiculous!" Sara Sims blazed at him. "He'd have to kill Daddy, and Dunk, and Bo, and..."

Sheila considered. A glimmering of an idea was beginning to occur to her.

Andy was now poring over the family tree. "Or maybe it's your Uncle Aubrey. He's a sly dog—did you know he has a girlfriend?"

"A girlfriend?" Sara Sims was scornful. "Don't be silly. He's *old*." With that dismissal of passion after thirty, she turned her attention back to Sheila.

"Other possibilities, as I see it," Sheila told her, "are your Uncle Cline..."

"Not Uncle Cline!" Sara Sims's hair swung in outrage. "He wouldn't hurt Uncle Billy!"

Sheila shrugged. "What if Billy stood in the way of Merle, Faye, and Amy inheriting more? Or—in the case of Wart—what if he stood in the way of their getting *anything?*"

Sara Sims shook her head mutinously. "Wart just died, Sheila. Nobody killed him." Sheila knew from her tone that the family had come to a united conclusion on that.

"Well, what about your Uncle Bubba, or Roger?"

"Roger!" Sara Sims clutched at the name like a baby clutches its mother's hair. "He hated Mama, because she and Daddy had Nana's power of attorney and Roger thinks he ought to have it. And he was always nasty to Uncle Billy. Of course," she added, to be fair, "he's nasty to everybody. But I'll bet he killed them!"

"Nice family," Andy said to Lady, who was sniffing his feet.

Sheila frowned in his direction, then back at her list. "Those aren't strong motives for murder, though. Most people don't commit murder unless they think they can't get something any other way."

Sara Sims let that sink in, then she sighed. "Then the only death that would really benefit anybody is Grandma Sims's—but nobody has tried to hurt her."

"Because she hasn't made a will?" Sheila hazarded.

Sara Sims started to nod. Then, at the same moment, they all had the same idea.

It was Andy who voiced it. "Up to now, she's had somebody around to protect her."

# TWENTY-THREE

GRANDMA SIMS was well protected when Sheila and Sara Sims arrived about four. Sheila had been reluctant to go, but Sara Sims had assured her, "It's only neighborly. They'll be more surprised if you *don't* come than if you do." Seeing the crowd, Sheila understood what she meant.

A knot of sullen young men with leather vests, jeans, boots, and shiny bikes stood smoking under the old sycamore in the side yard. "Wart's friends," Sara Sims hissed unnecessarily. The young men looked sideways at the two women, but did not greet them.

On the porch, Bubba and Roger sat with Aubrey and Cline, talking with several men. From the amount of thigh slapping and laughter when the women approached the porch—and the immediate silence when they got within earshot—Sheila suspected they were not discussing last week's Sunday school lesson.

Inside, Erika and Merle shared the couch, bringing a roomful of women up to date. "We left the kids with my mother," Erika said when Sara Sims raised her eyebrows at their absence.

Evelyn, as usual, was in the kitchen. So were Faye and, surprisingly, Dudley, washing dishes.

Faye wore a beige skirt and soft white top so simply cut they had to have been expensive. Both showed curves Sheila had not suspected she had. She also wore a bright Guatemalan belt and green flats, and her eyes still shone from last night's date. Some of her gaiety occasionally rubbed off onto Dudley, but he looked wan, drawn, and a little feverish. Sheila admired him for coming at all after everything he'd been through in the past two weeks.

Except for Ruby, who was still on strict bed rest, only one person was absent. "Where's Bo?" Sheila murmured to Sara Sims.

She received a shrug. "Probably taking another bath after his morning at the police station. Bo can't stand anything that makes him feel dirty."

Sheila could identify with that. A professional detective, she suspected, would have joined Wart's friends under the tree. She was not a professional detective. She wasn't even a *willing* detective, and the thought of getting near those sweaty, tattooed thugs made her skin crawl.

"I'm glad you came, Sheila," Evelyn said, interrupting her thoughts. "Have a bite?"

Wart had been found early enough in the day for friends to get to the Winn Dixie and "run by with a little something." There must have been a sale on ham and potatoes. Sheila had never in her life seen so much baked ham and potato salad on one family's table. Before Sheila could refuse, Evelyn had already begun to pile a plate. "You want something too, Sara Sims?"

"I'm too busy admiring your dish drier," Sara Sims said, leaning against the table. "Never saw that man dry a dish in his life."

Dudley gave his daughter an embarrassed grin.

"Have you learned to cook, too?" she inquired.

"I'm not the chef," he asssured her. "Just chief drier of dishes and avoider of the front porch." Sheila could sympathize with that.

Faye dipped a finger into beet juice, drew a half-moon on his cheek. "Great Chief Dudley." Sara Sims laughed. He swatted her with the dish towel, then scrubbed his face.

"Have you ever noticed how people tease after a death?" Evelyn murmured to Sheila. "You can only cry so much."

Sheila wondered who in the family had really cried for Wart.

One, at least, was mourning. "This ain't the time for them shenanigans." Grandma Sims, almost hidden at the far end of the table, thumped her cane on the floor.

"We're sorry, Grandma Sims. You're right." Faye turned back to the dishpan and handed Dudley a dripping plate. "It's just such a gorgeous day outside today that I'm in better spirits than I ought to be." She gave Sheila a conspiratorial smile, looking as if any minute she would start to float a few inches off the floor.

"What's gonna happen to me?" Grandma Sims quavered, jutting out her chin. "Wart weren't good, but he stood by me." Her old jaw began to tremble, and she wiped one eye with a gnarled hand. "Who's gonna take care of me now?"

Evelyn cut ham into tiny pieces, mashed up some sweet potato, and set it before the old woman. "We'll take care of you, Grandma. You eat something now, with Sara Sims and Sheila. Sheila's company. You don't want company to eat alone."

Grandma Sims looked directly at Sheila. "You here again? That's good." She ducked her head, and began to eat.

Over the old woman's head, Evelyn winked and mouthed, "Keep her eating!" Sheila wondered if that meant she would have to keep eating herself.

Faye leaned over the sink, craned her neck to look at the young men in the side yard. "I wish they would go home, Dudley," she said in a low voice. "They worry me, standing around out there."

"I'll go ask if they want something to eat," Dudley suggested. "Maybe if we feed them, they'll leave."

"More likely, they'll move in," Evelyn grunted. "But it's worth a try. There's plenty here." Dudly whisked off his apron and hurried out.

For several minutes the kitchen was silent enough to hear snatches of conversation from the next room.

"...they're a handful," Erika was saying to one woman.

"...sick as a dog after chemo, but I'm better now," Merle was saying to the others. Nobody, Sheila noticed, either in the living room or on the porch, was mentioning Wart.

"I wish Merle'd give up that job," Grandma Sims said suddenly.

"It's her life," Faye protested gently. "If she didn't have it, she'd just sit and brood."

"Let her come to Ruby." Grandma Sims's eyes darted from Sheila to Sara Sims, then to Evelyn. Seeking an ally? "Let them take care of one another. Get Ruby off *my* back." Her lower lip quivered. "I can't abide being fussed over. Ruby's a fusser."

"Oh!" Faye gasped suddenly, peering out the window over the sink.

Sheila, about to put her plate in the sink, glanced out. Two of Wart's friends towered over Dudley with menace in their eyes. She bit her lip. Should she interfere? Were the men on the front porch aware of Dudley's danger? The old Chevy near the porch would screen their view of the gang under the sycamore.

Quickly she thrust the plate into the dishwater and hurried out the back door, down wooden back steps, and around the house through tall grass to the side yard.

"Hey! What's going on?" she called.

It got them off balance, as she had hoped.

"Beat it, lady," one man bellowed.

"What's going on?" she repeated, moving closer.

One of them took a step toward her, which was what she wanted. In an instant he was lying on his back staring up into the sycamore with a bemused look on his face.

Another man moved toward her, but a third held him back. "It ain't worth it, Mort. That's one tough bitch. Let's beat it." He hauled his friend to his feet. The entire pack turned and mounted their bikes, revved the engines, and roared away.

"Yeah, Sheila!" Roger called from the porch, making loud, hollow claps. His praise sounded hollow, too.

"Good work, little lady," Cline chimed in. His praise was real.

"I thought you needed help," she told Dudley.

He gave her an embarrassed smile. "I thought so, too. Thanks." He put a hand to her waist and led her toward the kitchen via the back door. She was grateful that he didn't make her run the gauntlet of the front porch.

Faye met them, twisting a dish towel in her hands. "Are you all right, Dudley? Sheila, you're just the bravest thing I ever saw! I'd have been scared to death."

A limp strand of hair dangled in his face. He swiped it back angrily. "Those hoodlums were smoking marijuana right in our yard! And when I told them to leave or we'd call the police—well, I don't know if they would have really hurt me or not, but I was having a bad moment when Sheila arrived."

"Wow, Sheila!" Cute Jimn's eyes shone, regretfully, with something akin to worship. "Teach me to do that!"

"Drugs!" Grandma Sims spat out biscuit crumbs with the word. "Bo said Wart was using drugs in this house. If I'da known, I'da given him a hiding, big as he was!"

"We all would have." Evelyn gave the counter a fierce wipe.

Sheila nudged Sara Sims gently. This was as good a time as any for the first question she'd primed the young woman to ask.

Sara Sims turned to the old woman. "Were you awake last night when Bo brought Wart home, Grandma? Did anybody come see Wart after that, or did he go out again?"

Dudley turned and spoke sharply. "Sara Sims, Grandma has enough to grieve over without worrying that somebody might have gotten into the house!"

The old woman sat like a basilisk, head thrust out, not moving a muscle except to blink her eyes and chew her food. Her gaze pierced Sara Sims, then moved to Dudley. "I ain't seen nobody."

Faye turned from the sink. "Of course not! Who could arrange to meet Wart here after midnight without making him suspicious?"

"Suspicious about what?" Sara Sims demanded. "They could have decided to get together to listen to music, or work on a truck, or talk carburetors."

"I guess so," Faye said uncertainly.

"Wart was cutting trees," Grandma Sims said. Something in her voice compelled them all to listen. "Men come by with pickup trucks. They'd mosey down back of the barn, then drive around back and cart off firewood. Wart thought I didn't know. I did, though. Billy seen him, more'n oncet."

"Wasn't that all right?" Evelyn asked. "Grandpa Sims used to sell a good bit of lumber, I remember."

The old woman jerked her head once. "Will made right smart out of lumber. But Wart was clearing where we got paid by the gov'ment to plant. We ain't supposed to cut them trees for another two years."

Dudley bent near her, appalled. "Are you sure he was cutting them, Grandma Sims? That's violating a government contract!"

She nodded. "It weren't right, but he was doing it—cutting 'em into firewood and selling it. When I ast him about it, he said he was clearing that land to plant. Just like it were his'n awready!" Her black eyes snapped with indignation and her dentures clacked.

For one crazy moment Sheila pictured Grandma Sims putting pills into Wart's cocoa to protect the government's trees. She resolved to have a look behind the barn as soon as possible.

Dudley echoed her thoughts. "I'll go have a look." He went out the back door. Evelyn heard the sound of new arrivals and went into the living room to welcome them—and accept, probably, more ham and potato salad. Faye, temporarily finished with dishes, drifted into the living room.

Sheila caught Sara Sims's eye and traced a dollar sign and a question mark on the tablecloth.

Sara Sims spoke softly. "What was Wart doing with the money, Grandma Sims? Did you know?"

She nodded. "Kep' it in a tin in his room, in the back of his closet, underneath his trashy books. He had more'n six hundred dollars in there Wednesday. I seen it."

"Is it still there?" Sara Sims nearly danced to her feet.

"Reckon it is. I ain't looked." The old woman bent to her plate.

Sara Sims held out a hand. "Come on, Sheila. Let's find out."

Billy's bedroom and the bathroom were between Grandma Sims's room and Wart's. Sheila tested the front window. It slid up and down without a sound, and the screen was merely propped into place. Even if the old woman's hearing had been excellent, she might not have heard Wart come home or let in a visitor.

"It's pretty raunchy," Sara Sims said, apologizing for the room.

It was. Wart's taste ran to posters of nude women with flowers in nonstrategic places and monster dogs leaping with fangs bared.

"Where's Bull?" Until now, Sheila had forgotten him.

Sara Sims looked about as if expecting him to appear. "I don't know. Maybe Uncle Cline shut him in the barn."

Along one wall ran what could only euphemistically be called a bookshelf. It held a collection of guns, ammunition boxes, knives, and one spiral-bound notebook. Sheila picked it up without much enthusiasm. Wart had not struck her as the journaling type.

He had been—of a sort. The book was full of drawings of monsters, pentagrams, swastikas, and obscenities, and of words scrawled unevenly without regard for lines or spelling. She sampled several entries:

It is hard to think with a headful of rain.

I am the Electric Messiah, the Destroyer, locked away in this dark room in this dark cintury. Is it any wonder the world sickens and dies?
We, the acid scarred victims of histery, of evil and hipocrisey, exalt criminals to office!
With roaring missiles and lovely bombs, destroy the rich, niggers, and the hidious. Burn children and torture women, forever and ever! Amen.
Noise, confusion, and teror. May they rein forever.

The last entry was cryptic, but sounded saner than the rest:

Two heads are better than one. At last it begins to happen. Not much longer now.

"Whew!" Sheila handed the book to Sara Sims. "Does any of that make sense to you?"

Sara Sims shook her head. "Probably something to do with his friends. A lot of them have these designs on their jackets." She tossed the book into the trash can.

Sheila retrieved it and put it back on the shelf. "It could be evidence—of something. I wonder what he expected to happen. Didn't he say something to Bo about waiting for a sign?"

"He was crazy," Sara Sims replied. Sheila was inclined to agree, but even craziness can have its own order.

Sheila looked at the guns again. "Would anybody besides Wart know if they are all here?"

Sara Sims joined her. "I doubt it. I haven't really been in his room before, just at the door." Her thoughts suddenly matched Sheila's. "Mama could have been shot with one of Wart's guns!"

Sheila nodded. "But I doubt that anybody could prove it now."

Nor, she thought but did not say, could they probably ever prove whether it had been Wart who fired the shot.

An exclamation made her turn. "Yuck!" Sara Sims was at the closet door. "Don't look, Sheila. You'll throw up."

She almost did.

The entire floor and shelf above were heaped with piles of books, magazines, and pictures, the most explicit pornography Sheila had ever seen. She cringed as she watched Sara Sims pawing through them seeking the tin box. It appeared, near the bottom. Sara Sims handed it up to her. "Open it!"

Sheila obeyed.

The box was empty.

## TWENTY-FOUR

SARA SIMS DASHED to the kitchen, blurting out the news. By the time Sheila reached the door, the old woman was standing at the table, brandishing her cane and screeching at the top of her lungs, "We've been robbed! We've been robbed! Somebody's been in the house and taken Wart's money!"

Sheila was reminded of Baby Bear's lament: "Somebody's been eating my porridge, and they ate it all up!" She stepped back to allow family members to gather around their matriarch.

Grandma Sims would not be soothed. The tin had to be held up and shaken several times, to make certain six hundred dollars had not miraculously stuck itself to the bottom. Wart's unsavory closet had to be turned inside out by Dudley and Roger, while Grandma Sims sat on the bed and muttered to the others, "Don't you look at this trash. It's pure filth!" She refused, however, to avert her own eyes.

"Burn them!" She commanded Roger when every book and magazine had been shaken out. "Burn them in the barrel right now!"

"It's illegal to burn trash these days, Grandma Sims," he told her. "Put them in a bag for the garbagemen on Monday."

"You burn them!" She bounced up and down in frenzy. "Right this minute, you hear me? I don't want them on my property!" Only when he had loaded everything into a large box and staggered toward the back yard did she stomp back to the kitchen.

There, however, she collapsed into a chair and gasped from exertion. "I need to rest. Faye, he'p me to bed."

"I'll help you, Grandma," Evelyn said. "Faye can keep things running smoothly in here."

Sheila, unassigned a post, returned to Wart's room to see if she could find anything else of interest, including the money. She found Dudley perusing the weapons on the shelf. "I must have told Wart twenty times he needed to register these things," he murmured, almost to himself. "I wonder if he ever got around to it?" He looked around the room and gave an involuntary shiver. "Not a pleasant place to be, a scene of death. Shall we?" He put out an arm and ushered her back to the small hall, then stopped, as if reluctant to join the others. "Sara Sims informs me you are an amateur detective." He was trying not to sound patronizing. He almost succeeded.

"I've had some experience," she admitted, cautious. "Do you know if the police found any evidence of what killed Wart?"

He shook his head. "Not that I've heard. He may have had a heart condition we didn't suspect. His father died of a bad heart at thirty-five. The coroner's office said they would run several tests, but results may take weeks to get back."

"What have the police come up with on your wife's murder?"

"Nothing much. They are looking at people in other places who have committed similar crimes." He hesitated, then said in a soft voice, "I don't want Grandma Sims to hear me, Sheila, but it was probably Uncle Billy. Martha Sloan said some pretty foolish things that Sunday you came to dinner. If Uncle Billy thought she was going to harm Grandma, there's no telling what he would do. But there are other possibilities, of course." He pushed up a sleeve and checked his watch. "In fact, I have to call the detective very shortly. There's a man in South Carolina who has been killing women in subdivisions. Maybe he killed Martha Sloan, too." He gave Sheila a pat on the arm. "I think we can leave this up to the police, Sheila, but if you get any ideas, let me know and I'll pass them along. And I do appreciate what you are doing for Sara Sims. She admires you tremendously. Did she take you out to dinner last week, like I told her to?"

"She brought me flowers. They were lovely."

He looked puzzled. "I told her to treat you to dinner!"

"Oh, the flowers were enough of a treat." Sheila caught a glimpse of his daughter's face through the kitchen door. She had overheard, and the look on her face gave her away. Sheila knew who had eaten that dinner. Sara Sims turned and went quickly out the back door.

As on Monday evening, Dudley seemed to be having trouble actually leaving. "I'm sending Bo over to spend the night."

"Good idea. Sara Sims was afraid it was going to be her."

He chuckled. "She and Grandma would have each other scared to death by midnight, then we'd all have to come." He looked in at one of Wart's more savage pictures and shook his head. "Bo had better sleep in Billy's room."

When Sheila returned to the kitchen, Dudley behind her, Evelyn was asking. "When does Amy get home?"

Faye handed her a dripping plate. "Tomorrow. She was coming in time for the lake party. Amy never missed a party in..."

"Is the party still on, Uncle Dudley?" Roger pulled out a chair and sank into it, heaping a plate as he sat. He speared a beet from the bowl, ate it from the fork, and speared another. Sheila was glad she didn't like beets.

"Maybe you ought to put it off until July Fourth," Evelyn suggested, giving Roger a maternal frown.

"We can't think about death all the time, Evelyn," Merle called from the living room. "It might do us all good to think about something else for a day."

Dudley chewed for a moment, thinking. "The boats are ready, and the food is there. I suppose if anybody wants to come, they can. Bo will come up anyway, I'm sure, and probably Sara Sims."

"And Amy," Faye drawled.

"Count us in." Roger had practically inhaled his food. Now he stood. "Oh! I came in for matches for Grandma Sims's bonfire. Keep your ears peeled for sirens. I don't want to spend Memorial Day in jail." He took matches from a drawer and headed for the back door.

"I'll just check on Aunt Ruby, then I need to go home for awhile," Dudley said. The two men left together.

For several minutes Faye murmured to Evelyn by the sink. Her voice finally rose on the end of a sentence. " . . . spend the summer playing, she can think again! She's going to take care of Mama while I take a cruise, and that's all there is to it." Sheila was astonished at how this sister nettled Faye out of her usual gentleness.

The phone rang. Faye jumped for it. At the greeting, her voice grew soft. "Why, hello!" Sheila moved to Faye's abandoned dishpan and the last three glasses. "Aren't you sweet!" Faye exclaimed. "A quick bite now would be perfect.... Me, too." She whispered. She hung up and said, "I'm going out for a little while, Aunt Evelyn."

Hope was written all over Evelyn's freckled face. "Somebody special?"

"Maybe." Faye's blush deepened. "I'll let you know one day."

She paused in the living room to kiss her mother and say when she'd be back. On the porch she kissed her grandfather and waved good-bye to his friends. "You all be sweet, now, you hear?"

As she went to her car, one old man rasped, "What's happened to Faye? She's gotten herself beautiful."

"Always was," her doting grandfather replied.

Faye's leaving signalled a general exodus. Three neighbors rose and began lingering farewells. In a few minutes Dudley's silver BMW left Ruby's, followed by Erika's blue Caravan. Sheila knew she should leave too. Nobody else seemed concerned about Wart's sudden exit from the family, and they were probably right. Nevertheless, she wanted to have at least one look around outside before she went.

When Evelyn finally went into the living room to sit a while, Sheila slipped out the back door, keeping a wary eye and ear out for Bull and cursing her own foolishness for wearing a skirt to this particular house of mourning. The older women all wore double-knit pantsuits and sensible shoes. Sara Sims wore jeans and running shoes. Only Sheila, Grandma Sims, and Faye wore skirts, and Grandma Sims and Faye had more sense than to go for a stroll through high grass and brambles.

Sheila, however, had a purpose behind her stroll. She was heading, slowly, toward Roger, who stood beside a smoking fifty-gallon drum.

He stood with his back to the house and his head bent, intent on one of Wart's magazines.

"Hello!" she called when she was still several yards away.

He whirled, holding the magazine behind his back. She heard him drop it into the barrel, then he took one step back to shield the box and remaining books from her gaze. Surreptitiously he wiped the hand that had held the magazine on the side of his pants.

"You ought to get some hot dogs," she greeted him.

"What do you mean?"

"The law, I believe, says no burning except to cook food. I have friends who have a weenie roast every time they clean branches out of their yard."

He laughed without mirth. "I wouldn't feel much like eating anything cooked over this filth. It might contaminate the food."

"Not the most savory of literature," she agreed.

"You saw it?" His brow rose in surprise.

She nodded. "Mrs. Sims asked Sara Sims and me to bring her the money can. It was in the closet, under all that." She waved toward the barrel and its smoking contents.

He took another step back, as if to disassociate himself from a woman who had exposed herself to pornography and survived.

The wind, shifting direction, blew black smoke into her face. She stepped nearer to Roger to avoid it.

A stick lay near the fire drum, one end charred from past use. He poked the fire, giving Sheila a quick look from the side of his eyes. "Uh, when you were over at the new house this morning, you know the fella who left as you were arriving?"

As she remembered it, the man had just arrived when she arrived, and had left after she and Andy had heard the whole conversation. "Yes?" She wouldn't make this easy for him.

"Well, uh—" he poked the fire again, then turned and took a step toward her. He spoke rapidly, in an undertone. "I'd rather you didn't mention him. You understand?"

Sheila nearly laughed. Who did Roger think could hear him, standing totally isolated in the middle of an empty yard? She wasn't ready to promise yet. "Sounded like he was giving you a rough time."

Roger shrugged. "Yeah, well, he didn't have all the facts. My situation is improving, but he didn't know that. So just don't mention it, okay?"

She mirrored his shrug. "Sure, if you'll tell me a few things."

"Like what?"

"Like, about Wart. Did Sara Sims say he used to work for you?"

He relaxed. He'd obviously expected something else. "Almost everybody in the family has worked for me one time or another. Wart, Bo, and Dunk were my summer framing crew until Dunk left and Wart decided to plant the farm again."

"I take it you didn't agree with that decision?"

"You're durned tooting I didn't. Good carpenters are hard to find, and Wart was damned good."

She watched him poke the smoking fire. "Not always easy to get along with, I'd imagine."

"Oh, he hadn't learned yet that you can't kill everybody who disagrees with you, but he didn't give me much trouble. I let him work his own way, and kept blacks away from him."

"Did he really ever kill anybody?"

"Not that I know of, but he threatened several. I was always having to stop him from fighting with somebody or other."

"Even his cousins," she agreed. "Sara Sims was furious that he wanted your great-grandmother to give him the whole farm."

Roger slammed the stick against the barrel so hard its end snapped off. "Dumbest idea in the world. Ten million dollars' worth of real estate, and he wants to turn it into a farm." He spat into the high grass beyond the barrel.

"It *was* a farm," Sheila pointed out.

"Sure, when Sherman came through. Hasn't grown much since Grandpa Sims died. It's silly to farm land needed for houses."

"People have to eat," she said, deliberately seeing how far she could push him.

"Not on my land they don't!" He spat again, bent to the box and began to shovel handfuls of books and magazines into the faltering flames—having decided, she concluded, that she was not enough of a lady to be worth shielding from life's sordid side.

"Your land? Well I like that!" Sara Sims had come across the grass so silently that neither Sheila nor Roger had heard her until she was within earshot.

"Well, then, our land." Roger upended the box and let the final few books fuel the flames. "I've been wanting to talk with you and Bo about that. The way I figure it, and Faye agrees, Grandma Sims ought to give the land to our generation. There's only Ruby left in hers. In the next one, Merle probably won't live as long as Grandma Sims, and

Daddy's never sober. I think all of us together ought to sit down with Grandma Sims and ask her to make a will leaving everything directly to us."

"In six equal parts?" Sheila asked, with malice aforethought.

Roger gave her a quick, suspicious look. "Not that it's any of your business, but no, I think it should be divided in thirds, for her grandchildren, or maybe half for Granddaddy's descendants and half for Aunt Ruby's."

Sara Sims was quick in math. "You mean either one third for you, one third for Faye and Amy to share, and one third between me, Bo, and Dunk, or one fourth each for you, Faye, and Amy, and one fourth for Mama's kids to share?"

He shrugged. "Why should the rest of us suffer because Martha Sloan decided to overpopulate the world?"

"Why, you . . ." Sara Sims stepped forward, fist raised.

He grabbed her wrist and forced her back. "I am the only Sims left! In some countries I'd get the whole damned pie!"

"Aunt Ruby's more a Sims than you are, and so's Uncle Bubba!" Sara Sims blazed. "Not that you believe that. He is trying to get poor Uncle Bubba declared incompetent," she spat out to Sheila, "and give himself power of attorney to put the store up for sale. I heard Daddy talking to him on the phone about it just this week."

"You sneak!" Roger's voice rose to a squeal. "I ought to sue you for invasion of privacy!"

"I wasn't sneaking, I was doing my wash. I can't help it if Daddy doesn't close the door when he talks on the phone."

She turned and held out a hand to her friend. "Come on, Sheila, I want you to see the barn." As they walked away, she turned toward her cousin. "You are a rat, Roger Sims. If anybody else dies in this family, I surely hope it is you!"

# TWENTY-FIVE

"I DIDN'T REALLY WANT to show you the barn," Sara Sims admitted when they got inside. "I just couldn't stand any more of Roger. And about that dinner..."

"Forget it. Andy and I had fun. And as long as we're here, why don't you look around for anything you don't remember being here before?"

Sara Sims got busy. Sheila picked up a stick near the door and began to poke the straw under where Uncle Billy's body had hung.

"Looks like Bo and Uncle Billy forgot this." Sara Sims held up a yellow water pistol. "They were using it for Cowboys and Indians last Sunday. That's all I see."

Sheila sighed. If the pistol had had fingerprints, Sara Sims had probably covered or smudged them. Nevertheless, she wrapped it in a tissue she had brought for just this purpose and dropped it into the large pocket of her skirt.

"What you doing here?" Bubba, at the doorway, had his back to the light, but chagrin was evident in his braced shoulders.

Sheila was prepared. "I dropped an earring Monday night. I hoped maybe we could find it."

"I'll find it." He reached for an old rake handle and began to vigorously beat at the straw. If there had been an earring, it would have been pounded through one of the wide cracks between the floorboards by his efforts. So might any clues to Billy Sims's death.

She took the handle. "Thanks, but we'll just look a little longer. You haven't found anything, Sara Sims?"

"Not a thing." Sheila was glad Bubba was too full of his own problem to wonder at Sara Sims's conspiratorial tone.

He glared from one to the other. "You shouldn't be down here. There might be snakes in the hay." Sheila resisted an urge to step to bare floor nearer the tractor. He licked his lips and darted a quick glance toward a high shelf in one corner. "Listen. Go back up to the house, tell Bo to come down later with one of Cline's yard rakes. He can sift around here for you."

"Is Bo back?" Sara Sims headed for the door.

"Yeah. He just got here. He's getting something to eat. And he asked for you."

The hint was so broad, Sheila would have had to be a fool not to get it. She would also have had to be a fool not to know what Bubba had hidden on that high shelf. His hands shook and he practically danced in his eagerness for her to be off. She chose to pretend to be a fool.

"I hate to bother Bo about an earring, Sara Sims, and it's you he wants to see. Go ahead. I'll look for a few more minutes." When Sara Sims trotted up the rough tractor track, Bubba leaned against the huge tire and shuffled his feet in frustration.

Sheila poked the floor where Cline had fainted. "It must be hard on you, losing so many people at one time."

"Yeah." He took another yearning look at the high shelf, then slid his eyes toward Sheila. "But like the Good Book says, the meek inherit the earth." He gave a nasty little giggle. "Meek old Bubba never amounted to much, but I've inherited the whole damn lot. Me, Roger, and little Tad are all that's left of the family now."

Another time Sheila might have debated his dismissal of the entire female line. Today she wanted to hear what he was working toward.

He was muttering, almost to himself. "No more silly Billy or fat-ass Wart, no more precious Martha Sloan." He glared under his gray curls. "All my life—all my *life*—all Mama ever saw was Martha Sloan. Martha Sloan this, Martha Sloan that. Bubba could cut the grass and carry in her groceries, but Martha Sloan got all the attention. Well, now there's no more Martha Sloan to get it.''

Sheila would have liked to leave then—walk straight out the door, get into her car, and drive home. Take a hot bath and put first-aid cream on the scratches on her leg. Make a cup of strong steaming coffee and let Beethoven symphonies surge over her. "Don't talk like that in front of the police," she warned him. "They might think you killed her."

He jabbed his hands in his pockets. Even through the fabric she could see how he clenched them. "I couldn't shoot her. She was my sister. You don't shoot your sister, no matter what she's like."

She believed him. Perhaps it was the wistfulness in his voice.

She pointed her stick toward the corner rafter. "You don't suppose Bo was right, do you—that somebody else hung poor Mister Sims up there?"

Bubba responded with a sound somewhere between a growl and a snort. "Who'd do a thing like that? No, Uncle Billy killed himself because he killed Martha Sloan. We all know it.''

She was startled at hearing it put so baldly for the second time in an hour. "You do?''

"Sure! We just don't want to say so to the police. He's paid his debt. Why stir up trouble?''

"You're putting the police to a lot of trouble.''

He waved that away as unimportant. "That's what they're paid for." He shifted himself to a more comfortable position against his tire and prepared to expound on this startling revelation. "Normally, now, there wasn't a speck of harm in Uncle Billy. But Martha Sloan could rile a saint. She used to make Uncle Billy madder'n anybody, because he didn't know when she was mad at him or just in a general bad temper. Martha Sloan was the meanest woman with the sharpest tongue in Georgia. And she was getting worse. Why, at the end she was threatening Grandma! That's something Billy would never tolerate. He worshiped his mama."

He burped, excused himself, and jabbed a finger at Sheila to emphasize his next words. "I tell you something. When Uncle Billy shot Martha Sloan, he did the world a favor. A favor," he repeated, jabbing the air. Then he let his hand drop and turned his head away, but not before she had seen tears in his eyes. "He had no cause to kill himself. None at all."

Sweat beaded his forehead and his hands were beginning to shake. Sheila took pity on him. "Maybe you were right— I'll ask Bo to use a rake to look for my earring. Thanks for the idea." She heard him scuttling toward his shelf before her shadow was out the doorway.

Roger was no Eagle Scout. He had abandoned the barrel, although it was still smoking. She tramped back through the grass to peer into it, afraid a burning ember could drift out and set something on fire. But he hadn't been as careless as she had feared. This barrel refuted the proverb "Where there's smoke there's fire." Only the magazines had burned. Now charred books with curling pages lay among bizarre scraps of breasts, buttocks, and shoulders.

She saw, between the pages of one book, a piece of pink paper. Carefully she reached for it. The paper was hot, but not even browned. She blew on it a few moments, then— since she was in full view of the kitchen and reluctant to examine her find until she had more privacy—put it in her pocket with the water pistol. Further poking of the fire yielded nothing else except a particularly dreadful bondage picture, still unburned. Marveling at how many uses a rake handle could have, she pushed it toward one remaining ember and watched with satisfaction as it curled, then burst into flames.

"What are you doing?"

Sheila, startled, turned. Bessie Sims stood nearby, watching her with a wide, curious stare. Today she wore a lavender caftan and bright blue beads.

"Making sure this trash gets good and burned," Sheila replied, giving the barrel a final poke for good measure. "Mrs. Sims asked Roger to burn it."

"I am Mrs. Sims, too," Bessie informed her. She moved over to peer into the barrel, stared without a trace of embarrassment. "That's not love." She shook her head. "Oh my, no! I know all about love." She turned and took Sheila by one elbow, spoke in a confiding, low voice. "My Harley was prettier than Bo, but I didn't love him because he was pretty. I loved him because he was straight and fine, and he made me happy. Not like that." She pointed to the barrel and tugged gently on Sheila's elbow, as if to dissuade her from looking for love in its contents. Then she dropped the elbow, turned, and looked about her in confusion.

"I came to the party. Nobody came to fetch me, so when Lillie lay down for a nap, I came. Are you Wart's girlfriend?"

Sheila nearly gagged. "No, I'm a friend of Sara Sims."

Bessie sighed. "Sara Sims doesn't know about love, either. Ask Faye. Sara Sims thinks love is broad shoulders and a swagger."

Sheila felt a need to reassure her. "She's young."

Bessie shook her head. "She's getting older every day. It is sad to grow old unloved."

Sheila smiled. Was there ever a grandmother whose grandchildren didn't grow up too fast?

Bessie moved across the grass, her long skirt graceful. She peered into the grass as if searching for Easter eggs, then returned, muttering, "...kind and fine, and eager to please." She raised those blue, blank eyes to Sheila. "You heard about my daughter?" When Sheila nodded, she said with a deep sigh, "Poor Dudley. Poor, poor Dudley."

Sheila wondered if she were still convinced Dudley had shot her daughter. She was also wondering what to do with the woman, and was relieved when Evelyn came to the back door and called, "Hello, Nana, come let me fix you a plate.'' Bessie turned and crossed the yard at a slow lope without a backward look.

Feeling a bit cobwebby after trying to follow that conversation, Sheila directed her steps to an overgrown tractor track curving around the barn.

By now the sun had almost set. Each step was an act of will, for she coudn't help remembering Sara Sims's folklore about snakes being more active at dusk. Weren't snakes cold-blooded animals who liked to lie in the sun? If not, could you beat a snake to death with a rake handle? She hoped so, and clutched hers firmly.

It was lighter behind the barn, for there were fewer trees. At the end of the track a few cows rested in a pasture. One stood near the fence, bawling. Sheila wondered who would milk now that Wart was dead. Someone would soon have to.

On her right sat a long stack of firewood, hidden from the house by a corner of the barn and several overgrown forsythias. The tractor road—now scarcely ruts through tall grass—curved around toward a gate that opened onto the small side road. A car had driven down that road after last night's rain. Tracks showed plainly in places where the ruts were mud rather than flattened grass. If the police decided to investigate Wart's death, they might learn something from those tracks—if they saw them before it rained again. She scanned the sky, relieved to see that only a few cirrus clouds feathered the upper regions.

"What are you doing way back here?"

She whirled, startled, and dropped her stick. Cline Shaw straddled the road, legs ending in stout Western boots, a bucket in one hand, stool in the other. He glared, clearly waiting for an explanation and just as clearly remembering that in their last chat he had ordered her off the property.

She decided to stretch the truth slightly. "Mrs. Sims asked Sara Sims and me to look back here. She thought Wart had been cutting timber that was planted by government contract, and she was pretty upset. On our way out to investi-

gate, Mr. Sims—Mr. Harley Sims—told Sara Sims that Bo
wanted her back in the house, so I came on alone.''

Did it sound as lame to him as it did to her? He turned
and considered the firewood with what seemed like genuine
surprise. "Looks like Grandma was right. I wonder what
Wart wanted with all that wood? Grandma doesn't have a
fireplace.''

"Mrs. Sims was worried that he was selling it.''

"Oh." He scratched one cheek and looked at the wood
some more. "Could be. Lots of these new houses have fire-
places. I never did see the sense of it myself, hauling wood
and then hauling ashes, when you could flip a thermostat
and get the same results.''

"A heat register isn't very romantic," Sheila pointed out.

"I guess not." Cline did not sound convinced that romance was worth all that effort. "Well, little lady, you can
report back to Grandma that you found a pile of wood.''
His tone held a grudging apology. "I've got to try my hand
at milking. Wart or Billy always did it—or Ruby, if they had
to be away. Now she says, 'Take that bucket and milk that
poor cow before she dies.' I've never milked a cow in my
life." He gave a self-conscious laugh. "But Ruby sure isn't
up to it, and not a soul up at the house knows how to milk
except Grandma, so I guess I'm going to get my first lesson.''

Sheila had been raised to be helpful, and could use some
Brownie points with Cline. "Shall I do it for you?''

He eyed her suspiciously. "You know how?''

She was already regretting her offer, but had to nod. "My
dad taught me when I was ten. I milked pretty often for the
next few years. I think I'd still remember how.''

"Well, you're a handy lady to have around the house.''
His tone was a shade below admiration, and he considered
her skirt and pumps with a jaundiced eye. "You're not exactly dressed for it, are you?''

By now straw stuck to her shoes and her skirt was streaked
with red Georgia mud that would never come out. "I'm as

dressed as I'm ever going to get. But you'll have to stay with me. Sara Sims has me scared to death of snakes. And where on earth is Bull?'' She sounded to her own ears like a simpering miss straight from the magnolia trail. Cline straightened his shoulders and tromped across clumps of grass like a grizzled Matt Dillon.

"Sure, I'll come with you, but I haven't seen Bull all day and we don't get many snakes around here. Not poisonous ones, anyway. An occasional copperhead, maybe, and now and then a rattler. Nothing much to worry about.''

An occasional copperhead and a now-and-then rattler sounded like plenty much to worry about. Sheila looked wsitfully at her stick lying in the grass. If she stooped to pick it up, Cline might think she planned to attack him. She moved as rapidly as the terrain permitted toward the pasture gate he was dragging open.

Now that he didn't have to milk, Cline was downright cheerful. "I guess that's the cow.'' He pointed to the nearly frantic animal.

"I guess it is.'' She picked her way through cow patties toward the skittish cow, making soothing noises as she'd heard her father do.

Cline stumbled behind, clanking the bucket. "They don't have but the one fresh just now.''

"Thank God for small favors,'' Sheila murmured to herself.

She settled herself on the tiny stool. Had stools been bigger when she was ten, or had she just been smaller? Positioning the bucket beneath the swollen udder, she reached for the first teat with a quick prayer. She had not milked for twenty-five years, and had never milked in a darkening field on a shaky stool. It was highly likely that she was about to make a fool of herself.

After an exploratory tug, however, she found that the rhythm came naturally. While a stream of warm milk pittered into the bucket, Cline leaned against the fence and chewed a piece of wild onion he'd tugged from beside the fence. "You do that fine!" Seeing other wild onions dotting the pasture, Sheila was glad she didn't have to drink this milk.

Cline glanced over toward the firewood again. "Wart must have started cutting that wood recently. I never saw it before. But then, I never have much cause to come back here."

He sounded friendly enough now. Sheila wondered if she could presume on their new chumminess. "You didn't happen to hear anybody back here last night, did you? It looks like there are some fresh tire tracks on the road to the side gate."

"I didn't hear anything." He chewed his onion in silence.

"Mrs. Sims seemed pretty upset about the wood. She seems to think Wart was clearing the land to plant as if the farm was his."

Cline tossed away the chewed onion and spat. "Not to speak ill of the dead, but Wart always did think the farm was his. Since he came back from the marines, anyway. I guess he figured none of the rest of the family would want to farm it, and until that Sunday when you came to dinner and Martha Sloan spilled Dudley's beans, Wart would never have thought it might be sold and the money divided. He never thought of land as money. He was a lot like Grandpa Sims in that." Cline trailed off and leaned against the fencepost contemplating a distant cornfield.

At last the udder was empty. Sheila stood, arched her stiff back, picked up the bucket, and patted the cow's warm flank. "Feel better, girl?" She handed Cline the bucket and lifted the stool. For an instant she stood drinking in the beauty of pasture, fields, and dark gray sky. "Wart was saying last night that he wanted to make this farm a pick-your-own place."

"Wouldn't be a bad idea," Cline replied. "You can make good money with those places. And you know, Wart might have made a good farmer in time. Maybe even a good man, given a few years. He got a little lost when he had to give up the marines, and he'd taken up with some unsavory characters, but time and a family of his own might have worked wonders.''

Trudging behind him to the gate, Sheila did not reply. She would have pitied any woman married to a man with Wart's taste in friends and literature. Ahead of her, Cline chuckled. "But between you and me, Ruby's pumpkin shed and Wart's pick-your-own together would have had Martha Sloan whirling in her grave. Watch your step, now." He shoved away a curious cow and opened the gate.

He spoke too late. Sheila had already felt her right instep sink deep into a fresh, still-warm cow patty.

## TWENTY-SIX

"IT IS POSSIBLE, I suppose," Aunt Mary said with a crest-fallen air, "that young Wallace could have been murdered for his money."

"Don't sound so disappointed!" Sheila chided her. "Most people think Wart died of a bad heart or drug overdose. Only you and I even wonder if he was murdered. I suppose you have your heart set on a more involved case than murder for six hundred dollars?" She expected no reply and got none—except for a slight tightening of the network of wrinkles around Aunt Mary's lips.

Swirling her glass, Sheila admired the amber liquid. How glad she was to be sitting in this rose and ivory living room instead of in Grandma Sims's kitchen, sipping sherry from crystal instead of sweet tea from a jelly glass, listening to Chopin instead of to Merle's health report. "I am such a snob!"

"Nonsense, dear. It is just easier to think constructively in congenial surroundings."

Sheila wiggled her toes (clean and pink from a hot shower), snuggled deeper into the terry-cloth robe she kept at the apartment, and tried to think constructively. It was no good. She let her head loll against the well-padded chair back and closed her eyes.

"The hour of Wallace's death is suggestive," Aunt Mary said in a thoughtful tone.

Sheila opened one eye. "Call him 'Wart,' Aunt Mary. I keep forgetting who Wallace is."

Aunt Mary shuddered and shook her head slightly.

Sheila gave her half a smile. "All right, Wallace it is, but he really was a short, squat toad."

"To return to my former point, dear, midnight is not an hour when most decent people would be abroad."

"Most decent people would not be committing murder, Aunt Mary."

"Pshaw. Murderers take care to look respectable, Sheila. You know that as well as I do. We should be looking for the person who seems most normal after all that has happened."

"Roger," Sheila said promptly. "He was gauche and greedy before, and he's gauche and greedy now. Or Merle—she's too sick to pretend to be anything but herself. Or Faye. In the middle of all this mess she is falling in love. So is Aubrey, apparently."

Aunt Mary considered the possibilities. "Does Faye strike you as the type of woman who could go straight from a date with her lover to kill someone?"

"Does one need to be a type to do that?"

"Of course, Sheila. Lady Macbeth could have done it. So, from your description, could Martha Sloan Tait. Gussie Mae Curtis, on the other hand, would be too engrossed in putting down every detail in her diary and getting her hairnet on straight. She couldn't possibly kill someone unless she set aside a whole evening for the purpose."

"I see. Considered in that light, I don't think Faye could have killed Wart, either."

Aunt Mary's use of the word "lover," however, clarified one change in Faye. Her teasing of Dudley and Cline's friend on the porch had been competent, even daring—the jesting of a woman who finally has been desired and satisfied by a man.

Sheila felt a sudden stab of fear for her, followed by a dose of common sense. Like most other women, Faye would probably prefer to love and lose than never to have loved at all. Especially right now, when love was rich and new.

"Where on earth is your mind?" Aunt Mary demanded. "I have asked twice about the rest of the family."

"I only met these people two weeks ago," Sheila protested, "and I was groggy with antihistamine then."

"What about Dudley, Martha Sloan's husband? A husband is such a good prospect for killing a wife."

Sheila chuckled. "Is that why you never married? But Dudley, alas, has an alibi all day the day she died. He also gained nothing, since she never inherited anything from Grandma Sims." She rose and padded to the window to look at Atlanta's twinkling skyline. "We may be making a mystery where there is none. The family believes Billy shot Martha Sloan and Wart died of an undiagnosed heart condition."

"Perhaps so." Aunt Mary could not quite conceal a little sigh.

Sheila shoved her fingers through her thick hair. "Frankly, Aunt Mary, I am ready to forget the Sims family ever existed."

"I don't know why you are so tired, Sheila. You have scarcely done a thing thus far."

Stung, Sheila replied hotly. "I've milked cows and burned trash today, and...wait a minute!" She padded into the back bedroom, fumbled through the pocket of her filthy skirt, brought the water pistol and pink piece of paper and laid them in her aunt's blue linen lap. "There! See if they mean any more to you than they do to me."

Aunt Mary held up the water pistol and raised her eyebrows.

It was as good as a question.

"Bo and Uncle Billy played Cowboys and Indians a lot, using water pistols. They played the day before Uncle Billy died, and may have left the pistol in the barn."

"'May have,' dear?"

"That's what Sara Sims said when she found it."

Aunt Mary reached for her pad again. "But you didn't ask Bo, dear? See what he says about the pistol and the barn. Now what is this paper?"

"It was in a book of Wart's."

"What book, dear?"

"You don't want to know, Aunt Mary."

"The publication date might tell us something." She jotted down another note on her pad. "Tomorrow, bring the book here. We'll see if a friend of mine at the library can tell us when it was sold."

Sheila snorted. "To preserve a friendship, Aunt Mary, and your reputation, I'll try to check on that one myself—if we decide the date is important."

"Plastic explosives, electrical blasting caps, timer...," Aunt Mary read aloud. "It's a list to make a bomb, dear."

Sheila sighed. "I was afraid of that. Are you sure?"

Aunt Mary nodded. "Yes, dear."

"Should I ask how you know?"

"No." Curled in the corner of her couch, feet tucked beneath her, Aunt Mary looked as if she scarcely knew how to make an omelet.

Sheila gave her a quick hug. "Someday, please tell me the story of your life. All about how you made bombs in your wild youth."

Aunt Mary patted her mouth with her fingertips. "How exhausting that sounds, Sheila. It is getting late. Before you go, the question before us is whether Wallace recently made a bomb in *his* wild youth—and if so, where it is at this moment."

Sheila regarded her soberly. "Should we call the police at once to suggest they poke around tonight for anything that ticks?"

"I don't think so, dear. If Wallace had set it before his own death, it would probably have gone off by now. First thing tomorrow you can go back to the farm and look around."

"Great. And if the bomb doesn't get me, there is always Bull, or the snakes. Farms are more dangerous than I ever supposed."

SHEILA WOULD HAVE loved to spend the night in Aunt Mary's guest room and eat Mildred's special Sunday pecan waffles. A dog owner, however, cannot afford the luxury of casual sleep-overs. It was well after twelve when she wearily pulled into her own parking space.

She was surprised to see a light in her window. Cautiously she opened the door. Lady pranced around her feet, yipping a welcome. The kitchen light was on. Sara Sims, wrapped in Sheila's blanket, head on Sheila's pillow, lay on the living room floor, face streaked with tears.

Sheila shook her neighbor gently. "Were you waiting for me?"

Sara Sims jerked upright, then her shoulders slumped. "Where have you been? I've waited for hours!" She made no apology for having used the key Sheila had given her for emergencies.

"I went to my aunt's for dinner. Has something else happened?" Remembering Wart's bomb, Sheila feared the worst.

"Ye...ye...yes!" Sara Sims burst into tears. Lady leaped and barked in renewed frenzy.

"What is it?" Sheila's voice was sharper than she had intended.

Sara Sims's sobs increased. "It's Kevin. He's..."

Before she could finish, three knocks sounded on the door. It was Andy Lee, in pajamas and bathrobe. "I heard Lady through my soundproof floor. What's wrong?"

Before Sheila could answer, Sara Sims wailed, "I'm going to die!" She joined them, trailing her blanket and dripping tears.

"Let's go in, Princess Trail of Tears." Andy supported her as she stumbled toward a chair. "Get her some water, Sheila."

As Sara Sims gulped it down, Sheila abandoned all hope that they would ever make a pair. No man in his right mind would fall in love with a woman whom he usually saw with swollen eyes, tear-stained cheeks, and a runny nose. And what woman could love a man who wore a purple and green plaid bathrobe?

Andy went to the kitchen and fetched a box of tissues. "Blow!"

Sara Sims obeyed, loudly.

"He...he..." She stopped, bewildered.

He raised both eyebrows. "I presume you are referring to the man called Kevin?"

"He's not 'called Kevin,'" Sara Sims sniffed. "It's his name. But he...he's calling everything off!"

Sheila was too tired to play games. "There wasn't really anything to call off, was there? I mean, you weren't engaged."

"He wanted to be. Remember? But I said I thought we ought to wait a while first. Why did I ever say that? I love him so much! But tonight he said...he doesn't want to see me again! He said he's too old for me, and I'd be better off without him." Again she collapsed into sobs. "I don't want to be better off without him. I want to be *with* him!"

"The rat!" Andy winked at Sheila over Sara Sims's shoulder.

Sara Sims sat up and shook her head. "Don't insult the rats!" Her voice now held a spark of temper, Sheila noted with relief.

Andy patted her back. "He's not worthy of you, my dear. Count your blessings."

Sara Sims sniffed, gulped, and stared into space. Whether she was taking Andy's advice, or facing the enormity of her losses, Sheila didn't know, but Lady could wait no longer.

"I'll be back in a few minutes." Sheila reached for the leash.

She returned to find Andy had put on music. Pachelbel again. Sheila wondered if she would ever hear the *Canon in D* without thinking of the two of them.

"Most people get so caught up in the canon," Andy was saying, "that they never hear the wonderful ground bass."

"What's a ground bass?" Sheila asked, hanging up the leash.

"A short repeated motif in the bass clef," Sara Sims replied. "But I hadn't realized there was one in this canon. Are you sure there is?" she asked Andy.

"Of course there is. Listen!" He stopped the music, sang eight notes, repeated them, then lowered the needle again. Now Sheila could hear it, too.

Sara Sims looked at him suspiciously. "How did *you* know that?"

"I play the bass fiddle," he said, "or, rather, play at it."

Her eyes widened. "Really? I play the violin! You ought to come over some Sunday and…" She stopped and her eyes filled with tears. "If I live so long."

Andy caught Sheila's eye and handed Sara Sims another tissue. "Definitely a two-blow situation."

After blowing her nose, she looked at him through wet lashes. "Why were you still up?"

"Oh, just puttering about doing this and that." He had, for no reason Sheila could see, turned pink.

Sara Sims pounced. "You were waiting up for Sheila! Admit it!"

"Well, it's not always safe for a woman to be out at night."

Sara Sims blew her nose again. "You're in love with her!"

"He is not," Sheila said tartly. "He's just a good neighbor who is about to go home to bed." She gave Andy what she hoped was an eloquent look.

If so, it did not speak to him. "Come on, Sheila, you can't plan to toddle off to bed and leave the lady in tears."

"No, but I plan to have a woman-to-woman chat. Your presence somewhat inhibits that."

"Oh, don't mind me," he said with a grand wave. "I'll just sit here and be a bump on a log."

"I don't care if he stays or goes." Sara Sims took a deep, rasping breath. "I'll never speak to another man in my life."

"Well, in that case, I'll go." Andy stood. "I don't mind being insulted, but I can't stand to be ignored."

It took Sheila another hour to get Sara Sims to the point where she could sleep. Even then she couldn't bear to be alone. At last Sheila made up her guest room bed and sent Lady in to sleep on her guest's feet.

As she climbed between her own sheets, she reflected that befriending Sara Sims was costing her hours of sleep, regular meals, and a fortune to replace ruined clothes. Sometimes it felt a whole lot like babysitting.

# TWENTY-SEVEN

*The Third Week*
*Sunday*

SHEILA WAS CLIMBING a woodpile. She was the size of an ant, or the pile was enormous. She had to get to the top, needed something on the other side, but the logs were slick with damp. She climbed, slid back, clutched frantically for small knots on the wood to keep herself from tumbling into a sea of manure just below. At last, with one mighty heave, she pulled herself onto the top log and, gingerly, knelt to look down the far side. To celebrate her success, a bell began to ring and someone began to pummel her, growling.

She opened one eye to find Lady on her chest, poking the covers with a long snout. The telephone was still ringing.

It was Bo Tait, distraught. "...tried and tried, but I can't get a thing! Aunt Ruby mustn't..." When she finally understood what he was talking about he was asking, "...just this morning? We'll make other arrangements by tonight. I don't know who else to ask. None of our friends have cows."

"None of my friends have cows, either," she murmured, only half aware of what she was saying. She had gotten to bed after two, been wakened twice by Sara Sims having fresh hysterics. She was in no shape to be alive, much less awake.

"Could you come soon?" he urged. "The cow is awful upset."

You'd be upset, too, if inept people had been pulling at you all morning, she wanted to tell him. Instead she shoved back her covers and fumbled for her slippers. "I'll be there in about an hour." Another day, another cow, she would have told Bo to call the Department of Agriculture or a vet. Today she wanted to get back to the Sims farm anyway.

It would have taken less time if Sheila had not felt it necessary to wake Sara Sims and ask if she wanted to come. She dressed to a rhythm of groans and wails about Kevin's desertion.

"Don't talk while we drive," Sheila told her. "This fog is so bad that I need to concentrate." The fog was bad—a thick gray swirl that filled every dip in the road and concealed oncoming cars. It was also the only excuse she could think of to ensure a quiet drive.

Snatches of her dream got mixed up with the mist, swirled through her thoughts, and drifted away before she could quite remember them. Something she needed to find. That was all she could clearly recall.

The fog had settled in Grandma Sims's yard and risen halfway up the house, but it hadn't reached the treetops. As she left the car, Sheila felt if she really tried she could push off from the earth and float up to where the air was clear. Down here it felt cool and clammy, smelled like sliced tomatoes and plowed earth. The cow's plaintive bawl echoed in the distance. A robin twittered in the big sycamore overhead.

Sara Sims sat on her side of the car without opening the door. "I don't think I can face anybody, Sheila."

"They don't know anything is wrong," Sheila reminded her. "Go in and have a cup of coffee. Grandma Sims is feeling pretty lonely right now, too."

Sara Sims reluctantly obeyed.

Bo slammed the door behind him and ran across the yard, shirttails flapping. "I'm so glad you'd come, Sheila. Hear her?"

"I hear her. Do you know where the stool is?"

"Sure. We left it out there." He made no move to lead the way. "The bucket's there, too," he added.

"Is Bull chained?"

He looked around, peered over both shoulders. "I haven't seen Bull since I got here yesterday."

He did not sound concerned. Sheila was.

"You'll need to come with me, Bo. If Bull comes home and finds me in with Wart's cows, I'll be in big trouble."

"Okay." He tucked in his shirt as they walked. This time, at least, she was properly clad in jeans and leather walking shoes. She was not afraid of snakes, either. No self-respecting snake would venture far into this cool air. As damp from the grass soaked the bottoms of her jeans, however, she realized that the only proper garb for farm chores was what Cline had worn last night: high waterproof, snakeproof boots.

She hitched the stool near the cow, spoke reassurance, and reached for the udder. The cow stepped away. Sheila looked up to find Bo, bent almost double, trying to get a good look at what she was doing.

"Go over by the fence," she said crossly. "You are making us both nervous."

He ambled over to a fencepost and leaned against it, whistling off-key, while she filled the pail.

Slowly the mist lifted. The pale blue sky filled with birds darting in search of breakfast. Sunlight warmed Sheila's shoulders, glittered off dew diamonds in the grass. She stood and stretched, handed Bo the pail. "I don't know what you do with it now."

"I don't either, but Aunt Ruby will. She's doing almost as good a job of running things from her bed as she does when she's up and about. She's already made Uncle Cline and me feed the chickens, take in the eggs, and make breakfast this morning. I am beginning to get a new respect for old Wart. He worked harder than I thought."

His eyes moved across the pasture to fields of corn. "Dammit, Sheila! I can hardly stand to think of all this—" he waved his free arm toward hardwood and pine forests nestled around grassy pastures and fields "—covered with concrete and stores. Money matters. I know that. But there are some things that matter more!''

He stopped, suddenly embarrassed. "So now you've had your sermon for today." He gave her a rueful smle. "You can skip church.''

She smiled back at him. "The congregation says, 'Amen.' The question is, how long can you stay on your soapbox, Bo? Most of my generation got off when the question was not money in general, but 'my money' and 'my job.' It's easy to be a crusader when you aren't having to give up anything yourself. If you crusade to keep this land a farm when it could make you a millionaire, you'll earn a sainthood merit badge.''

He rubbed one toe in the grass. "I don't know. I keep thinking of all the good I could do with a million dollars." His grin flashed again, honest and very young. "And places I want to see, things I want to do.''

She nodded. "That's when soapboxes get awfully high.''

He flushed. "And that's how each farm gets turned to concrete, isn't it? One at a time. I guess this is what they mean when they say 'Now the rubber hits the road.' ''

"Or 'Put your money where your mouth is,' '' she agreed, starting for the gate. He turned to follow, slipped on a wet clump of grass, nearly dropped the pail. She chuckled. "The proverb we ought to be worrying about is, 'Don't cry over spilt milk.' ''

He grinned. "Grandma Sims wouldn't cry. She'd cane me.''

As they reached the woodpile, Sheila remembered her dream—and Wart's bomb. Was that what she had been seeking in the dream? She was certainly going to have a good look for it here and now.

"Go on in, Bo. If there's a coffeepot on, find me a cup." She flexed her fingers, which were stiff and damp. "I want to poke about out here for a minute or two. Okay?''

"Okay, Sherlock. Sara Sims told me you were going to do a bit of sleuthing." He didn't sound any more impressed than his father had been. It was just as well. So far she was miles from solving any of the Sims family puzzles.

He headed down the tractor track, whistling the theme from the Pink Panther movies.

Sheila approached the firewood with caution, aware that snakes and spiders could be drowsing inside. The split pine was damp, as in her dream, darker where wet had seeped in, light pink and orange where moisture had not reached. A jay darted from an old oak and chattered at her. A mockingbird sang from the barn roof. Otherwise, the entire farm seemed to hold its breath.

The wood made a rough wall higher than her waist. As she peered over it, she lost her balance, grabbed for the top piece of wood, and fell heavily, scraping the side of her hand and bruising several ribs.

Lying in that awkward position, she found what she could not in her dream. Bull lay against the far side of the woodpile, feet straight up in the air, eyes open.

Gently she leaned over and reached toward him, trembling. What if he were only shamming death—suddenly bared his teeth? No, his coat was stiff and lifeless. Insects crawled over his muzzle and across his open eyes. He was as dead as his master.

Quickly she hurried around the end of the woodpile and searched for footprints or signs that the dog's body had been dragged. She saw none. Heedless of the damp, she knelt beside him. Now she saw that his throat had been slashed.

"Who did this to you, boy?" she whispered, even though no one could hear. As much as she had feared this huge dog, she was furious with whoever had killed him and tossed him into this forgotten spot. She was also curious. Who except family could have gotten close enough to Bull to kill him? Who would have dared try?

She stood and once again measured the woodstack against her body. It must be well over four feet high. Who was large enough to hoist him over? Experts might discover footmarks where someone stood with such a heavy carcass. They might find traces of hair on the wood. Sheila hoped experts would be willing to look.

She knelt once more to bid Bull farewell, and saw—caught between two powerful teeth—a scrap of brown. She rose, determined to persuade the police to look at the dog immediately. They might argue that Wart had killed the dog before ending his own life. Sheila was certain Wart would never have left the dog out here to rot. Someone had dispatched Wart's sentinel and discarded it. Had that person returned to kill Bull's master?

SHE TRUDGED TOWARD the house, deep in thought, stopping in the barn long enough to wonder if Wart had hidden a bomb there. Disquieting rustlings in the straw persuaded her to leave that to the police, too.

She hurried to the house. Her first impulse was to tell Bo and urge him to ask Detective Belk to examine Bull. But could she trust Bo—or Cline, Dudley, Roger, Bubba, or even Sara Sims?

She walked into the kitchen and met the jet black eyes of the only person of whom she was entirely sure.

"Have some coffee." Grandma Sims shoved a steaming mug in her direction. "Bo's coffee ain't as good as Wart's, but it's credible."

Sheila looked around. "Where are Sara Sims and Bo?"

"Gone to set with Ruby while Cline goes to church. It's preaching Sunday for us. Only happens oncet a month, so you got to catch it whiles you can. I told them I'd be all right, seeing how as you was coming by."

Sheila took a sip of coffee and tried to think of how to explain what she wanted the old woman to do. "Mrs. Sims, I have something to tell you that may upset you. I have just found Wart's dog Bull, down behind the woodpile."

"Did he come at you? He's fierce, old Bull is."

"No, ma'am, he's dead." Sheila used the term of respect automatically. Her Southern roots must be growing!

"I wondered if he might be." Grandma Sims rubbed a spot on the table again and again. "Otherwise he'da tore up the men that come for Wart."

"What men?"

"Them in the hearse."

Sheila was disappointed. For a moment she had hoped Grandma Sims had remembered someone being at the house last Friday night.

"I think the police need to see that dog, Mrs. Sims. I'm going to call and ask them to come examine him."

The old woman pushed back from the table and hoisted herself to her feet. "I'll call. I can't see to dial, but if somebody dials for me, I can talk all right."

"I'll dial for you," Sheila agreed.

The man who answered was reluctant at first to call Detective Belk on a Sunday, but Sheila had told Grandma Sims to insist. Insist she did. Aunt Mary could not have gotten better results. Within the hour the big detective himself arrived.

Ten minutes later he was back in the little kitchen, drinking coffee and telling the old woman what he had found. "The dog has a piece of leather in his mouth. Probably a glove, although the lab will have to make a positive identification. Looks like when somebody in leather gloves held his collar to slash his throat, the dog took a nip out of the glove."

"Wart never wore gloves," the old woman quavered. "Not even when it got nippy."

"Would Mr. Sims have killed his own dog?"

She blinked, fixed him with those piercing eyes. "Mr. Sims? He's been dead nigh on thirty years."

"I mean Mr. Wallace Sims, ma'am."

"That's Wart. You just call him Wart."

"Very well. Would Wart have killed his own dog?"

"No siree! He plumb loved that dog. Onliest thing he ever did love, after his daddy and mama both died."

The big detective sighed and stirred in his chair. "It is possible, ma'am, that we are going to find evidence that your grandson was murdered. That someone killed his dog to keep him from sounding the alarm."

A triumphant smile spread over the old face, and she turned her sharp eyes to Sheila. "I knew Wart never died from a bad heart! His color was better'n mine. Now tell him how Billy never killed himself, neither."

The detective turned to Sheila. "As I recall, you aren't really related to the family."

She gave him a rueful smile. "No, I'm the friend who brought Sara Sims home the night her mother died. I brought her over on Monday to deliver a cake, and we found Billy Sims hanging in the barn. This morning I came over to milk, and found the dog."

He shot her a suspicious glance. "Well aren't you Johnny-on-the-spot! Or should I say Jane? Do you milk here regularly?" His eyes looked skeptically at her L.L. Bean jeans and SAS shoes.

"Only in an emergency," she assured him. "My name is Sheila Travis," she added, prompted by a pencil he held over a pad.

He wrinkled his high forehead. "Now where have I heard that name before?" He sucked in one cheek, thinking.

"You don't happen to know Lieutenant Owen Green in Atlanta's Homicide Division, do you?" she asked, hoping he didn't.

He snapped his fingers and pointed one at her like a pistol. "You're the woman who hounded him until he investigated Dean Anderson's suicide?"

"It wasn't suicide," she reminded him. "It was murder."

He gave her a long, thoughtful look. "And now you think old Mr. Sims and young, er, Wart may have been murdered, too?"

She made a quick decision. "I think, Detective Belk, that the best thing would be for you and me to go catch my aunt before she leaves for church. She will never forgive me if she's not there to help me explain. But first, you need to search the house, if Mrs. Sims doesn't mind."

"Search?" Grandma Sims turned her head this way and that. "What you want to search *for?*"

Sheila rose from the table. "A bomb."

Now she had the big detective's attention!

# TWENTY-EIGHT

*Monday—Memorial Day*

SHEILA HAD CHERISHED the illusion that telling Detective Belk all she and Aunt Mary together knew about the Sims family deaths would relieve her of further responsibility for the family itself. Sara Sims dispelled that illusion early Monday morning. Too early, from Sheila's point of view.

She had risen to walk Lady. Returning, she planned to put her pajamas back on and climb into bed with her second cup of coffee and *Armchair Gourmet,* which she had still not found time to finish. Instead, Sara Sims appeared at her door.

Pert in white shorts, a bright green top, and sandals, she regarded Sheila with disapproval. "Aren't you ready yet?"

Sheila raised one eyebrow. "Ready for what?"

"The party! Up at the lake. Remember? We've talked about it lots of times."

"*You* have talked about it." Sheila hoped she had put enough emphasis on the pronoun.

"But you have to come!" Sara Sims danced in her eagerness. "Even Kevin is coming! I called him yesterday and reminded him he'd promised, and he said yes. Oh, Sheila!—" her voice dropped to a whisper "—I just know today he's going to change his mind about—you know. Once he sees us all back to normal."

She continued in a louder tone. "Besides, Andy's coming, too. You have to be there to round out the numbers."

"You mean to chaperone you with two dates? Not on your life. I am planning to spend most of this day in bed with a book."

"You can read at the lake. Daddy probably will, and Faye and Merle, if they come."

"All the old people." She didn't say it. She didn't have to. Sheila shook her head. "No, not today."

Sara Sims's eyes filled with tears. "You really do have to, Sheila. We're all going to be thinking about last year, and how Mama and Uncle Billy and Wart were there. But if there are people who aren't family..."

Sheila had no intention of falling for sentiment that turned on like a tap. She had started to shake her head again when Andy Lee ran up the stairs wearing shorts in a particularly vile red and purple pattern with a green shirt. "You ready, Sheila?"

Kevin came out of Sara Sims's door, stunning in tan tailored shorts and a butter yellow polo shirt. "Hurry, Sheila. I want to get all the sun I can!"

His tone settled it once and for all. She had opened her mouth to refuse when the telephone rang behind her. She said over her shoulder, "Saved by the bell," and closed the door behind her.

The husky voice on the other end filled her with immediate dismay. "Aunt Mary, what on earth are you doing up this early?"

"I've been up most of the night, Sheila, thinking and planning. I don't think we should leave this case entirely to that nice Mr. Belk. He seems a fine man, but a bit plodding, didn't you think? And from what he said, every police officer in north Georgia is occupied today with those marches up in Forsyth County. Mr. Belk could take forever to solve this thing." She paused, and Sheila could see her taking a dainty sip of the one cup of black coffee she permitted herself each morning, then lying back against her lace pillows. Up all night indeed!

"Detective Belk will do fine, Aunt Mary. He knows everything we know, and has all the facilities he needs to investigate. And I have an appointment this morning with a good book and my bed."

"Pshaw! You can't lie down on an important job, dear. Now I've been thinking. Didn't you say most of the Sims family is going up to Lake Lanier for a picnic today? If you could get yourself invited..."

"I've been invited," Sheila told her, "and turned them down. I really don't think—"

"That's your problem, dear. You don't always think clearly. Now here's what *I* think you ought to do."

Ten minutes later, Sheila reluctantly agreed.

THEY WERE STILL CROWDED around her doorway when she returned. "Okay," she sighed. "I'll go—if I can drive my own car. I will *not* be folded into Kevin's backseat again. Give me time to dress."

"You ride with her," Kevin told Andy. Sara Sims started to protest, then nodded.

As he climbed in beside Sheila fifteen minutes later, Andy looked at the book she had pitched into the backseat and shook his head. "Can't you find better light reading than a cookbook?"

She handed him two nonspill mugs of coffee. "To each her own. Besides, a man who likes to eat as much as you do ought to read that. It makes cooking easy."

"Maybe so." It was clear his mind was not on the conversation.

As she followed Kevin's silver convertible for the half-hour drive to Lake Lanier, Sheila scarcely noticed Andy's scowl. She was too busy fuming at Aunt Mary for practically ordering her to go. "It's vital," the husky old voice had assured her—preparing, Sheila knew, to stay in her own bed for a couple of hours with the morning crossword and a mystery.

At last, however, Andy could be silent no longer. "If Sara Sims doesn't get back on her side of that car, I'll break her neck." He ground his teeth.

Sheila raised one eyebrow. "And I thought you were waiting up for me Saturday night."

He flushed. "Well, I was—sort of. I didn't like to barge in on her until you got home."

She grinned. "Showing admirable restraint."

A carpet of pine needles served the Tait lake house as a drive. The house itself was weathered cedar, with a deck overlooking the water. Sails made vivid triangles of color against blue sky, dark green pines, and almost black water. A few motor boats buzzed like flies. A ski boat bobbed by the Tait dock. A small sailboat was pulled up on the grass.

Dudley's sandals, cut offs, and plaid shirt proclaimed him a man on vacation, but his shoulders slumped with weariness and he could scarcely muster a smile to go with his welcome speech. "We don't stand on formality here," he told the three guests. "Beer and Cokes are in the refrigerator when you want them, chips and dip on the counter. I'm smoking a turkey and we'll eat about three. Men change in the bunkroom to the left, women in the master bedroom to the right."

He padded back out to the deck, where a book lay face down on the chaise. Sheila followed Sara Sims to leave her bathing suit, which she had no intention of using in May waters.

"Here you are," Sara Sims said at the door, and left.

Faye was in the bedroom, pulling her hair back with a yellow ribbon. That touch of color, however, was the only sign of the new Faye. She wore no makeup, and her brown bathing suit was demure enough for a nun. Only her body moved in a new, experienced way.

"Hello, Sheila!" She smiled—the pallid, old-Faye smile. She stepped to the right. "Need a mirror?"

Sheila shook her head. "I'll leave my things here, but I really don't plan to swim."

Faye sighed. "Me neither. But I hope I can get some sun. My tan is fading." She pulled an eyelet cover-up over her suit. Sheila wondered if Fay would shed the cover-up in public, even to get sun.

Fay moved around the room, gently touching the bed-spread, the curtains. Catching Sheila's eye, she flushed. "I love this house. We've been coming here since I was four-teen. It's...it's almost like a holy place to me. So peace-ful."

The peace was shattered. "You aren't dressed!" Sara Sims accused Sheila from the doorway. She herself was sleek as a seal in a bright green two-piece bathing suit.

Sheila raised one eyebrow. "You're big on green today. Did you change in the men's dressing room?"

Sara Sims laughed. "No, I have a cubbyhole next door to the boys. And Andy said the other night that green would suit me. I think it does." She pranced to the mirror.

"You look adorable," Faye assured her, moving out of the way.

Sara Sims preened. "If this doesn't change Kevin's mind, I don't know what will."

Faye's eyes widened. "Is Kevin here?" If she had clutched her cover-up to her neck, her meaning couldn't have been clearer.

"And Andrew Lee, too," Sara Sims said with satisfac-tion. "You'll just have to shed your girlish modesty, Faye, and realize these men are used to seeing women in bathing suits. Come on! The others are already at the water." She started to go, turned back to Faye. "Is Amy here?"

"Of course. Does she ever miss a party?" Faye bent to pick up and fold her clothes, hiding her expression, but her tone of voice expressed enough dislike for anyone to know how she felt.

As soon as Sheila reached the deck and saw Amy, she thought she understood. Amy was everything a younger Faye had not been—alive and popular. She looked like Princess Fergie in miniature. No more than five feet tall, under a hundred pounds, she had flaming red hair, freck-les, and a zest for life that made the air around her seem to shimmer with energy. She was tossing a ball with little Tad and Michelle, laughing as hard as they. She waved an arm to draw Andy and Kevin into the game. Sara Sims hurried down the steps and across the grass to join them.

"Planning to play ball?" Dudley asked Sheila, laying aside his book.

"No, I thought I'd join you, if I may." She chose a chaise and wiggled into the cushions to get comfortable.

"What a lovely place," she murmured. The sun glittered on the lake, but the deck, shaded by towering pines, was dim and quiet. In the water, Roger did laps while Erika made a splash of slim white body, blue bathing suit, and yellow towel on the gray dock.

At the edge of the water the ball suddenly went in. Amy dived after it, followed by the others. Soon shouts of "Marco! Polo!" filled the air. Roger, Sheila saw, swam under the dock and joined in. Erika dutifully rose and went to play with their children in shallow water.

Faye came onto the deck, carrying a towel and a pillow. "Hello, Uncle Dudley." She drifted to the rail, touched it gently, looked at the frolic below. "I was going to sun with Erika for a while."

Dudley smiled up at her. "You are free to join us, if you like."

She sighed. "No, I really need some sun."

He nodded. "Be careful not to burn, now."

She smiled back. "I'm being careful today, Uncle Dudley." She moved gracefully down the steps and across the lawn. On the dock she sat on her towel before shedding her cover-up, hesitating over each button, then arched her back before lying gracefully back on the bright towel. Sheila wondered if she realized that that was far more sensual than if she had merely flung it away. In any case, she was not visible to the men playing in the water below.

The morning passed peacefully. Sheila read awhile, drowsed awhile, read a few more chapters. About eleven Dudley rose. "Beer?"

He returned with two cold cans, and they returned companionably to their books. The only sounds were screams of delight, most often from Amy, as the swimmers splashed and ducked one another.

Faye came back about eleven-thirty, modestly clad, and settled on a third chaise with *Sonnets from the Portuguese*. Almost immediately Amy called from the foot of the dock steps, "Can we start skiing, Uncle Dudley?" She was like a water sprite, dripping wet, green eyes dancing. She almost danced herself in her eagerness.

Faye glowered down at her sister. "Don't bother us."

Amy's mouth set in a stubborn pout. "I'm not bothering you, I'm asking Uncle Dudley if we can ski."

"Do you ski, Sheila?" Dudley asked in an undertone.

She shook her head. "I would like to try your sailboat later, though. I've been thinking of buying myself one that size."

"Sure." He smiled at her. "I'd like to take you out. The wind will be better in late afternoon, though."

While they were speaking, Kevin had joined Amy, tight blue trunks moulding his tanned body. "You coming, too, Faye?"

She shook her head. "She doesn't ski," said Amy.

"You could ride in the boat," he persisted.

Faye shook her head again. "I'll watch from here." She turned away, wearing a small, private frown.

"We can. It's okay!" Amy dashed down the grass toward the boat and the others followed—Roger in his new red bathing suit, Andy and Bo in technicolor knee-length pants, two excited children with their mother, Sara Sims and Amy both in green, one nicely round and one slim and boyish. Kevin waved at Faye from the dock.

They went laughing and jostling, full of the joy of playing, this one more time, like the children they had all once been. Sara Sims had greatly exaggerated the grief that would haunt this family gathering. Dudley alone seemed unable to relax. All morning he had picked up his book and put it down again, sat staring across the water, chewed his lower lip nearly raw. As the boat started up, he gave an uncon-

scious sigh so deep that both Sheila and Faye looked up.
"Sorry. I'm a real party pooper today."

Sheila gave him a sympathetic smile. "You are really
tired, aren't you?"

Faye spoke hotly. "No wonder! He carries this whole
family. Dudley and Aunt Evelyn take care of everybody, and
he's plumb worn out. He didn't need to have everybody up
here today, but they wanted to come." From the other side
of the house a car door slammed. "And now here come the
rest."

Dudley stood with a wan smile. "Then I'd better gird up
my loins to welcome them."

LUNCH WAS A CULINARY, if not a social, success. Evelyn
brought potato salad, a congealed salad, and a banana
pudding to augment Dudley's smoked turkey. Erika had
made deviled eggs and a broccoli casserole. Faye had baked
an enormous chocolate cake. Aubrey arrived with a nervous grin, another chocolate cake—and Gussie Mae Curtis. Merle had sent Bubba to the Winn Dixie for a relish tray
and sourdough rolls, which she kept insisting were almost
as good as her own. Sheila wondered why she bothered to
apologize. Nobody in this gathering expected her to make
homemade rolls.

The young adults carried their plates back down near the
water. Their elders dragged chairs onto the deck where they
could enjoy the pleasant breeze without getting too much
sun. Sheila chose the latter group, having had enough of
Sara Sims for one day and enough of Roger to last a lifetime. She was surprised, however, that Faye stayed, as well.
The adults were mostly silent, saying little to compete with
the laughter floating up from the waterside.

"It's a shame Uncle Cline had to stay home," Evelyn said
at one point, with a sigh. "He loves it up here so."

"Mammaw couldn't come," Faye reminded her, "and
somebody had to look after Grandma Sims, too. He can
come next year."

Evelyn nodded. "I know. Seems funny to have the picnic without him and Aunt Ruby, though."

Bubba looked up from his turkey. "And without Martha Sloan nagging us, and Uncle Billy dribbling grease down his chin."

Another uneasy silence fell.

Nobody, Sheila noticed, mentioned Wart. She wondered if Merle was thinking she would probably not be at the next Memorial Day picnic. If so, she hid it well. She and Aubrey were the only two in the family who made a determined effort to give the guests a cheerful lunch.

When the last bites of cake and pudding had been eaten and plastic cups of tea drained to the ice cubes, Aubrey plucked up the knees of his tan linen pants, hitched himself close to the edge of his chair, and smiled around the circle. "I am so glad to be able to introduce all of you to Gussie Mae, here. She is very special to me, and this family has always been like my own, ever since I first came into it."

Expecting an engagement announcement, Sheila was surprised when he stopped. He gave Gussie Mae a pleading smile and reached over to give her soft hand a pat. Sheila knew, then, that Gussie Mae had not yet said yes. Aubrey gave her one more pat and sank back into his seat.

Sheila was so busy thinking up scenarios for how Aubrey might persuade the wealthy widow to marry him that she missed the sound of approaching feet. Around the corner of the deck tripped a trim little figure wearing white linen, a huge white straw hat, and an air of utter helplessness.

"I beg your pardon." The husky voice seemed far too deep for her tiny body. "I wonder if I might use your phone? I was out for a drive and my car stalled, and I just can't seem to get it started again."

She stood and waited, a picture of demure female ineptitude. Then she saw one of the persons present. "Why, Gussie Mae Curtis! What a fortunate circumstance to run into someone I know!"

Two voices spoke simultaneously. "Why, hello," said Gussie Mae Curtis, surprised, and Sheila said, astonished, "Aunt Mary, what are you doing here?"

# TWENTY-NINE

AUNT MARY TURNED, eyebrows raised in delight. "Why, Sheila! Is this the Tait place? How very fortunate!" She moved across the deck like a duchess and extended a hand to Dudley. "Mr. Tait? I am Mary Beaufort, Sheila's aunt. I knew your wife. Please accept my condolences for your loss."

Even in shorts with his shirttail out, Dudley gave her a courtly welcome. "Thank you, Miss Mary. Sheila has been a big help to our family these past weeks. Please have a seat and let me get you a glass of tea, then we'll take a look at your car."

"I'll get it, Dudley." Evelyn went inside. Aunt Mary took a chair in the shade, setting a large shopping bag beside her.

Sheila watched her aunt carefully, hoping for at least a clue as to why she had come. This was not the plan. Had she discovered something since morning? Or just finished her mystery novel and decided to add a little excitement to her life? Where had she gotten that shopping bag? Probably borrowed it from Mildred. Aunt Mary did her shopping by phone. And what had she done with Jason, her driver and an excellent mechanic? Aunt Mary had never driven a car in Sheila's lifetime.

Not one to be troubled by her own falsehoods, the tiny woman accepted her tea (in a real glass, not a plastic cup), then favored one person with an especially charming smile. "We have never met, but don't I remember seeing you on television?" She could not have sounded more impressed if he had received an Emmy.

Aubrey Wilson reacted as Sheila knew he would. Far less foolish men went down before that smile and those fluttering lashes. He inched his chair toward her and put out a slender hand. Before he could speak, Gussie Mae laid a possessive hand on his forearm. "Let me introduce you, Mary. This is my fiancé, Aubrey Wilson."

Aubrey turned to her, delighted and surprised. "Why, Gussie, honey, I didn't know you were going to—"

"—tell anybody today?" she finished for him. "Just family, dearest." She preened and gave her new family a smile all around. Then she rose, put out a hand to her old friend. "We really must be going, Mary. We have wedding plans to make. I hope we'll see you again soon." They said farewells and departed.

"Looks like Uncle Aubrey's getting what he deserves," Bubba growled. Sheila suspected that was the general sentiment.

With the air of one making a delightful discovery, Aunt Mary turned back to Dudley. "You know, Mr. Tait, it seems to me that my coming to your house this afternoon may be providential!"

Sheila hid her expression behind her cup. Aunt Mary did have a tendency to confuse her own plans with those of the Almighty.

"Sheila has been telling me what your poor family has endured these past weeks." Sympathy dripped from Aunt Mary's voice like molasses from a biscuit. "We have been giving it a lot of thought, and have come to some conclusions that I would like to share with you."

"Of course." Sheila felt sorry for Dudley, trapped by his desire to please into a situation he would certainly prefer to avoid.

Amy had come up for another piece of cake. As soon as Dudley assented, she waved one arm and shouted, "Hey, guys, come on up here. We are finally going to talk about it!" After a startled pause, all the young adults except Erika picked up their litter and came warily toward the deck. Erika and the children went wading.

"I don't know if you know," Aunt Mary continued, "but Sheila has considerable experience in solving crimes involving murder."

At the moment Sheila was contemplating committing one. This was not at all the way they had planned to go about this. "Subtle" and "tactful" had been Aunt Mary's own words on the phone.

Amy's freckles grew oranger as her face grew pink with excitement. "Are you a detective? Have you found out who killed Aunt Martha Sloan? I really hated to miss..."

"Amy!" Faye rebuked her, and gave Sheila a look of equal rebuke.

Amy shrugged. "It's the truth. I did." She shoved Bo over and joined him and Andy sitting sideways on a chaise. Sara Sims and Kevin shared a bench. Roger leaned against the deck rail, arms clasped over his bare chest.

Aunt Mary gave the youngest cousin a nod of approval. "A wise man once said, 'Know the truth, and the truth shall set you free.'"

No one spoke for a moment, then Bubba leaned forward and said bluntly, "We know the truth, ma'am. We just don't like it."

"Oh?" She arched her brows and inclined her silver head.

He flushed and cleared his throat, looked around the deck as if assessing who might be hearing this for the first time. "Uncle Billy killed Martha Sloan, Miss Mary."

Amy made a small sound of surprise. Bo moved in protest. Bubba went doggedly on. "Uncle Cline took him over to watch TV Tuesday, because Uncle Billy's TV was broken. Billy had been worried since Sunday that Martha Sloan might hurt Grandma. She wouldn't have, of course," he hastened to add, "but once Uncle Billy got an idea in his head, there was no getting it out. So he shot her." He paused, but when no one else spoke, he defended his case. "Why, if you had seen how strange he acted the next Sunday—remember Faye? Remember Roger? You weren't there, Dudley, but he wouldn't stay in the same room with

Cline or Ruby, wouldn't look anybody straight in the eye. If Faye and Sara Sims, here, hadn't taken him off our hands, he'd have driven us plumb crazy.''

''Don't!'' Sara Sims's face was white. ''Maybe he did kill Mama, but you don't have to tell the world!''

Aunt Mary shook her head. ''No, he did *not* kill your mother. Tell them, Sheila, about the note.''

Sheila had not planned to do anything of the sort, but every eye on the deck was trained in her direction so she did. ''It could have been a confession,'' she concluded, ''but I think it was put there by someone to whom he wrote it, someone who was afraid of what Billy had seen and decided to silence him.''

''Yes!'' Bo said, pounding one palm with a fist. ''I knew it!''

Aunt Mary reached into her shopping bag and handed him a clear sandwich bag. ''Have you ever seen this before?''

Bo's eyes were puzzled. ''It looks like a water pistol Uncle Billy and I used when we played Cowboys and Indians.''

''When did you last see it?''

Bo thought. ''The Sunday before he died. I had this yellow one and Uncle Billy had the blue one.''

''Did you leave it in the barn, or wipe off your prints?''

''Of course not! Why should I? I just tossed it onto the porch.''

''There were no prints on this gun when your sister handed it to Sheila last Saturday—except your sister's own.''

Bo stared at his sister. ''Sara Sims? You didn't . . . ?''

''Of course not!'' Her indignation matched his own. ''I found it in the straw, down behind the box where the cat had her kittens. If there aren't any other prints on it, somebody wiped them off.''

''So what happened?'' Bo asked. ''You think somebody else played Cowboys and Indians with Uncle Billy, lured him into the barn, and then—'' He could not finish.

"I can see it now." Roger raised his voice to a falsetto. "'Time for a hanging, Billy. Put your head in the noose, right here.' Then wham-o!" His laugh was nasty.

Horror stared at him from every seat.

Aunt Mary nodded somberly. "I think we ought to at least consider that possibility." She turned to Amy. "Your grandfather, for instance..."

"Pawpaw!" Amy gaped. "He wouldn't kill anybody!"

"Perhaps not, but he's been discussing large investments with a stockbroker." She pulled a sheet of paper from her shopping bag and said, aside, to Sheila, "Charlie and I breakfasted together today, dear. He brought along a few things." While Sheila was wondering if Charles Davidson had climbed in to share her usual breakfast in bed or if Aunt Mary had risen and dressed for the occasion, her aunt was already saying to the others. "Mr. Shaw has been discussing investing ten million dollars. Do you know how he planned to get that much money?"

Most people did not move. Roger swore. Evelyn, however, chuckled. "Uncle Cline always has been a dreamer." Her green eyes twinkled. "He was probably getting ready to give us all advice."

Bubba nodded. "He's thought he had to take care of family finances ever since my daddy died and I—" he gave Evelyn a quick look, "—I started drinking. I'm ready to take the cure now, though. Somebody's got to take charge." He ignored Roger's sudden movement. "It's not fair for Cline to have to do it. Or Dudley, either. Look at him! He's a mere shadow of his former self. Man," he said to his brother-in-law, "you need a long, sunny vacation."

Dudley nodded. "I'm going, Bubba, in a couple of weeks."

Evelyn wanted to clear up one possible misunderstanding. "Uncle Cline won't really get to invest any money. Aunt Ruby will take care of that."

"Where would anybody in this family *get* any money?" Amy demanded. "You talk like we're millionaires or something."

"Didn't Aunt Merle or Faye tell you?" Sara Sims asked. "Developers want to build a mall on Grandma Sims's farm. They could give her ten million dollars!"

Finally, Amy was speechless.

"Unraveling this case," Aunt Mary said, almost to herself, "has involved a lot of guessing and some painstaking thought."

"Do you think you *have* unraveled it?" It was the first time Merle had spoken. Sheila had thought she was asleep.

"Oh, yes, I think so." Aunt Mary daintily sipped her tea. "But several people made it difficult by lying. Which one of you is Bo?"

Bo raised his hand, then quickly dropped it back on his thigh. "I don't lie, ma'am," he assured her with a look of candor.

Aunt Mary raised her eyebrows. "Oh? I thought you said you were in Athens all day the day your mother was killed. Weren't you really at the house that morning?"

His gaze dropped, and he began to trace the pattern on his bathing trunks with one forefinger. He said nothing.

"Your clothes were on the drier," blurted Sara Sims.

Bo glared at her. "Thanks, Sis. Thanks a lot."

Dudley half rose in his chair. "Bo had nothing to do with Martha Sloan's death!"

Bo raised his head and met Dudley's gaze. "No, but I was there, sir, right after you went to work." Tears came into his eyes, and he swiped them away angrily. "Mama threw some clothes in the washer for me while I ate breakfast. We...well, we had a fight. A hell of a fight."

"When did you leave, son?"

"I stormed out about nine-thirty, before my clothes were dry, and drove back to Athens. But I didn't kill her. I swear it."

"If Uncle Billy didn't do it, nobody in the family did,"
Bubba said. His tone added, "And that settles it."

Aunt Mary reached into her bag again and pulled out a
small pad. She consulted it, then looked around the circle.
"Whoever shot her, it would help if we could identify the
gun. Detective Belk gave me the make, model, and serial
number. Does this mean anything to any of you?" She read
from the pad, then looked around again.

Amy padded over to read the page, biting her lower lip.
Finally, with a defiant look at her mother, she said, "I think
it was one of Wart's. If I saw it, I could tell—at least, if it's
one he had last Christmas."

"How?" Merle asked. She was looking pale and very,
very weak.

Amy knelt, buried her head in her mother's thin lap. "He
was teaching me to shoot, Mama. I begged until he said he
would, if I'd clean every one of his blasted guns."

"Oh!" exclaimed Faye. Amy ignored her.

Merle rubbed her younger daughter's wiry hair. "You always have done what you thought you needed to, honey."
She gave Faye a worried look, but Faye had shifted her attention from her trying sister toward Erika and the children, down near the water.

Amy stayed where she was, but she looked up at Sheila.
"I think that's a gun Wart got when he was in the marines,
from a guy named Corker. Corker came to see him a couple of times, remember?" She turned to the others for con-
firmation. Sara Sims and Roger nodded, but nobody in the
family looked particularly pleased with Amy.

"Who would have had access to Wallace's guns?" Aunt
Mary inquired. "Surely he kept them locked?"

Amy shook her head. "He just piled them on a bookshelf in his room. Anybody who went to Grandma Sims's
could go to the bathroom and grab one before they went
back to the living room. He didn't register them, either."

"Wart," Sara Sims reminded them all, "was not someone who took law and order very seriously."

"You might go down to police headquarters tomorrow and see if you can identify the gun, Amy," Evelyn suggested.

The girl had regained some of her spirit. "I don't even know where police headquarters is. Can you tell me, Uncle Dudley?"

Dudley looked dazed. It took him a moment to reply. "Yes, Amy. Yes, I can. We'll go together first thing tomorrow." He sat lost in thought, as if working things out, then he turned to Sheila. "Is it possible, then, that Wart killed my wife, killed Uncle Billy because Billy saw him, then took his own life in remorse?"

There was a moment of silence. From the waterside Sheila heard little Tad scream at Michelle, "Fall down! I killed you! I'm the bestest Ninja Turtle of all!" Before she answered, Sheila wondered why a nice Baptist mother like Erika let her children pretend they were ninjas. Didn't nice Baptist mothers know that ninjas used to be Japan's most ruthless assassins? Perhaps, she thought wearily, divine justice neutralized ancient evil by turning it into friendly turtles.

The evil at hand refused to be neutralized. She could feel pain welling up inside her, yearned to stand up and go home now, before they had to delve deeper.

Bo answered before Sheila could. "I don't think so, Dad. Yesterday Sheila found Bull behind the woodpile, with his throat cut. Wart certainly didn't do that. It looks like somebody got Bull out of the way so they could get to Wart."

The ripple rose to an uproar. "Bull? Who'd kill a dog? Who *could* do it? Bull would kill anybody who..."

Bo shrugged. "It had to be somebody who knew Wart left his front window unlocked so he could come and go. Probably," he looked around the deck soberly, "one of us."

"It was somebody wearing leather gloves," Sheila said. "Bull had a piece of leather in his teeth. Do you own a pair, Kevin?"

# THIRTY

TWO VOICES SPOKE as one. Sara Sims said, "Yes," and Kevin said, "No. Why do you ask?"

Roger looked from one to the other. "Oh-ho! There seems to be a discrepancy here. Why did you say yes, Simsy?"

"I . . . I was mistaken." Sara Sims faced him defiantly.

"If I may change the subject for a moment?" Aunt Mary intervened, "I would like to ask Mr. Bradshaw about a business called—" she consulted a paper she held, "—B & S. I believe you and Wallace Sims were the principal partners."

Kevin looked at her in astonishment. "How did you get those? I have the only copies . . ."

She smiled at him. "I only have the name, Mr. Bradshaw, but perhaps you will be so good as to tell us about it?"

Kevin chose his words carefully. "It's . . . it *was* a business Wart wanted to start. I had a little money to invest, so I was going in with him."

"'All I need is *to* sign'!" Bo exclaimed. "That's what Wart said, not 'All I need is *a* sign.' He was talking about signing papers."

Dudley addressed Kevin mildly. "You were putting up money and Wart was putting up—what?"

"Not much, yet," Kevin admitted. "If his great-grandmother left him her farm, he'd have had that. Otherwise, he'd have had some of it."

Aunt Mary peered at him over her half-glasses. "My financial advisor says that the developers who approached the county commission about the Sims farm were contacted recently by B & S about property. Was that also the Sims farm?''

Sara Sims's eyes blazed. "Were you planning to steal our farm, Kevin Bradshaw? Is that why you stopped talking marriage?"

Kevin shifted uneasily and looked at his feet. Sheila answered for him. "No, Sara Sims, he started backing out when he found out you had brothers to share your inheritance. If I'm not mistaken, he started looking for what he felt were greener pastures. You should have put Amy on that family tree you gave him."

It took Sara Sims only a moment to figure that out. "Faye?" she asked Kevin, outraged. "You'd have married Faye?"

He still refused to look at her. Sara Sims turned accusingly to her cousin. "You wouldn't have, would you?"

Faye shook her head. "Never," she said fervently.

Sara Sims caught a hidden meaning. "You went out with him!"

Faye's color rose. "Once, the Monday night Uncle Billy died. He asked me while we were shopping for Mama's dress." She gave Sara Sims a penitent smile. "I'm sorry, honey. He said you and he were just friends, and he was so sweet that day that I decided to go. After all, he is more my age than yours. But I found we are very different." She shuddered delicately and drew her cover-up closer around her.

"Ice Maiden," Amy muttered. No one paid her any attention.

Sara Sims turned to Kevin in fury. "You asked her out while buying a dress for *my mama's funeral?* You bastard!" She thought of one objection to the story. "But you were in Macon that Monday. You called me about four."

He shrugged. "I called you from my car phone on my way home. I left Macon about three."

Sara Sims flew at him and pummelled him with her fists. "You took her out to dinner, then came to Grandma Sims's to find me?"

Kevin held her wrists in a grip of steel. "I needed to see Wart about something."

Sheila had forgotten Andy Lee until he lunged toward Kevin and caught him by the throat. Aunt Mary reached out to restrain him.

"Andrew, please stop choking Mr. Bradshaw. I have a few more questions. And stop gaping, Sheila. Andrew Lee and I had lunch together last week. He wrote that delightful book beside your chair, *Armchair Gourmet*."

Sheila continued to gape. Andy backed off, panting and glared at Kevin. Amy snatched up the book and stared at the cover. "You didn't write this! It was written by a woman."

Andy shrugged. "Anne Delly, Andy Lee. Depends on how you say it."

"Is it a dirty book?" she asked suspiciously.

Sheila chuckled. "No, and it's still a bestseller."

Sara Sims gave him a look of grudging respect. Andy pulled her to her feet and walked her over to where he had been sitting. "Move, woman," he told Amy. "Sara Sims needs your place."

Aunt Mary turned back to Kevin. "I am still a bit confused about this business. Were you investing in a pick-your-own farm, or planning to sell the farm to developers?"

Her tone encouraged Kevin. Here, it told him, is someone who wants to understand. He relaxed, explained how clever he was. "You don't need a hundred acres for pick-your-own. Wart could have had fields at the back, and the developers could have had the front. Everybody would have been happy."

"*We* wouldn't have been!" Now it was Roger who grabbed Kevin, and sent him crashing to the deck. Kevin rose, shaking his head to clear it, and his fist met Roger's jaw with enough force to slam Roger's bare back against the edge of the railing. Roger yelped in pain, then, trembling with rage and shame, shouted, "Get the hell out of here!"

Kevin started to the door, but Bo jumped up and caught his arm. "Not so fast. Maybe you killed Uncle Billy and Wart!"

Kevin jerked away from him and backed toward the door. "I never! I had no reason to kill Wart!"

"No," Sheila agreed. "That would have been killing the goose before it laid any golden eggs. But Sara Sims, why did you think Kevin had leather gloves?"

Sara Sims's loyalty was gone. "I gave him a pair."

"I lost them." Kevin muttered.

Sheila shook her head. "I don't think so. I think you wore them Friday night when you killed Bull. And I think you know something about Wart's death."

He sidled closer to the door. "I didn't kill him, I tell you!"

"Of course not," Aunt Mary soothed him. "But why don't you just tell us what you know?"

Kevin glowered from near the door. "Okay, but it isn't much. I went to see Wart late Friday night. He said he'd have the papers signed by then. He took me in through his window, and he was staggering around, talking funny. All of a sudden he collapsed in a heap on the floor. When I checked his pulse, he was dead! I didn't know what to do. If I called the old woman, she'd think I'd killed him. But I hadn't. I swear it! He must have taken something before I got there. I panicked—got the hell out of there!

"Then I got to thinking. If the police found those papers, I might be in trouble. So I went back. But Bull wouldn't let me in without Wart's say-so. I had my leather gloves in the back of my car, and a hunting knife, so I killed the dog and flung it over a woodpile behind the barn, because I didn't want it found and I sure didn't want blood all over my car." Confronting disgust on all sides, he shrugged. "Somebody would have had to put Bull down. He wouldn't obey anybody but Wart. In a way, I was doing the family a favor." Never had Sheila found him more repugnant.

Her feelings must have shown in her face, because Aunt Mary gave her a warning look before asking, "What did you do then?"

"I went back into the bedroom and got Wart onto his bed, so it would look like he'd died there. Then I took the papers and left."

"You took a couple of other things, too," Sheila added. "His money, for instance..."

"...and bought me a bracelet!" Sara Sims flung it at him. It gleamed between them on the deck.

Finally Kevin had the grace to flush. "Okay, so I'm part creep. But I'm no killer. Wart died from something he'd eaten or drunk, but I didn't give it to him. I'll swear to that."

"You may have to," Sheila assured him grimly.

He turned. "Where are you going?" Sara Sims demanded.

"To get my clothes. Do you mind?"

"Yes, I do! I mind a lot of things! Don't ever let me see you again!" She made it to the last word before bursting into tears and hurling herself into Andy's ready arms.

"Before you go, Kevin, there's one more thing." Sheila held him with her tone. "Detective Belk wants to talk with you. I called him before we left and suggested you might have taken a bomb from Wart's room, too, and sent it to the Forsyth County march. When I called his office again about two, they'd questioned the neo-Nazi marchers and found it—before it exploded."

Kevin froze. Aunt Mary smiled at him. "They're waiting for you at the road, dear. I saw them when I came in, and told them we'd send you along soon."

He whirled, started for the steps and the convenient power boat. Roger and Bo leaped as a team to block his escape. With a shrug he turned back to the house. "You may not believe me, but I did that for Wart. A memorial of sorts."

When he had gone, Aunt Mary told Sheila, "Good work, dear. That had not occurred to me. Now! Now that that's cleaned up," she sounded as if she had scrubbed an entire house, "the police can concentrate on who killed Martha Sloan Tait."

"Don't *you* know?" Amy demanded, disappointed.

Sheila and Aunt Mary nodded in unison. "Oh, yes, we think we know," Aunt Mary told Amy, "but the police will have to gather proof. That may take them a few days, even a few weeks. They will need to talk with people, examine sites, check stories. But they will get what they need in the end. As a lawyer, Mr. Tait will know better than I what they will look for—and how thoroughly. And how unwise I'd be to say more at this time."

Dudley had been gazing at Sara Sims with compassion. Now he nodded without a word. The events of the afternoon had seemed to shrink and fade him. He looked as ill as Merle.

Bubba pulled himself to his feet. "Let's go, Evelyn. I think when the police have done all the looking they can do, they will still find Uncle Billy took Wart's gun and killed Martha Sloan, and Wart died of natural causes." He pulled on his windbreaker. "Evvy and I have work to do. We've decided to put the store up for sale. Our house, too. We'll buy something with wheels and travel a bit. We ought to have enough money to hold on until Social Security kicks in."

"You can't do..." Roger began angrily.

Bubba ignored him. "You coming home, Merle? You look plumb worn out."

She pulled herself up with difficulty. "I think I will, Bubba. I am getting a little tired and we've got Wart's funeral tomorrow." Her color was bad. Pain stood in her eyes. Before she left, she gave each of her daughters an embrace. Then she hugged Dudley, Bo, and Sara Sims. Sheila wondered if Merle had deliberately omitted Roger, or merely forgotten him. By now she was beginning to feel pity for the man. Had he always been the family pariah, or brought it on himself by his own behavior?

When they had gone, Aunt Mary looked at the young people. "I am sorry not to be able to satisfy your curiosity, my dears, but you really will have to leave it up to the police. Why don't you ski or swim while the sun is still hot? Sheila and I must be going soon, too."

A chorus of protest rose, but Dudley waved them away. "I think Miss Mary is right. It won't do us any good to sit around talking about this. I, for one, am very weary. Please go back to the boat."

Soberly they stood, looked at one another and—with that instinct common in herds and young adults—moved as a body across the deck and down the grass.

When they were out of earshot, Dudley sighed. "You really do know, don't you?"

Faye put out a hand to stop him. Instead, he took hers and held it gently. He looked at her a long minute, tenderness in his eyes. "You can't buy happiness with murder, dear one. We both should have known that." Retaining her hand in his, he looked from Sheila to her aunt. "How much do you know, and how?"

"Everything!" Aunt Mary declared. Sheila wished she had hedged a bit, or waited to have this conversation with Detective Belk present. Why was Aunt Mary settling herself more comfortably in her chair and speaking as if they were all having a cozy chat? "We know that you, Faye, shot Mrs. Tait, and you, Mr. Tait, killed the others. We figured that out from putting together snippets of what various people said. Tell them, dear."

Did Sheila have a choice? "Your secretary, Dudley, said you were too busy Tuesday to kill anybody. Sara Sims later exclaimed that she made it sound like you could have killed people any day but Tuesday. That was right, wasn't it, Faye? You chose Tuesday because you knew Dudley would be publicly busy all day? Then that evening you went to Roswell to the swim meet. You didn't even get tested to see if you'd fired a gun. We figured out from what Wart said to Bo that he planned to sign papers Friday night. That pointed to you, Dudley.''

Aunt Mary went on without waiting for Faye's reluctant nod. "What really suggested to Sheila Faye was involved was Andrew Lee's pointing out a ground bass in Pachelbel's canon on Saturday night. You are both musical. I am certain you know to what I refer. In this case, as in that canon, there is a recurring theme: You, Faye, were falling deeply in love, yet you were reluctant to bring your new love to meet the family. You claimed you did not want to intrude your happiness on their grief, but that was nonsense. What better time to bring a little happiness into a family's life? Surely there must be another reason why this particular man could not be paraded with pride. Besides,'' her old brown eyes were shrewd, "you were not always considerate. You left your mother alone on Mother's Day to have dinner with the family. You let Sheila deliver a parcel to your great-grandmother rather than miss orchestra rehearsal. You told Evelyn you were planning to take a cruise this summer even though your mother is near death. We began to consider alternative reasons for your reluctance to bring this man home. Only one made sense. You are a good actress, dear, but you gave yourself away to those who knew how to look.''

Faye bit her lip and stared out over the water, eyes full of unshed tears and jaw set in what looked to Sheila like fury.

"Sometimes,'' Sheila pressed, "you called him 'Dudley' instead of 'Uncle Dudley.'''

At last Faye broke. "Do you know how hard it was being near him, wanting to put a little softness in his life, and having to play a part—always the part!—of a concerned cousin? This man is worth ten of my whole family! I *hated* having to sneak around. I wanted to climb Grandma Sims's sycamore and tell the entire county that Dudley Tait loves me! He does, and whatever happens now—"

She broke off, picked up Dudley's hand, and kissed it again and again. He turned toward her and stroked her hair gently. At last she slumped against the back of her chair and closed her eyes.

He turned to Sheila. "How long do you think it will take Detective Belk to get the evidence he needs?"

"Maybe a week," she told him, "maybe less. He'll need to find people who saw you together, ask Faye's principal to confirm that she called in sick the day Martha Sloan was shot." She turned to answer Faye's quick indrawn breath. "Your mother said you'd had a headache. It just took me a while to realize what day that was."

She turned back to Dudley. "Belk will have to try to get enough sense out of your mother-in-law to prove you had no real business with her the day you killed Billy, but needed an alibi. He'll have to get the lab reports on what killed Wart, and he'll have to get the signed papers from Kevin to prove Wart signed them after he left Bo and before he saw Kevin. If you drew them up, that will prove that you were with Wart at the right time to put something in a celebratory drink. That is what you did, isn't it?"

He nodded. "Martha Sloan always had pills around the house. Wart felt no pain, I assure you."

"But why did you kill *them?*" Aunt Mary asked it in much the same tone she would ask an artist why he painted birds instead of fish. "Surely not for money?"

He rubbed one hand across his eyes. "In a way, perhaps. With Billy and Wart gone, my children will inherit more."

Faye sat up again, and spots of color appeared on her cheeks. "He did it for me! Uncle Billy knew I killed Martha Sloan. He was lurking behind the bushes and saw me go in. He heard the shot, saw me leave, watched me throw the gun in the pond, and found her on the kitchen floor. He walked home..."

"...and killed a chicken," nodded Sheila.

Faye continued in a rapid, breathless voice. "When he told me on Sunday, and showed me what he had written, I thought I'd die. I didn't know what to do. So I came up here to see Dudley and admit what I had done. Now look what I have done to *him!*'' Tears ran down her cheeks and with her free hand she gently touched his ravaged face. "He killed them to protect me!"

Dudley took her hand and kissed it. "As you killed Martha Sloan to protect me, my dearest." He turned back to Sheila and her aunt. "My wife was getting a bit peculiar, like her mother—but with none of Nana's gentleness."

"She was getting downright hateful!" Faye cried. "Meaner and meaner! You saw how she was when you came to dinner, Sheila. I couldn't stand it any longer! Poor Dudley—all his life with her picking at him, taunting him...." She looked across the water and spoke in a flat, sad monotone. "I didn't really plan it, it just all seemed to happen. When I went to tell Grandma Sims good-bye, I saw Wart's guns on the shelf. One of them was loaded. I took it with me—I didn't know why. Tuesday I woke up with a headache, and while I was lying in bed, I remembered Martha Sloan saying she'd be home all day baking. I drove over there, thinking I would talk to her, but when I got there—" She pulled her hands from Dudley's and covered her face, shoulders shaking.

"You did take the gun," Aunt Mary reminded her.

Faye raised her tear-stained face. "Yes. Afterwards I thought I was glad. But I'm not. Oh, I'm not!" Again she shook with sobs. Dudley turned and held her in an awkward embrace.

Sheila felt swamped by their pain and hopelessness.

In a moment Faye raised her head again and spoke with rising hysteria. "We never did anything wrong before that. We rode to symphony practice together, and went out for coffee afterwards, but all we did was talk. We didn't even say 'I love you' until..." Dudley placed a finger over her lips to stop her.

Sheila remembered how reverently Faye had touched Dudley's bedspread, how she had glowed Saturday morning. If they had consummated their love Friday night, was it before or after Dudley left for an hour to kill Wart? Poor, poor Faye!

Aunt Mary must have been thinking along the same lines. "You still haven't told us why you killed Wart," she reminded Dudley.

"Billy said something that made Wart suspect Faye. Wart told me he planned to use it to persuade Grandma Sims to leave him the farm, in exchange for keeping his mouth shut. Blackmail, pure and simple." He shook his head. "Killing Uncle Billy was the hardest thing I've ever done. Killing Wart felt like extermination. He had lost all humanity."

"That," Aunt Mary told him, "is never for us to judge."

"No," he admitted with a wan, wry smile. "Nothing he did was as bad as my killing poor Uncle Billy."

"That, too, is not for us to judge. I, for one, leave judgment of people to a higher authority." Aunt Mary bent to pick up her shopping bag and purse.

Sheila resolved to remind her of that lofty sentiment the next time Aunt Mary criticized her coffee drinking or dating habits.

They all stood. "Sheila can drive me home," Aunt Mary told them, "and we can send someone later for my car."

Sheila presumed they would send the same person who drove Aunt Mary's driver away.

She gave Dudley a long, level look. "You won't do anything foolish like trying to leave the county, will you?"

He shook his head. "We won't leave the county."

They put out hesitant hands. Aunt Mary clasped them both between her wrinkled ones. "My dears," she said in her deep voice, "I cannot tell you how sorry I am."

ON THE WAY TO THE CAR, Sheila asked, "Why did you decide to come instead of letting me feel them out the way we'd planned? Belk could have done all this in a few days."

Aunt Mary looked up into a lofty pine. "I remembered that the Lord requires two things of us, Sheila, to do justice *and* to love mercy. And I remembered meeting Dudley Tait once. He struck me as a man of honor. I thought I'd come see for myself." Lips pursed into a network of wrinkles, she climbed into the passenger seat.

Sheila got behind the wheel, but she did not start the car.

Aunt Mary spoke under her breath, as if reciting a strange litany. "Faye could have left town. She could have tried harder to find someone else to love. Wart could have locked up his guns—or not have had guns at all."

Sheila reached over and touched her arm gently. "Let's blame it on the lack of gun control laws, shall we?"

Aunt Mary nodded. "Guns are such hasty weapons, and the results so often irreversible." Her old voice trembled.

Sheila opened the door. "I forgot my bathing suit. I'll be right back." Aunt Mary deserved to have her weep in private.


DUDLEY AND FAYE were no longer on the deck. Sheila stood for a moment at the window, saw them walking slowly down the grass, heard them calling a greeting to Erika and the children.

"I'm a Ninja Turtle, Uncle Dudley!" Tad piped.

"You're the best there is," Dudley replied.

He helped Faye into the sailboat, pushed off, and hoisted the sail. The boat nosed slowly away from shore.

Laughter spilled up from the dock. The younger members of the party were so engrossed in watching Amy try to dump Bo off his skis, they didn't see the small sail crossing the wide lake.

Alone by the window, Sheila watched. When it reached the horizon, two small figures merged in an embrace. The boat sailed past a distant island, outlined by the sunset.

She watched until they disappeared from view.

FROM THE TUESDAY six-o'clock television news:

A sailing accident yesterday claimed the lives of Gwinnett County Commissioner Dudley Tait and his niece,
Faye Baines, bringing the holiday weekend death toll to
seven. Skiers in nearby waters noticed the overturned
sailboat and alerted authorities. The bodies were re-
covered early this morning.

This family has been plagued with disaster in recent
weeks. A funeral was scheduled today for Wallace
Sims, a cousin of Miss Baines, who died last Friday
evening of unknown causes. His funeral was post-
poned until Thursday, when a multiple service will be
held.

Authorities speculate that the sailing accident re-
sulted from a lack of life vests in the boat, and the fact
that neither victim was a strong swimmer. Boaters are
urged to make *certain* sufficient vests are on board before leaving shore.

# EPILOGUE

ONE WEEK LATER Sheila turned into the familiar rutted drive at dusk. Grandma Sims sat in a cane-bottomed rocker with her walker beside her, watching the road. Sheila parked under the sycamore, crossed the yard, and sat in the next rocker, careful not to disturb the old ebony cane hung over the porch rail.

"I brought you an angel food cake, Mrs. Sims."

The old woman nodded. "I'm much obliged." She rocked in silence for several minutes, one hand rubbing her aproned lap. "You he'ped me, like you said you would. I didn't know it would cost me so dear, though."

Sheila sensed that no response was expected.

"Dudley and Faye was carrying on, warn't they." It was not a question, and Grandma Sims did not turn her head to look for an answer. "I guessed it, far back as Christmas. Merle did, too. We seen the way she looked at him. Bessie seen them out back at Ruby's one Sunday night—that time you come to dinner. She come haring over here to tell me. Said they had it bad. Poor Faye, she'd never had a man before, and Dudley—being married to Martha Sloan woulda been a trial for any man."

Again she rocked in silence, making a soft sucking noise. Then she seized her cane and thumped it twice on the floor in anger. "They hadn't oughta killed Billy, though! Poor Billy would never have tol' what he saw Faye do. He was scared to death Cline would find out and whup him. Cline set such a store by Faye, you know."

Sheila turned, startled. "You knew what Billy saw?"

"Sure I knew. Billy come right home and tol' me. I didn't believe him, of course. Made him so mad he went out and killed poor Ruby's favorite hen. Later, when I decided he was telling the truth, I didn't see how it could he'p anything to tell. Who'd put a retarded man on the stand in a murder trial? And it woulda killed Merle and Cline." She paused, shaking her head at the memories. "But I was wrong. Billy died because of what he knew. My poor old silly Billy." She lifted one corner of her apron and wiped her eyes.

Then she carefully hung the cane back over the porch rail and turned to Sheila with her customary spunk. "But what's done is done, and at least my Billy won't ever be simple again. I 'spect you'd like to know if I'm gonna sell the farm to those pesky developers after all this."

Sheila was surprised by the abrupt change of topic, but she nodded. "Yes, I do wonder."

Grandma Sims cackled. She reached over and gave Sheila a playful pat. "Well, I'll tell you and put you out of your misery. I'm leaving everything to Ruby! Every speck of it. I called me a lawyer today and told him to draw up the papers. Are you surprised? I can see you are."

She spat into a can she had tucked in beside her. Sheila smelled the sweet, thick smell of snuff. "Ruby's fat, and she's ugly," her mother said frankly, "and I don't always value her like I should. But Ruby's like her daddy. She loves this land. My Will used to say, 'We don't own the land, we just use it for a while. And they ain't making no more of it.' When he run old red clay through his fingers, he was like a preacher at communion." She reached into her pocket and brought out a tiny can, gathered snuff with a small stick and put it in her mouth. When she got it tucked in where she wanted it, she spoke again, almost to herself.

"Money don't matter to Ruby. She's a contented woman. She's got everything she wants, 'cept'n one—Merle's health—and money can't buy that. If it would, I'd sell the farm myself!" Sheila had never heard her so fierce.

She turned and pinned Sheila to her chair with those burning black eyes. "Don't you never tell Ruby about Faye and Dudley—nor Cline, neither. It would like to kill them both. They got good memories. You leave them be. That policeman you brought out here, he come back and talked to me some more. He thinks Wart killed Martha Sloan and Billy, too, then killed hisself.''

Sheila nodded. "My aunt and I gave him that impression Monday night, I'm afraid, and failed to mention anything that could change it.''

Grandma Sims nodded and spat into her can again. "Wart's memory ain't much to anybody but me. I can stand to carry it.''

They rocked companionably in silence. Finally the old woman said again, "I'm much obliged for the cake. I been eating ham so much lately I'm likely to oink. And Ruby, bless her heart, never did learn to bake a good angel food cake. I bet you never baked this 'un, neither, did you?'' She patted the bakery box that Sheila still held on her lap and her black eyes twinkled.

Sheila chuckled. She had come to cheer up this feisty old woman? Who was she trying to fool? "No, Mrs. Sims, I bought it. I'm like Ruby. I never learned to bake angel food cake, either. But I have learned where to buy a good one.''

"That's okay. You learned to see what's what, too. That's a gift, girl, a pure-tee gift.''

As again they rocked in silence, Sheila's shoulders relaxed, her breaths came deep and slow. Grandma Sims leaned forward and pointed with her cane across the azaleas. "See them leaves out there near the road? Yellow daisies. Come September, they'll bloom. Only grow close to Stone Mountain. Nowhere else in the whole world! We've had them in the yard since I come here as a bride, eighty years ago next month.''

She rocked and Sheila waited.

"If they put stores here, they'd bulldoze my daisies like they was trash, wouldn't they?'' The black eyes searched Sheila's, made her feel like she had suggested the bulldozers herself.

"Yes, ma'am, I'm afraid they would.''

"Then they'd put up buildings full of real trash and work folks up to buy it." She spat contemptuously into the azaleas, spurning the can beside her.

"I'm too old to fight, girl. Too old to care much, even. But Ruby will care. And she'll pass on the farm to somebody else who'll care. Amy, maybe. Or Sara Sims. They both got gumption. We always did have strong women in this family. The men never amounted to much." A smile lit her creased face, and her eyes snapped. "They was some handsome ones, though. Bo, and Harley, and my Will. That's worth something, ain't it?"

She heaved herself to her feet and reached for her walker. "How 'bout you and me having a piece of that cake? It makes my mouth water to think about it. And you can tell me all about this young man you've found for Sara Sims. I'd like to see them settled before I'm gone. I surely would."

Sheila smiled at the humped old back. "You probaby will, Grandma Sims." She scarcely noticed what she'd said. She felt right at home.

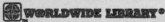

# FOUR ON THE FLOOR

## RALPH McINERNY

### A Father Dowling Mystery Quartet

*First Time in Paperback*

### THE FEROCIOUS FATHER
Mr. O'Halloran had lots of fund-raising ideas for St. Hilary's—plus an unidentified corpse in his car trunk. Had the Mob followed Mr. O'Halloran to town?

### HEART OF COLD
Branded a thief, old Ray has paid his debt to society. But when he is abducted, Father Dowling must prove that crime is all in the family.

### THE DEAD WEIGHT LIFTER
A body is deposited at St. Hilary's, and Father Dowling must find out who the man is and why he died.

### THE DUTIFUL SON
Father Dowling agrees to help a man by exhuming and reburying the body of an infant who died years ago. But the body in question proves to be something quite different.

"Excellent short adventures, crisply written, with surprising twists."     —*St. Louis Post-Dispatch*

**Available in October at your favorite retail stores.**

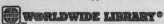

# HARD WOMEN

## *BARBARA D'AMATO*

### *A Cat Marsala Mystery*

*First Time in Paperback*

### A DAY IN THE LIFE

Does anybody care about a dead hooker? That's the question Chicago journalist Cat Marsala is wrestling with. The hooker, Sandra Love, is sleeping on Cat's couch in exchange for the inside scoop on life as a prostitute. Now she's dead in a gutter outside Cat's building and nobody seems to be in a hurry to solve the crime.

Except Cat. Digging into the netherworld of prostitution, from the streetwalkers who trade sex for food, to the enormously high-priced independents, Cat's search for a killer takes her deep into the motives and motivations of hard women—and men—on both sides of a dirty game.

"A heroine for the '90s."—*Houston Chronicle*

**Available in August at your favorite retail stores.**

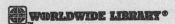

**WORLDWIDE LIBRARY®**

HARDW

# CAT'S CRADLE
## CLARE CURZON

First Time in Paperback

### A Mike Yeadings Mystery

## OLD LORELY PELLING WAS AS QUEER AS TWO LEFT BOOTS....

She's a reclusive eccentric with a checkered past and dozens of cats, and her shooting death is first believed accidental, the result of local boys' target practice. But Detective Superintendent Mike Yeadings of the Thames Valley Police Force believes darker motives are behind the death of the old woman.

The villagers are astounded that Lorely has named her neighbor's children sole inheritors of her estate. For Yeadings, it means unraveling the tangled skein of deception, scandal and desperation in Lorely's long, frustrated life—and the secrets she shared with a killer.

"All the right ingredients." —*Booklist*

**Available in September at your favorite retail stores.**

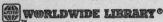